WREN

IT'S A
Wonderful
Lie

HEAVEN ON EARTH SERIES

MYSTIC OWL

AN IMPRINT OF CITY OWL PRESS

IT'S A WONDERFUL LIE
Heaven on Earth, Book 1

MYSTIC OWL
A City Owl Press Imprint
www.cityowlpress.com

Cover Design by MiblArt. All stock photos licensed appropriately.

Edited by Lisa Green.

For information on subsidiary rights, please contact the publisher at info@cityowlpress.com.

Print Edition ISBN: 978-1-64898-124-1

Digital Edition ISBN: 978-1-64898-123-4

Printed in the United States of America

To my husband, Michael, my rock, my supporter, my angel. Thanks for making me soar. Love you, 3000.

1

EDEN

No one in real life went to a tree lot and came out unscathed. What the greeting cards and Christmas carols didn't mention was the sap clinging to your fingers like some alien lifeform sucking the happy from your soul. And if the sap failed, the pine needles that embed into your skin pierced whatever remaining dignity you had left, until you Grinched-out on some poor unsuspecting seventy-year-old lady just wanting to get a poinsettia plant for church.

I felt really bad about that and ended up buying her five more. I also loaded them into her car.

Then again, most people didn't wait until Christmas Eve to buy their tree. I normally didn't either, as I expected to be on my honeymoon in Barbados with Grayson right about then. But after I walked in on him stuffing his neighbor's turkey—metaphorically speaking—on Thanksgiving Day, I hadn't been in the Christmas spirit much. Everything in my life slid in a downward spiral, including my favorite time of year.

I decided to sulk my way through the holidays. In the midst of drowning my sorrows in two cartons of eggnog that morning, I succumbed to the ridiculous urge to buy a live tree. For the last couple of years, I'd put up a gorgeous prelit one that played Christmas songs as it rotated. Grayson bought it for me and tied a ring to one of the branches when he proposed. But thanks to my drunken eggnog rage, that one was now smoldering in a snowbank on my front lawn. So I figured, why not get a real tree?

Fighting between last-minute shoppers and Scrooge-like employees regretting their decision to work retail, I took a breather and stood near the exit of the lot. As I stared at the overwhelming tree choices, the soft whimper of a crying child interrupted my pity party. I found a boy, probably no more than ten, standing at the cashier trying to buy a wreath. Tears clung to his little frozen cheeks as he walked away, bowing his head.

"What's the matter?" I asked the cashier and pointed to the child.

"He didn't have enough money." She shrugged and picked up her phone.

I walked over to her. "How much was he short?"

She huffed as she tore her attention from the phone, glowering at me like I'd asked her to donate a kidney. "About thirty cents."

Burying my annoyance, I shook my head as I laid down my credit card and bought the damn wreath. Poor kid. I raced after him, slipping and sliding over the snow-covered ground.

"Here you go," I said between gasps of breath as I caught up to him, fighting to keep upright.

He turned around, and tears poured out of his wide eyes. Why was he crying even more? I hadn't scared him with "stranger danger," had I? I probably should have rethought my "Flight of the Bumblebee" approach.

I handed him the wreath, wheezing like I'd just gotten chased by zombies, which I was sure didn't help the fright factor. I decided to throw getting back into shape onto my list of New Year's Resolutions I wouldn't keep. "I'm sorry, I didn't mean to scare you. I just know you were short a little money, so Merry Christmas."

"Thank you," he whispered. "Momma always told me there were angels. I never thought I'd get to meet one."

A twinge of warmth cracked my cold heart. "Oh, sweetie, I'm no angel. But sometimes people can do nice things too."

"She's gonna love it. I always save my allowance and buy a wreath for her grave at Christmas. Gran hasn't been able to pay me as much for my chores like she used to. Thank you." He wrapped the arm not holding the wreath around my waist, gave it a squeeze, and ran off toward an elderly lady standing in the parking lot. She gave me a nod and a smile as the boy held up the wreath with pride.

I fought my own onslaught of tears as his words hit me, packing a punch to my already emotional state as the sudden ache to talk to my dad overwhelmed me. No matter what problem I had going on in my life, Pops somehow made it better, and I knew I'd get through it. But I didn't have that luxury anymore. He died six months ago, carving a giant hole in my heart that had only widened with Grayson cheating on me.

At least my mom was still alive—if only we were speaking. She had warned me about Grayson the minute we started dating. In my infinite wisdom and invincible twenty-nine-year-old mind-set, I ignored her. It snowballed into a source of contention between us. When we announced our engagement, she even refused to come to the wedding, and I shut her out of my life.

I had yet to tell her I called off the wedding, mainly because I'd be riddled with I-told-you-sos, and I needed that right now like a hole in the head.

Swiping my tearstained face, I made my way over to the myriad of trees and tried to make a quick decision. I had to get out of there fast. I couldn't "people" anymore today. I would either end up a blubbering mess under the blow-up lawn ornaments or in jail from high-fiving the heartless cashier right in the face who couldn't fork over thirty cents to help a kid buy a Christmas wreath.

In my unstable mindset, I made the poor choice to go for the nine-foot Douglas fir. As I yanked the leaning tree from the fence, little did I know I held a death trap in the palm of my sticky hand. The laws of physics mocked my existence as the tree toppled over, taking my five-foot, six-inch frame with it.

It's completely true how your life flashed before your eyes in those last seconds of mortality. Mine happened to be stuck on repeat of Grayson stuffing Suzie as I cursed his name in all six languages I spoke. If he hadn't cheated on me, I'd be in Barbados as Mrs. Jilani, not splattered on the floor of Trees-R-Us as the jilted Eden Credere.

Instead of hitting the cold, snow-covered ground, something strong cradled the back of my head, radiating a warmth that caressed my skin and soothed what should have been my shattered bones. I would have sworn there were no customers around me as I hid my ever-blackening soul in the back forty of the tree lot. No one could have caught me that fast. Then again, one hundred pounds of Douglas fir swallowed my face, so my vantage point skewed a bit.

"Thank you, Lord," I whispered on the breath that whooshed out of my lungs.

A melodic yet husky chuckle vibrated around me, filling me with the same warmth that held my head in some bubble of safety. Maybe I did hit the ground, and the warmth was a pool of my own blood. It wasn't out of the realm of possibilities with as much rum and eggnog as I'd consumed earlier.

"Believe me, I am *not* the Lord." A voice surrounded me, and heat tingled straight to my toes, as if his tone resonated just for my ears.

"Oh good, because if you were, I'd be really upset that I'm meeting him in yoga pants and no makeup." Sometimes the things that came out of my mouth missed the sanity filter in my brain.

Another chuckle vibrated against me before it halted, followed by a sharp intake of air. "You heard that?"

With pine needles burrowing into my closed eyelids, I couldn't be sure I was actually talking to another person and not just myself. "Heard what?"

"What I said. I didn't mean for you to hear it." Worry strained his words as he softened his voice.

"You didn't exactly whisper it, and seeing as how you caught me like a ninja, you had to be nearby. Which reminds me, I still have a tree on my face. I don't suppose you'd help get it off me? I'll buy you a coffee or a beer or something."

"I'm so sorry. Of course. I...I was caught off guard. Let me help you up," he stammered.

"Well, I suppose anyone would be caught off guard while having to dive for some stranger being eaten by a tree. Unless you're like a lumberjack and see that kind of thing all the time." The spiked eggnog I'd had for breakfast now seemed like a really bad idea as the stupid tumbled out of my mouth in droves.

His harmonious chuckle returned and enveloped me again, like tiny ripples of pleasure bouncing off my body. I loved this man's laugh, and I hadn't even seen his face. In the span of thirty seconds, I'd developed some freaky fetish where all I wanted to do was have him laugh near me so I could swaddle in the warmth and happiness of his voice.

Shit, what the hell did I put in that eggnog? Was it expired?

"Hold still," the mystery man said.

He eased me to the ground. Cold snow soaked the back of my head, my hair sucking it up like a slushy. I cursed the blasted New Jersey winters in three ancient tongues. I'd probably pay for that later, but as an archaeologist, I rarely got to use all the dead languages I studied. Now seemed like a good time.

The tree whisked away from my face, and I blinked my eyes open. The gasp that followed sucked in so much cold air, an erratic series of hiccups erupted. Another sign I was more than likely drunk—Thor hovered over me, or at least he could have passed for his twin brother. Thick blond locks of hair danced across his broad shoulders in the light breeze, framing his marble-smooth, chiseled face. The bluest eyes I'd ever seen sparkled like an ocean, and if I stared into them long enough, I was sure they'd take me to a whole other world. Those eyes looked hauntingly familiar. Where had I seen them before?

"You've got quite the naughty mouth, Eden," he said, warming me with his voice and a smile that probably dropped a lot of panties. He slid his arms under my back and lifted me from the ground as if I weighed nothing. Boy, would he have a backache in the morning.

"How do you know my name? Have we met before?" I blinked again, reassuring myself I hadn't passed out and that I was indeed alive, awake, and in Thor's arms.

"Um, your driver's license was on the ground. Must have fallen out when the tree landed on you." He glanced away from my inquiring stare.

Hmm, plausible, since I had stuffed my debit card and license in my pocket instead of carrying a purse today. I only planned on getting a tree and going right back home. I dared not go anywhere else on Christmas Eve with all the crazies on the road.

I slipped my hand into my pocket and found both cards there. Did he put it back? Surely I would have felt it. But it had been a while since I'd had a man's hand in my pants. Grayson and I stopped having sex about six months before the marriage that never happened. He wanted the wedding night to be special. Yeah, so special because he was basting the neighbor.

Wait, he said I had a naughty mouth, meaning this dude knew I cursed in a dead language. Or maybe he assumed it was cursing, since Aramaic and ancient Greek sounded a lot like my angry Italian mother.

But I was dying to find out. "So, what, you speak Aramaic?"

"I do, among many other languages." He smiled again, and my insides melted with the heat of a thousand suns. An educated man —those were hard to come by. The last three guys before Grayson were bartenders. Grayson owned a bar. I sensed a theme.

"What did I say, then?" I forced the words over my lips before all my thoughts turned to mush at the warmth coursing through my body.

"I can't repeat it. I don't curse."

"Aren't you just an angel?"

He choked on a cough as he eased me from his arms until my feet touched solid ground. "Are you injured?"

"Just my pride," I said, reaching for the tree that I would enjoy inflicting revenge upon come Boxing day. But the minute I clenched my hand around the center, a stabbing pain radiated up my arm and a yelp burst from my lips.

"What's wrong?" my knight in jeans and flannel asked.

Bark scraped my fingers as I jumped back, and the tree slammed against the fence. With a wince, I cradled my arm like a baby. "I think I broke my arm or something."

In a moment of sheer brilliance, I gave the trunk a hearty kick with my furry boot. It helped ease the stabbing in my arm, but only because a new pain jolted through my toes. I couldn't win today. I blamed the eggnog.

"Let me take a look at it," Thor said, sliding his fingers up the sleeve of my jacket. "We should probably get you to a hospital for an x-ray to make sure it's not broken."

"I'll be fine. I just want to go home. Stupid tree. Stupid Christmas. Stupid Grayson. I'm a walking catastrophe." Tears stung my eyes as they leaked over my cheeks, probably all the rum oozing out of me. I wasn't normally a drinker, despite my dating history, but the eggnog-rum smoothie numbed the ache in my heart, so I hadn't wanted to stop.

"We'll take that one and a tree stand," Thor said to the cashier as he pointed to the tree of horror and opened his wallet.

I limped over to him, channeling Quasimodo. "What're you doing?"

"Getting your tree so we can take you to the hospital and then home." After tossing the checkout lady a toothpaste-commercial smile, he turned to me and held out his hand. "Where're your keys? I'll bring the car around for you."

I hitched a shoulder and narrowed my eyes. "I'm not giving some strange guy the keys to my car! Are you insane? 'Tis the season to get carjacked, buddy."

He shook his head with a laugh. "Would someone who wanted to rip you off pay for your tree and a stand?"

"Probably not, but hey, criminals are getting smarter these days. Spend fifty on a tree and get a forty-thousand-dollar car in return." I huffed.

"Your car is *not* worth forty-thousand dollars. In the condition it's in, six max, if you had gotten the sunroof."

"Who the hell are you, some kind of stalker?" Without thinking, I swatted at his shoulder with my bad arm and instantly regretted it as another wave of pain did its best to render me unconscious with each intensifying throb.

"I saw you pull into the parking lot in a 2005 Toyota Matrix that needs new tires." He raised his hands in defense before reaching for my arm, running his warm fingers along my skin. Whatever mojo he had going on soothed my inner beast, and all I wanted was for him to never stop touching me.

I had to stop thinking about him like that, or I'd be going home with more than a tree tonight. And I needed to get involved with another guy as much as I needed a Brazilian wax from Sweeney Todd. Note to self: too much eggnog caused raging hormones. I realized then just how much I had been missing in my relationship with Grayson if a simple touch from a stranger lit me on fire. Yet oddly enough, this stranger didn't seem like a stranger. He might not have been familiar to my eyes, but something in my heart felt like he was.

"You're really frustrating, you know that?" With a pout, I handed over my keys to some strange hippie-lumberjack that oozed sex from every pore. He probably just rubbed CBD oil along my arm to calm me down, but at that point, I didn't care anymore. I only wanted to be back in my house, drowning myself with more eggnog and rum to erase the giant hole in my heart, swallowing my life.

He jingled the keys. "I'll be right back."

I needed a better excuse to tell my insurance company when he didn't come back with my car than an eggnog lust-fog caused me to lose prudence. "I don't even know your name, and I just handed over my car keys. Who does that?"

"It's Theliel." A dimple pitted his cheek as he smirked.

With such heavenly eyes and perfect skin, I could probably get pregnant from looking at him. He must moisturize. A mixture of jealousy and desire swirled together inside me as I stared at his handsome face, unable to look away. Somehow, just gazing at him calmed me. His entire essence felt like an old familiar sweatshirt you loved wearing for comfort and warmth, or a favorite blanket as a child. He was walking serenity. How could one man be so friendly and comforting while wafting sexiness and throwing off pheromones like an underwear model? He was a walking contradiction.

I rolled his name over my tongue, but it jumbled into a rum ball. "The...Thelio...Theo. I'm just going with Theo."

He tossed his head back with a laugh. "I'm fine with Theo. Try not to injure yourself anymore while I'm gone."

My inner defiant toddler stuck her tongue out as he dashed away, and I leaned against the chain link fence. What kind of name was Theliel anyway? He did look like Thor, so maybe he was a Norwegian Viking.

I lost myself watching his thighs flex with each step, threatening to bust the seams of his jeans. A white cotton T-shirt hugged every ripple of his chest. The man didn't have a six-pack, he had an entire case of muscles. His red-and-white flannel barely fit over his massive arms. How was he not even cold? Of course, he did put off enough heat to warm my house, or at least my bedroom. Maybe he was some descendant of a Roman god, or Athena and a Yeti had a love child—he did have a lot of hair. He probably even looked magnificent in a man bun.

My heart sped every long minute that passed. Sure, there were a lot of cars in the parking lot, but he was in good shape. How long did it take to drive around? I chewed a nail in my worry but jerked back when I hit a spot of sap and licked the roof of my mouth like a dog with peanut butter. Blech. Would this day never end?

2

THEO

I GRIPPED EDEN'S STEERING WHEEL AND MULLED OVER WHAT JUST happened. I needed to be more careful with her. Several times I almost tipped her off, getting swept up in my interaction with her. I shouldn't have done it. I knew that, and the repercussions for it would be stiff.

But she caught me off guard, lost in thought, and in a split second I was there, catching her, saving her. I didn't even know it myself until she heard me answer her. Corporealizing was frowned upon, though not wholly banned, per se. Sometimes, it was necessary.

Warmth tingled the hair on my neck, and I glanced at the rearview mirror to the back seat. "I see you, you know."

"What did you do?" Kasbiel asked.

"What do you mean?" I furrowed my brow.

My age-old friend and mentor sat back and folded his arms. "Does she know?"

I shook my head. "I don't think so. I'm being smart. This isn't my first rodeo."

"Yeah, but if you're not careful, it could be your last. That was completely unnecessary, Theliel." Judgment colored his normally topaz eyes a shade darker.

He was one to talk. He'd appeared to many of his charges before, so the fact that he schooled me on it now irritated me.

Oh, that feeling was new—irritation. The tingle in my blood, a revving of adrenaline, and the desire to counter his scolding brewed inside me. But I forced it down and focused on the need to get to Eden instead of proving my actions right in his eyes.

"It was my call. Don't you have somewhere else to be? I have to get her to the hospital. She's injured." It was far harder than I imagined to keep the irritation out of my tone. I forced the words out evenly and soft, but with urgency.

"I'm just looking out for you, making sure you think things through before you make any rash decisions. They're tempting, I get it. I've been there. But you're here for a purpose, and it's not your own. Remember that."

He was right. I didn't like it, but he *was*. Kasbiel had always been the voice of reason.

I nodded. "Understood."

"One choice changes everything. All I'm saying is think it through." Kasbiel's straight-lined lips curved into a smile. "And what's with the lumberjack look?"

I rolled my eyes. "It's not like I had an hour to decide wardrobe when it happened. I had less than a second to come up with something and get to her in time. I don't think she minds."

Kasbiel tilted his head. "That's what worries me."

I glanced back at the mirror, but he vanished. Putting the car I gear, I swung around to pick Eden up.

A red knit hat covered the top of her head. Her long, dark-brown hair rode the crisp breeze, dancing in waves around her heart-shaped face. The color of it reminded me of the espresso she liked to drink. I loved her smile the most, and her laugh. I missed her laugh. She hadn't done so in a long time. So much sadness lived in her deep-brown eyes now, and a harsh, cynical temperament had taken up residence in her soul. I worried that if she continued letting the darkness poison her, she might never let the light back in again.

Maybe that's what made me do it. I could have easily kept her safe from afar. But maybe I wanted to save more than just her body from harm.

I hopped out of the car and assisted in tying the tree to the roof. The ever-independent Eden hobbled to the front seat and got herself inside before I could help her. She was an enigma. She desperately longed to have someone take care of her, to put her first. But when someone tried, she pushed them away, wanting to do it on her own. Maybe it was not wanting to inconvenience others. But I suspected it was more fear of letting her guard down and trusting.

"How's your arm?" I asked as I slid into the driver's seat.

"It's okay. My wrist aches though." She stared out the window as we pulled out of the lot. "I don't think I need a hospital. One more bill to have to pay. I'll take a couple of aspirin when I get home and call it a day."

"I'd rather you get checked out and make sure you didn't break something. If it's money you're worried about, I'll take care of it." I glanced her way, but she never looked back at me.

Her grant had been denied for her latest archaeological excavation. It was her dream dig in Egypt, so she funded it with her own money, and some of Grayson's friends, who'd invested in his bar, invested in her dig. When the wedding got called off, so did her cash supply. The dig folded, as well as any paycheck from museums on standby waiting to house what she uncovered. If she didn't find a new grant soon, she would be forced back into teaching history rather than discovering it. Another wound on an already sliced-open heart.

Of course, she was oblivious to the fact I knew all of it. It killed her to have to ask for help. So she bore the brunt of it in her heart, refusing for the world to witness her weakness.

"You already paid for my tree. You don't need to be paying my bills." She finally looked at me. "Who are you, anyway?"

"A friend." The lamest reply in the handbook, but I got caught in her gaze and it captivated my thoughts.

"Uh-huh. Whose friend? Grayson's? Seriously, I want you out of my car, right now." She reached for the handle, but I clutched her good arm and pulled her back.

"No. I'm not friends with that poor excuse for a human being."

"But you know him? Who put you up to this? Was it Margret? Barbara? Jessie?" After she listed off every would-have-been bridesmaid, she leaned back in a huff. "I bet it was Ama—"

She stopped short, and pain streaked through her eyes filling up with tears. She was about to say Amanda, her best friend since kindergarten. Amanda succumbed to depression while Eden was in Egypt. Every single day, Eden blamed herself for not being there for her when she needed her most. What she didn't know was that she had saved Amanda's life so many times before without ever realizing it. She just wasn't meant to this time.

"No one put me up to it. Well, that's not technically true. But I'm here to help, trust me."

"Trust you? I don't even know you."

That was the hardest part of the job, right there. She didn't know me, but I knew her inside out. "Well, get to know me. We'll probably be in the ER for a couple of hours." I pulled into the drop-off lane of St. Mary's Hospital. "I'll park the car and meet you inside."

She blew out a terse huff as she opened her door. "Fine. Just don't run off with my car."

"Really?" I shook my head, laughing it off. How much more did I have to prove to her I wasn't there to steal the stupid car? Maybe the rum was wearing off and she needed some caffeine. She really needed to lay off the eggnog.

After parking the car, I made sure no one was in view before conjuring a couple of peppermint mochas and then walked into the waiting room. Huddled in a corner, Eden sat with her arms wrapped around a middle-aged woman. I watched her console this stranger with warmth and tenderness as if she'd known her all her life. Matted salt-and-peppered hair clung to the woman's face from her tears, and Eden brushed it back before gently rocking her through each convulsing sob.

I walked a little closer but gave them space.

"I've been there, sweetie. I lost my dad six months ago and my best friend a month later. It was one of the hardest times I ever had to go through in my life," Eden said, rubbing a hand along the woman's back. "So you cry and let it out. One of the mistakes I made was not allowing myself to grieve, thinking I had to be strong for everyone else. You're allowed to be sad. You're allowed to cry." Eden handed her a tissue.

"Thank you," the woman choked out, dabbing at her eyes with it.

Eden cupped the woman's hands in her own and looked into her eyes. "The one thing you do have to remember is you still need to live. But don't let anyone tell *you* when it's time to move on or tell you it's too soon. Not everyone grieves or heals the same. Okay?"

The woman nodded. "Thank you so much. I don't even know your name. You're like an angel, just showing up when I needed someone."

A worried smile ghosted Eden's lips. "The name's Eden. Sometimes you don't need an angel. You just need a friend."

A nurse popped her head between the swinging doors of the waiting room. "Mrs. Vargas, we're ready to release the body to you now."

The woman swallowed hard, and Eden gave her hand a tight squeeze. "You need me to come with you?"

Mrs. Vargas shook her head. "My son is on his way. He should be here any minute. But thank you. Really, thank you, Eden. Angel or not, you're just what I needed."

Eden let out a soft sigh as she watched the woman disappear

behind the double doors with the nurse. She glanced over at me almost in shock, like she didn't expect me to actually come back. She tucked a leg under her as she adjusted herself in the chair.

"Did you know her?" I asked.

"No. She was sitting in the corner, crying by herself. I knew that sob. I've lived it. Someone close to her had passed. I felt compelled to sit with her and try to comfort her since she was alone. Turns out her husband had been in a bad car accident this morning and didn't make it."

"That was very kind of you," I said, handing her one of the mochas.

"I wish I could have done more. No one should have to go through that alone, especially on Christmas Eve." She blinked and took the drink. "What's this?"

Your favorite. But I couldn't say that, or she'd think I was a stalker again.

"Peppermint mocha. I figured 'tis the season, right?"

"Thanks, I love peppermint." She took a sip as a smile lit her face. There it was. That's where she lived, in that warm smile that radiated love across her beautiful face.

I returned the smile and took a seat next to her. "This is much better than rum and eggnog."

"Says you. I was perfectly happy with my eggnog-rum smoothie this morning." She turned and stared me down. "Wait a minute, how did you know I had eggnog?"

"You may have mentioned it a time or two at the tree lot." Glancing away, I took a sip of coffee and hoped the incident blurred a bit by now, making the details fuzzy. I couldn't very well tell her I was there, in her kitchen, and watched her down it, fraught with worry. Or that I was the one who knocked the decanter off the counter to stop her from having another one, not her.

"I'm a hot mess, aren't I? First, I nearly die, then I almost lose my license and credit card, and now I don't even remember rambling on about my breakfast. What other poor life choices have

I disclosed to you in the last hour?" She sighed and took a long drink of the coffee.

"Whatever else you mentioned will not be told to another soul. I promise." I gave her the Scout's honor. She took the bait, giving me a clear way to explain myself should I slip up again.

"At this point, I don't even want to know. I think the world would have been far better off had you just let me fall. Lord knows, I could have saved you a heap of trouble and inconvenience."

I leaned forward, resting my elbows on my knees to get closer to her. "What the Lord knows is that life is a gift, but no one said it would be easy. All our trials and tribulations shape us into who we're meant to become."

She narrowed her stare. "Oh no, you're not one of those religious cult people, are you?"

I shook my head with a chuckle. "Just speaking from the heart."

"I no longer have one. I'm beginning to think that love is only a dirty trick played on us to achieve continuation of the species. I'm pretty sure I'm on to something. I've become a self-loathing, man-hating, cynical person. Really, you should run while you can. At this point, I'll let you keep the car to get away faster. I'll only bring you down and probably ten of your cousins. Everything I touch lately just goes to crap. I lost my dad, my best friend, and my fiancé. I also lost my work grant, which means I'm also about to lose my house. Add in that my mom and I are no longer speaking...and I have no clue why I'm even telling you this." She dipped her head and stared at the top of her coffee cup, running the tip of her chipped red nail around the plastic cap.

"Probably because you needed to tell it to *someone*. I told you, I'm a friend. And didn't you just tell that woman that sometimes you need one?"

A single teardrop plunked against the top of her cup, and she sniffed, raising her head to rest it against the wall behind her as she closed her eyes.

Something hit my heart, a twinge, a spark, a prick of sadness. I wished I could take it all away, but I knew that wouldn't help her. She had a lesson to learn from this, and I had to lead her there. That was my part.

I'd experienced empathy for charges in the past. Though, I'd never felt the need or desire to take away all their pain before. I knew there was a reason for everyone to go through their trials, having to experience heartache or difficulties, and if they'd only see what lay on the other side—that what they had to go through was the way they could get there—they'd better understand and cope. But as they said, hindsight was twenty-twenty. If they knew, they wouldn't learn. So I'd never really been invested in the moments before the discovery because it was the journey they learned the most from.

"My dad died in July. Then my best friend took her own life a month later." The words wobbled out of her mouth between sniffs. "My mom got pissed at me when I got engaged. She didn't care for my fiancé, refusing to even come to the wedding, and stopped talking to me completely when I didn't want to move back home after Pops died." A laugh escaped between sniffles. "Guess I don't have to worry about that now because I caught my fiancé cheating on me at Thanksgiving."

Grief consumed people. If she would only realize her mother still loved her—she just had to take a step to get there. Two stubborn, defensive people couldn't have a discussion if neither was willing to listen to the other. Frustration turned into ugly words. Ugly words turned into hurt. Hurt turned into defensiveness, neither one willing to reopen themselves up to possible new wounds.

"I've pretty much alienated the rest of my friends. They all warned me about Grayson, but I didn't listen. I trusted him over them. Isn't that what you're supposed to do with a life partner? Trust?" Sadness consumed her eyes, and the weight of the pain in her heart about did me in.

I tried to find words that would comfort her or advise her.

"That's the way it's supposed to work, yes. But I'm sure if you talked to them—"

"Eden Credere?" a nurse yelled out.

"Here," Eden replied and jumped up, but the foot she'd been sitting on wedged beneath the armrest of the chair, and she nearly toppled to the floor.

I clamped an arm around her waist to catch her. Peppermint mocha launched into the air and painted my white T-shirt a muddy brown as it came back down.

"Betty, call for the janitor," the nurse bellowed to the lady at the reception desk.

"I'm so, so sorry, Theo. You're drenched!" She pressed her hand to my chest, not caring that it was covered in latte.

The moment she touched me, the air around me thinned and a flicker of lightning jolted my heart. Breath caught in my lungs and choked me. Breath—something so unique and powerful humans took it for granted. Something I'd never experienced before. Never in all the times I'd gone corporeal had something like that happened. My legs froze, and I braced myself with my free hand against the wall. Heat thrummed in my veins, sending a wave of dizziness through my head.

What did she do to me?

As the moment passed, my lungs unseized and I gasped, clutching at the spot where her warm fingertips brushed my heart.

"Are you okay, sir?" the nurse asked, stepping closer.

I managed a nod and forced myself to stand. "Yeah, just shock from the hot coffee, I imagine."

"Did I burn you?" Eden gripped the bottom of my shirt and lifted it, inspecting my chest. Soft fingertips slid across my skin, and a shudder ricocheted through my body, rattling straight to my bones.

Words stuck in the back of my throat. I'd spoken in every language ever known to man, and a few that weren't, yet all I could do was shake my head as a fog filled my mind.

"It's a little red. Maybe you should have the doctor look at it. Why don't you come with me into the room?" Eden grabbed my hand and pulled me along after her.

Everything clouded for me. I had a purpose. I had something to tell her, show her. She needed to learn that she had so much ahead of her, so much meaning to her life, despite her feeling like everything had derailed. There was a plan for Eden she didn't see coming, and couldn't until she'd been built up through the difficult times.

I had one job to do—get her back on track and breathe life into her dying soul.

I'd known her all her life. I witnessed her birth, her first tooth, her first steps, her first day of school, and her first boyfriend. Though she'd never known it, I held her hand as she rode her bike for the first time and wrapped my arms around her when she lost her father and best friend. I knew all her weaknesses and all her worries. But I also knew all her strengths and potential.

No one knew her better than I did, because I was her guardian angel.

I was supposed to be changing her, but now I wondered if she weren't changing me instead.

3

EDEN

I BLEW IT. TOTALLY AND COMPLETELY BLEW IT. BECAUSE WHY NOT toss your hot coffee on a gorgeous guy who saved your life, drove you to a hospital, and bought you said coffee, and then render him mute after scalding him with it?

"Lord, just take me now, please," I whispered as I climbed onto the hospital bed.

"What? No!" Theo dashed to my side. "Why would you say that? I mean, not that He would, you know. I'm sure He's got his own plan for things, in His own time." He cleared his throat and paced in front of me, running a hand through the top of his hair.

Great, now he thinks I'm suicidal.

Someone needed to blow dart me and knock me out. But if I were being honest with myself, I didn't really want to be alone on Christmas. I found myself enjoying his company, probably way more than I should, and because fate had other plans, any possibility I'd have to spend Christmas with him spilled out with my peppermint latte.

"Well, at least you're talking to me again." I popped a smile and calculated dry-cleaning charges in my mind.

He spun around and shook his head, like I ripped him from

some profound meditative musing. "Huh? I'm sorry. I'm just feeling a little out of sorts." He clamped a hand across his chest. "My heart's racing." Theo leaned against the wall and tilted his head back. "It's making my head spin a little."

His brows arched and concern filled his eyes, like he was trying to process what he'd said. He ran his hand along his chest again, clutching it over his heart, like he counted each beat, or maybe I gave him a third-degree coffee burn.

"Oh, that's probably the caffeine." That explained his anxiety— the dude couldn't hold his coffee.

He blinked like he didn't quite understand but nodded. "Yeah, that's probably it." He nodded again. "That would explain a lot. Guess I didn't realize it. Maybe they put an extra shot in mine."

The room curtain swished open, and I melted into the bed as the devil in a white lab coat walked in. "It's a vampire," I whispered to Theo.

"What?" He whipped his head up and stared at the phlebotomist. "Oh, got it. Blood work." A smile finally lifted his lips.

My heart fluttered like a butterfly on crack at the sight of it. It reminded me of someone. But for the life of me, I couldn't think of who.

I really liked his smile, and worry drown my heart that I'd permanently erased it with the Great Christmas Eve Coffee Debacle. But now that it was back, his smile melted me inside out with an almost magic glow to him, so pure and sincere. He oozed a serene happiness I wanted to cling to.

Theo leaned into me, sliding his hand under mine, and a fizz of warmth sparked through me, familiar and calming. He cupped the top of my hand with his other as the needle broke my skin. I inhaled with a hiss and looked the other way, burying my head against his latte-soaked shirt. The scent of peppermint and coffee inundated me, but I didn't care. I hated needles and blood. I never could watch anyone get their blood drawn, let alone my own get sucked out of my body and into a tube. But Theo stood at the ready, as if he anticipated the need to shelter me from it.

"It's over," he whispered and pressed his finger under my chin, directing my head up. "The vamp has left the room."

"Thanks. It's almost like you knew I needed to hold your hand. That was really nice of you." I bit my lip, and my heart slid to my stomach.

"Of course I knew." He smiled for an instant, but it slipped behind the worry in his eyes. "I mean, I know a lot of people don't like their blood drawn. I kind of figured it's already been a rough morning, and you might need a little comfort." He cleared his throat, stepped away from me, and paced again.

The curtain whisked open one more time, and a guy no older than me approached my bed. At first I thought he must be an intern, until I read his name badge, Dr. Rayce Carr, and I giggled. "You must have had a rough childhood."

"You've got a nice laugh, Ms. Credere. I take it you checked me out." He quirked a brow.

"I admit, I didn't make it past the name badge, Dr. Carr," I replied. "But now that you mention it, let's have a look at you. Can you do a spin for me, so I can assess what we have here?"

Rayce tossed his head back and laughed. "That's a new one, and I haven't even given you morphine yet." His laugh echoed through the ER, thin and tinny. Nothing like Theo's warm, rich one that wrapped itself around me like a tender caress. "As much as I'd be happy to have you look at me, my job is to look at you right now. Let's see what we've got." He slipped my hand in his and rotated my arm side to side. "You probably just sprained it. I can order you an x-ray if you really want one, but trust me, it doesn't appear to be broken or fractured."

I side-eyed Theo, who never took his gaze off the doctor as he folded his arms.

The doctor mouthed the words, *is he your boyfriend,* and tipped his pen toward Theo.

I glanced at Theo and back at the doc with a shake of my head.

A sly smile curved over the doctor's lips. "I'm going to prescribe you some pain pills for tonight and tomorrow. After that, switch to acetaminophen or ibuprofen for pain as needed." He leaned in and handed me two prescriptions, one for the pills and one with his phone number circled on it. "You need anything, you give me a call." Tossing me a wink, he sauntered out of the room.

Theo thrust his hands to his hips, and his lips tugged to one side of his mouth as he stared at the curtain still rippling from the doctor's exodus. "What kind of physician flirts with his patient during an examination? If you could even call what he did an exam. He just wanted to give you his number." His attention focused back on me. "You should have demanded an x-ray."

I rolled my eyes. "He was totally not flirting with me. Dr. Carr was just putting me at ease and being friendly."

Wasn't he? Did I miss a flirt? Yeah, he gave me his number, but it was probably to his after-hours answering service, if I had some kind of wacky reaction to the drugs he prescribed. Surely it wasn't his actual cell phone number. I mean, I'd been out of the game for a while. Grayson never flirted. He walked right up and pretty much took what he wanted. I guess I fell for the whole alpha male charade, which turned into alpha-hole.

"He absolutely was flirting with you. You're an intelligent, fun, beautiful human being," Theo said, walking back to the side of my bed.

I blinked as I processed the words coming out of his mouth. Did he just call me beautiful? And how would he even know if I was intelligent or fun? We'd known each other for all of maybe two hours. I stared at Theo's face, still unnerved by Dr. Carr.

"Seriously, I have no makeup on, I'm in torn yoga pants, and I have pine needle imprints all over my face. There is no way he was flirting with this." I fanned my good arm up and down my body for emphasis. "And he's right. He was able to bend my arm and wrist. While there's definitely pain, it's probably not broken. I don't see the big deal. You're the one that wants an x-ray. I just wanted to go home, remember?" I arched a brow. "Are you jealous?"

His eyes bloomed into wide circles of shock. "What? That's not even in my genetic makeup! Don't be ridiculous."

Well, that was stupid. Of course he wasn't jealous. We didn't really know each other. The more I thought about it, the more embarrassment riddled my soul that I thought Theo was upset at the phone number. He seemed far more concerned for my wrist than anything else. Maybe he didn't want me to sue him for rescuing me, thinking my injury was caused when he saved me from hitting the ground. Purely a precautionary tactic.

So what, then, had Theo's undies in a bunch? Which brought to mind the thought, did he even wear undies? Because those jeans left little room for anything besides my imagination. He had to go commando, unless he did have on tighty-whities and that was the source of his irritation.

In the scheme of things, the fact I just had a doctor give me his digits and a hotter-than-Hades knight-in-glaring-flannel at my side, things could be worse. They *were* a lot worse about two hours ago when I set out on my little adventure this morning.

Of course, in reality, I could be in a coma somewhere after I hit my head in the tree lot and this whole thing was nothing but a fantasy in my mind. But surely if this were a fantasy, there'd be a lot less flannel involved, or clothing in general.

Theo's lips opened, as if he were about to say something, but a nurse slipped in through the curtain carrying a tray and paper work, stopping him short.

"Okay, Ms. Credere, we've got your release paper work and your pain pill. Here's one to take home for tomorrow and a script for some prescription-strength ibuprofen for the remainder of the week. Follow up with your regular physician next week."

I popped the pill and signed the release with my left hand, which resembled more of the kindergarten version of my hand-writing than normal.

"Are you responsible for her?" the nurse asked Theo.

He stepped up. "Yes."

"Don't let her drive or operate machinery for the next two days." The nurse trained her gaze over the length of him, and the urge to yank her hair and scratch her eyeballs overtook me. "She's a lucky girl."

"I won't even let her go near the blender." He raised a hand, and that panty-dropping smile curved over his lips. Was he flirting with her?

"Hey, right here, folks," I said, slapping my good hand on the bed to distract them.

Nurse Vixen turned on her heel and gave Theo a wink as she sauntered out of the room, swaying her hips like a hippo. I rolled my eyes so hard my head hurt.

"Yeah, now who's flirting," I murmured and swung my legs over the side of the bed to sit up.

"That wasn't flirting," he countered and eased an arm around my waist as I slid off the bed, planting my feet on the floor.

"Oh no? She just did a mating dance with her hips all the way out of the room."

He canted his head. "Is that a hint of jealousy in your voice, Eden?"

"No." I pursed my lips, narrowing my eyes. Something fluttered in my heart at the thought. Was he trying to get back at me for the doctor? I tilted my head to match his own. "Why, do you want it to be?"

Silence answered me as he tightened his arm around me and walked me out of the room. "Let's get you home before the pain pill kicks in."

⚜

Theo

I had no response to her question because every answer in my head was a lie. I offered only silence as I mulled over the word floating in my mind—jealousy. Angels didn't get jealous. If we had emotions, it was some form of love and concern. We had nothing to be jealous of, as we had the perfect life, or semblance of life in the aspect human beings thought of it. No war, no famine, no sickness or injury. Only happiness, love, and purity. We existed, but for a different purpose. We were created beings, just not human ones.

I didn't think that going corporeal would have such an effect. I'd done it to hundreds of charges, since the dawn of time. But as I thought back on it, it was always for only an instant. A simple wave or a smile to someone who felt invisible, letting them know they were seen in a world where loneliness suffocated them. A word or two spoken in a grocery store or in a hallway, when kindness mattered to soften their hardened heart. A fraction of time carved out to give a helping hand that would change their outlook and keep them going. Strangers helping strangers, more often than not, weren't strangers at all.

Yet today I made a choice, one I hadn't even realized I did, when I shifted and showed myself to Eden. I stayed corporeal far longer than any time before in thousands of years. Perhaps in doing so, some aspect of humanity crept in and affected me.

I had stared at the doctor as the essence of his attraction to Eden drifted off his aura in waves. But he didn't know her. He didn't care about her. He only desired to drown himself in the euphoria that his bodily pheromones produced at the sight of her. The lust in the doctor's eyes spoke volumes about what he wanted from her, and it sank like a rock in my gut. I wouldn't call that jealousy, but concern.

What she needed was someone who knew her and would fill her body, mind, and soul. Someone who would guide her, love her, be a partner with her in life. Not another person who would use her and discard her.

I tightened my hold along her waist as I guided her to the car. I curled my fingers into the softness of her body, and an odd tingle coursed through me. I liked how she fit the curvature of my arm and nestled against me. It made sense, now, why people craved each other's touch in the human world. The tenderness of the moment between two people so close filled my soul with warmth and happiness. Something angels didn't get to experience on that kind of level.

"You're avoiding my question," Eden said as I drove out of the hospital parking lot.

"I'm concerned. That's all." I forced the words out of my mouth and watched from the corner of my eye as her smirk fell to sadness.

Did she want me to be jealous? A twinge hit my heart, and a foreign heat flooded my body all the way to my cheeks. Thoughts inundated my mind about what that could mean.

"I don't understand why. I don't know you. You don't know me. What concern is it of yours what happens to me?" She stared out the window.

Part of me wished I could tell her. Part of me knew, for her sake, it would be better not to. Once I put her to bed at her house, I'd have to leave. There was no point in trying to make her understand.

Maybe I'd check out the doctor a little more before leaving. Then, at least, she wouldn't be alone for Christmas. Even though she was never truly alone, as I would always be watching, until the day she departed her Earthly body and I took her hand one final time to lead her home. That would be the day she'd get to see the real me, per se. She wouldn't see me as corporeal or human as she did now, but in my true angelic form. No wings, no halos, no gold-and-white robes, just the essence of light and purity that we were created to be.

"Why do you try so hard to push people away? I'd like to help you." It bothered me that she was angered by my actions. The only approval I ever required was not of this realm. But suddenly, the mere thought that I'd hurt her lay heavy on my heart.

"If only you'd let me see your underwear," she said, slumping in her seat.

I arched a brow. "What?"

"Scrunch...wedgie." More garbled words rolled off her tongue.

I hitched a shoulder and glanced at her as we pulled into her driveway.

"Hey, I didn't...you...my house...know my house...how I live... this house...mine." She lifted her finger to point, but it flopped down against her lap.

A chuckle rumbled in my chest. The pain pill must have kicked in. It would work to my favor, and I could sneak out without her knowing I'd even been there. She could chalk the whole event up to a figment of her imagination from the drugs.

I scooped her into my arms and carried her to the house but forgot about the locked door. Since Eden was short of passing out, I closed my eyes, and with a click and a creak, the door pushed open and I carried her inside.

I eased her onto the bed and worked to get her out of her coat and boots. Static zapped my hand as I pulled off her knit cap. I jumped back and shook my fingers. *That actually hurt.* But angels didn't feel pain, so what was that?

"I like...your...face."

I glanced at Eden staring up at me from the bed. A smile twitched on my lips, and I forgot about the pain in my fingertip. "I like your face too."

"No...your face." She paused, and her finger swayed in the air as she tried to point. "Sexy."

Did she call me sexy? My eyes widened, and something shot through me, some kind of fizzy tingle, like the static on my finger, only inside me, right through my core. I swallowed hard as a tremble ripped through my hands. Raising them to eye level, I stared at them shaking like an earthquake, and I dropped to my knees beside the bed.

What was going on?

"So beautiful...like an angel."

I froze. Did she know? Had she figured it out?

My heart stopped. All time around me stopped as she pressed the palm of her hand to my face. A flash of heat ignited inside me at her touch. It spiraled in my chest until it burst through every limb like an explosion.

"Skin...perfect...glowing...do you moisturize?" Her eyelids slowly closed and then she forced them back open wider and shook her head. But her lids drooped once more as she succumbed to the medication, and her hand dropped against her stomach.

I stared at her for a moment, lost in the serenity on her face. I longed to touch it as she did mine, aching to return the loving gesture as I drank in her beauty. She really was one of the most stunning human beings I'd ever seen.

So many people tried to hide behind makeup and clothing, uncomfortable in their own skin. I never understood the need to cover up the greatest gift these beings had been given, a human body—each one unique and miraculous. Yet they all seemed to want to look like each other and make themselves into something they weren't. No one ever really saw their own beauty. It was truly a shame.

Eden, she wore her own skin unabashedly. She had her insecurities, like all humans, but hers were more internal than external.

Humans—they were lucky and blessed, but also cursed. Angels and humans were created so differently, yet we coexisted. They knew *of* us, though many didn't *trust* we were real. Humans saw through a veil, a partiality, and it only lifted when they truly believed.

Ah, belief. The key to everything.

I looked across the room at the mirror on her dresser. Golden hair draped my shoulders, and blue eyes sparkled back at me from the reflection. A hard, chiseled jawline held tight to a set of lips pursed in a straight line. I'd never seen myself in human form before. Was this how Eden saw me? She called me sexy, something I'd never thought I'd hear in all my existence. But would she think my angelic form the same?

My angelic form couldn't be seen by human eyes, only by the soul. Watching in the mirror, I ran a hand through my hair. We could be whatever form we wanted in the blink of an eye. Something about this one held my gaze captive. For any given situation, we could conjure things necessary. We could be anywhere we wanted and back in an instant, well, a human instant, as time worked differently in the angelic realm versus the human one. We had such freedom to come and go, to help and aid, to sing, dance, be grateful for the wondrous things we'd been given. My only desire was to help others. My gaze caught sight of Eden in the mirror, and I looked back at her. We did such good in the world, and my soul overflowed with happiness—pure euphoria.

I loved being an angel. I couldn't have imagined being anything else. Until now...

For a second, I reached for her, caressing the aura around her cheek, careful not to touch her for fear of waking her. With a sigh, I forced myself up from my knees.

"Stay...don't go, my angel," she whispered and swiped at one of my hands, locking onto it as she yanked me onto the bed. "Stay."

My body flailed before I landed on the soft mattress next to her. A lump wedged in my throat. "I...I shouldn't. I can't."

"My Theo...hero...flannel...stay." She curled against my chest, and before I realized it, I had wrapped my arms around her.

The words "my Theo" replayed on a loop in my head. I was indeed her Theo, her Theliel, and always would be. She just wouldn't know it. My heart sank, filled with a heaviness I'd never known at the thought of having to leave her now.

I brushed away a lock of hair falling across her eyes. The sensation of her soft skin against my fingers sent another jolt to my heart.

A flutter.

A skip.

A heartbeat.

I had a heart! One that beat with a thunderous rhythm inside this corporeal chest. The realization hit me as I touched my lips to her head, giving her a tender kiss, as I'd seen countless people do over time, a gesture of love and care. The scent of her shampoo and her essence filled my nose, sending another shock wave of tingles through me.

I liked it.

I liked it a lot and wanted more. A craving welled up inside me, wanting to touch more of her, kiss more of her. It never made sense to me why people kissed, why they would hold the instrument they ate with to another being as an act of love. I couldn't fathom the lure of it. But the feeling of her warm skin against my mouth was indescribable. It excited my mind and left a pleasurable feeling in my soul.

I hovered over her face, my own mouth a breath away from hers. Eden opened her eyes and gazed into mine, angling her head until her lips brushed against me. A tingle flickered in my heart as I lay there, frozen, unwilling to move, shocked by the softness of her lips.

One kiss.

Just one real kiss and I promised myself I would leave. Finally allowing my body to move, I leaned in and pressed my lips harder against hers. I planned on pulling back. My mind screamed at me to. But she tilted her head and her tongue lay against the seal of my closed mouth. I gasped at the feeling, warm and wet against my lips, and she slid it inside my mouth. It wandered, looking for its companion to meld with. She swept her tongue against my own, and that fire reignited, burning hotter than I thought possible. Heat surged through my veins, and that spark fed my heart as it hammered in my chest. Our tongues danced, entwining as we slanted our lips and melted together in the fire of our souls.

It was everything. Everything I'd dreamed of, and more that I hadn't. She broke me in two with her kiss, shattering every wall, seeping inside me until we were one. A soft moan escaped her, burying itself between our tongues as we kissed, and it surged that euphoric feeling through me to my core. My fingers sifted through her hair of their own free will, guiding her head movements, angling her so I could take it deeper. I did things I didn't know I knew how to do, like my body instinctively took over.

I filled that kiss with everything I was, and everything I wish I could have been. I longed for it to satiate the ache in both our souls. For I knew leaving her would be the hardest thing I'd ever have to do in my thousands of years of existence.

It was over too soon. Our lips parted, both of us needing air. That wondrous breath I once longed to know and feel, suddenly turned into my enemy, breaking our union apart. Her eyes closed, and a smile curved over her kiss-swollen lips. I could do nothing but stare at her, longing for more.

One kiss would never be enough.

Eden turned, and another soft moan escaped her lips as she shifted closer against me, pressing her lips to my chest. "Thank you, Theo."

My eyes snapped shut, and my heart thumped a thousand beats. Breath rushed in and out of my lungs, and I worried she'd notice as she snuggled closer against my chest. I ran my hand along her back, soothing her as the pain pill sucked her into a deep sleep.

I had to get out of there. I had to run. I knew with everything in me that this wasn't supposed to be happening. Kasbiel had warned me about a choice. Could this have been what he was talking about?

A million thoughts crossed my mind at once, yet I lay there with my arms around Eden. I didn't want to leave. I couldn't make myself. Our shared kiss, so pure and filled with love, it was the epitome of good. Surely that couldn't be bad, right?

I was an angel—I didn't do bad. I only did *good*, only wanted *good*. Right then, being next to Eden, having her in my arms felt *good*, better than anything I'd ever experienced in my entire existence.

But that very thought told me all I needed to know—angels didn't feel.

But I did now.

I felt everything.

And I didn't want it to stop.

4

EDEN

I ROLLED OVER, AND SOMETHING HARD HIT THE FLOOR WITH A LOUD *thunk*—my head as I fell off the bed. Blinking myself out of my stupor, I glanced around the room, my bedroom, to be exact. The fog in my brain swirled with a bunch of images that made no sense: a tree, a man, a latte, and a kiss. The pictures replayed over and over, and a smile lit my lips. It was one of those dreams that felt so real I could have sworn it happened.

I indulged in the thoughts as I shut my eyes, reliving the happiness filling my soul. Some ridiculously handsome lumberjack rescued me, again, and covered me in kisses. I'd seen him before. Many times. The minute I woke up, I knew. I would recognize him anywhere. I mean, when one dreamed of someone every night of her life, why wouldn't she?

But the more conscious I became, the more he faded, until he vanished completely.

Once again, the man of my dreams vanished into nothing, and I was left with an emptiness that swallowed my heart, but I couldn't figure out why. I knew I had a dream, a really good dream, but for the life of me, I couldn't remember any details other than a bunch of vague things like coffee, a man, and a tree. Yet somehow, they all fit together and made sense in my brain.

Rubbing the back of my head, I pushed up from the ground but winced at the pain shooting along my arm at the pressure. What did I do now? I thought I hit my head, not my arm, when I fell out of bed.

I stumbled to my dresser and scared myself at what stared back at me in the mirror. My brown hair stuck out in every direction like I'd spent some serious time with a light socket. With a yawn, I grabbed a tank top and my fuzzy Christmas pajama pants with little reindeer on them and headed for the shower.

After a thorough cleansing, that relentless throbbing struck again as I ran a brush through my wet hair. 'At the thought, a glimpse of a man with long blond hair and a brown-stained T-shirt flashed through my head. Then a tree, me under it, warm hands, rich laughter, coffee, safety, arms, love all balled together. I jumped back, dropping the brush on my foot. Pain inched its way across my toes, and I pictured myself kicking a Christmas tree.

What the hell?

I needed coffee. And a psychiatrist.

I wandered out to my living room. In front of the window stood an enormous Douglas fir. The image of the tree in my face flashed before me, and I stumbled backward until I hit the sofa. Stairs creaked down the hall, and adrenaline burst through my heart, tingling its way through my frozen limbs. I scrambled around my living room, looking for something to defend myself with. All I could come up with was spray bleach. I dashed to the kitchen and grabbed the bottle from the counter.

But what thief *brought* a tree instead of stealing one?

Heavy boots lumbered across the hardwood floor until a man came into view. I held up the spray bottle, nozzle turned to stream for max effect, and took my best *Charlie's Angels* stance.

"Who the hell are you, and why are you in my house?"

The man turned around. His long, flowing blond hair whipped

around his shoulders, and he looked at me with a quirked brow. "What are you doing, Eden?"

I blinked. The assailant knew my name. I blinked again and dropped the bottle. It was him. The man, the one from my dreams I could never remember. He stared at me with such a quizzical expression a laugh popped from my throat.

"You," I whooshed out in more of a mumble than a word.

"I was getting your Christmas decorations down from the attic. I didn't want you trying to carry the heavy boxes with your sore wrist. I'm sorry if I woke you." His sad eyes and sullen lips oozed regret and remorse.

"I'm sorry. I don't...who are you?" I took a tentative step closer. "You remind me of someone. But that can't even..." I shook my head and ran a hand through my hair. Pain in my wrist shot back another memory of being in the ER and a cute doctor. "My wrist. Pain. Pills. Oh, sweet baby Jesus." The heat of embarrassment splattered over my cheeks.

"Did you sleep okay? You've been out for several hours. It's nearly five o'clock." The hot lumberjack nodded toward the clock above me.

"The—Theliel," I whispered. I didn't know where it came from, but the name burst from my lips.

"Yes?" He tilted his head.

"You're him, aren't you?" I braved the question as all the memories of the morning rushed back, this time in proper order.

That sexy brow lifted, and a smirk spread over his face. "I am. But you like to call me Theo."

"No, I mean the one from my dreams!" The urge to run my hand along his incredibly marbled cheek overwhelmed me, but I pulled back my arm as I stepped closer to him, inspecting him.

"I don't know what you mean. I'm sure when the pain pills knocked you out, you probably recounted the events of the day in your head as you slept." He shrugged.

"No—I mean, yes. But not just today. I mean every day. Every damn day of my life. You're him. You're the one who I see in my sleep. You're the one who I can't remember when I wake. It's you. You're here. I just don't understand how."

"You dream of me?" The box dropped from his hands and clunked to the floor. I prayed it wasn't the one holding all my antique ornaments.

We both glanced at the box on the floor and dived to clean up the contents. Our hands touched and a spark lit our fingertips, but I chalked it up to static electricity. We pulled away and stared at each other, and for the first time, I really looked at his face. I remembered those blue eyes when he removed the tree from my face. But what I didn't remember was how they sparkled in three different shades. I remembered the warmth of his hand along my head as he caught me when I fell. What I didn't remember were the size of them: large, long, and so soft—not the hands of a laborer. I remembered the way his hair flowed around him, like he stepped out of a shampoo commercial. What I didn't remember was that every single strand was a different shade of gold. Or that his skin almost glowed. Or that he smelled like coffee.

Oh, wait, I did remember that part, the part where I launched a latte at him. I thrust my hand to his chest and nearly knocked him over. "You should take that off."

He blinked and stared at me as he tried to steady himself. "Wh-What?"

"The shirt. I'll wash it for you. You shouldn't have to wear a stained shirt for the rest of the day. Unless you're leaving right away...I mean you don't have to. If you want to stay, I'll wash you...I mean your shirt. I'll wash your shirt and you can wash yourself, if you want to shower." I cleared my throat and released my grip on him.

"I'll be fine." He glanced down at his shirt. "Do you think I should? Shower that is. Do I smell bad? I didn't even think about it. I don't want you to have to go to any trouble." The lost look in his eyes pierced my soul, like he'd never had anyone offer to help him before, and I ached to take care of him in any way I could. He'd already done so much for me, it warmed me inside to be able to do so for him.

"You don't smell bad. You smell like sunshine and peppermint, and a little like coffee. But you might feel better if you cleaned up." I slipped my hands under the hem of his shirt, and he sucked in a breath. I slid my fingertips along his chest as I pushed the material up his torso and over his head. I sat back, staring at his skin as smooth as silk, caramelized with a golden tan.

He stared back, his chest heaving powerful thrusts of air in and out of his lungs. I thought maybe he was asthmatic. I'd be happy to give him mouth to mouth.

"You smell like flowers and happiness," he said on the wing of one of his heavy breaths.

"Really? I thought I probably smelled like desperation and rum."

His laughter filled the house like a warm fire on a cold night. I loved his voice, his laugh, his essence. Everything about him calmed me and blanketed me in safety. Yet I had no idea who he was, only that he looked exactly like the man in my dreams, which would make me certifiably insane. But I just dumped the truth that I dreamed of him, and he was still there, shirtless, in my living room.

I tossed the last of the items in the box, and he picked it up, placing it near the tree.

"I'll show you to the shower." I guided him through my bedroom into the master bathroom. "Towels are in the cabinet over there. I'll go toss this in the wash and put on some coffee. I promise not to spill it on you again."

He smiled. "It's really okay. You don't have to go to all this trouble."

"No trouble at all. You do your thing, and I'll be out here watching...I mean waiting...doing something to occupy my time so I don't think of you naked in the shower." I turned and ran out of the room before any more ridiculous words jumped out of my mouth.

~⚭~

Theo

The minute Eden shut the bathroom door I forced out the breath wedged in my lungs. I stepped back and plunked down on the toilet seat. She didn't bring up our kiss, so maybe it was lost in the fog from her pain pills. An ache sliced through my heart at the thought she could forget something so amazing. But perhaps it was better that way. If she didn't remember it, maybe it would be easier when I left. I would be the strong one, having to live with the memory of it for eternity. Yet her words tumbled in my mind, over and over. She'd dreamed of me. Not just today, but every day she said. How was that possible?

For the last twenty-nine years, she'd been my charge, but I'd never revealed myself to her before today. Yet somehow, she knew me. Maybe not in the deep sense that I knew everything about her, but the simple fact I'd been in her mind as long as she'd been in mine shocked me. That had never happened before in my thousands of years of existence.

I shook my head and walked to the tub. How did this shower thing work? I had to admit, I'd been in the bathroom with Eden when she showered. I had to be there in case something happened, like if she slipped and fell, or if the water would be too hot and scald her. But I never paid attention to how she turned the contraption on. I turned the knob, and water shot out of the spout above me, and a yelp burst from my lips. Cold. Ice-cold.

"Everything okay in there?" Eden shouted through the door.

"Uh, just fine. Wasn't expecting it to be that cold."

"Turn the knob all the way around to get to the hot water."

I glanced at the little triangle pointing to the blue line on the metal plate and then found the red line for hot. "Ah, that's how you do it. Got it. Thank you."

Her giggle echoed against the door, and I knew she waited just on the other side for me. Did she want to watch me? Showers did seem fun, with all the soap bubbles and steam, and how she would caress herself, running her hands over her body. She seemed to enjoy it. Some days more than others.

I knew I had to go soon. This had to be why were instructed to never stay corporeal very long. I was starting to acclimate to this body, to enjoy being in it and experiencing things with Eden. I just needed to see her through the night to make sure she was okay and think of some plausible explanation so she wouldn't get hurt by me leaving.

The rush of the hot water bit my skin, but the sting felt good, not bad. I relished it. I turned it farther, sucking in a hissing breath at the first strike of the hotter water. But as my skin adjusted to the temperature, I found myself cranking it hotter and hotter until it couldn't go any farther, and the enjoyable sting faded away. Perhaps that's what happened to all humans in life. When they had something good, they always wanted just a little more, and a little more, and a little more until they'd pushed themselves to the end where there was no more, not ever happy with what they had.

With a sigh, I glanced around looking for something that resembled soap. A big white bottle with a pump hung on a rack to my left and I pressed it down, oozing a pearly white liquid into my palm. I shrugged and lathered it all over my body. My thoughts drifted to Eden and the memories of the times I'd seen her do the same, running her hands over her plump breasts and the folds between her legs.

My own hand traveled the same path, though my breasts were like a man's, flatter and firmer, and as my hand found its way between my legs, I jumped back at what I found. A penis. I had a penis! And it was huge, and thick, and standing upright, pointing at me.

How did I have a penis? Angels didn't have penises, or vaginas for that matter. When we went corporeal, it was in an assumed human form, but there was no need for genitals. Yet a very erect set of male genitals stood at attention, and I copped a feel. A breathy moan escaped from my lungs as I ran my fingers along its length, sending a wave of euphoria through my entire body.

I gasped as I tightened my hand around its firmness and lathered the soap with a pumping motion. The memory of our kiss, our tongues pressed together, our mouths breathing the same air played on a loop in my head. My hips rocked on instinct, alternating a rhythm with my hand. That euphoric sensation radiated through my core, from my head to my toes, and I slammed my other hand against the wall to keep from falling over in my zeal.

"Theliel!" a voice shouted from in front of me.

My eyes flew open. "Kasbiel?"

"What are you doing?" He hissed.

"I have a penis!" A jubilant smile lit my lips as I pointed with both index fingers to the hard flesh bouncing against my stomach.

"I can see that." He pursed his lips as he rolled his eyes. "That's why I'm here. You've gone too far, Theliel. You need to stop this, right now."

"I understand, now. This is why humans like sex so much. The feeling is incredible, Kasbiel." I gripped him by the shoulders. "We need penises! Who do we have to talk to, Gabriel or Michael?" The fascination running through my mind was like a child discovering a new toy.

Kasbiel shook his head and folded his arms. "It's time to go."

"What? No. I can't." I hitched back. "I can't just disappear on her." I fanned my arm to the door, hoping Eden wasn't still on the other side. "If I go without saying good-bye, it'll destroy her. She's been through too much. I'm just here to help. Trust me, I'm fine. I know what I'm doing."

"What you're doing is called jerking off in the shower. You're far from fine, Theliel. You're teetering on a fence you don't want to fall off of. If you do, you can't come back. Do you understand what I'm saying?"

His words punched me in the gut. "I know. I know. I get it. I now understand why they say not to go too long or touch our charges." I looked him straight in the eyes, partly to reassure him and partly to convince myself. "But I'll be careful. A couple hours more, and I'll make her Christmas Eve special and be gone. She'll get a fresh start with a new outlook on life."

"Uh-huh, and your penis?" Kasbiel pointed.

I shrugged. "I don't know how to get rid of it."

"Remember that choice I spoke of earlier? Think long and hard on it before acting. That's all I can say." Shaking his head, he let out a sigh and disappeared.

Guilt ate at my heart, and I pressed my hands to the wall, letting the last of the hot water cleanse my mind and body. He was right. As usual.

"Um, Theo," Eden said as she knocked on the door. "You okay in there? I thought I heard voices."

My head snapped up, and I cleared my throat. "Yeah, fine. Just, uh, singing." I rolled my eyes at my lame response.

"Okay, well, coffee's ready."

"Be out in a second," I replied.

Eager to see her again, I rinsed quickly, shut the water off, and dried—another fascinating and slightly wonderful experience. I wrapped the towel around my waist and opened the door. Eden collapsed into my arms from the other side. Her warm hands clawed at my chest until they gripped my shoulders as she steadied herself. I clung to the small of her waist, curling my fingers into her soft curves.

"I'm sorry, I was...I...um...you have a nice voice. Was waiting for you to sing." She cleared her throat and patted down my chest as she backed out of our embrace.

An ache welled up in me to pull her back into my arms, indulge in the sensation of her softness, the heat of her body pressed to mine. It clouded my head and choked my lungs.

"Eden," I whispered her name, and it sounded more like a prayer. I prayed she'd come back to me and put her hands on my chest again, but she shouldn't. It wasn't right. It wasn't fair to her.

She jerked to a stop but didn't turn around. "I'm going to be honest here, Theo. I'm so insanely attracted to you I can barely stand it. It's taking everything in me not to turn around and rip that towel off you. So unless you want me to, please let me walk out of this room with what thread of dignity I have left."

I gave her silence instead of an excuse, and she let out a sigh and all but ran out of the room. Perhaps words would have been a better choice. But the words I wanted to say, I couldn't. And I couldn't lie to her. Maybe I should've just told her who I was. Though if I did, it could change her future, her choices, her destiny. She needed to accept and believe. Have faith, not in me her guardian angel telling her these things, but in herself that she was loved, and that all things happened for a reason. Because without faith, there was no rock to stand on.

I had to also have faith. Faith that my job here was to help her see who she needed to be. Not that I was sent here to succumb to the free will of human beings. Like Kasbiel said earlier, I sat on a fence, teetering so very close to falling. Because everything in my heart wanted her to rip that towel off me and see what would happen.

5

EDEN

BECAUSE I HADN'T MADE ENOUGH OF A FOOL OF MYSELF, I HAD TO blatantly tell the hottest man on the planet I wanted to use him like a Sit 'n Spin. Either I rendered him mute with surprise or fear. But since he didn't call out my name, or throw me down on the bed and have his way with me, I had to assume it was fear or repulsion riding the thick silence in the air.

I ran out, holding back the flood of tears threatening to burst from my eyeballs. Embarrassment riddled me from head to toe, churning my stomach into a sea of regret. I prayed for a hole to appear in my kitchen floor and suck me into blackness. I collapsed in a heap at the table and contemplated how I would run away from my own house on Christmas Eve.

A large, warm hand pressed against my shoulder. "Eden."

The voice that once soothed me now tied my stomach in knots. I wasn't sure why because while I was truly embarrassed at my awkward come-on, it felt more like something else stirred the whirlpool of anxiety brewing inside me. Something deeper, more rooted, a nagging in my gut that all but shouted "Danger, Will Robinson." But I couldn't figure out what. I knew it wasn't Theo himself, as he'd proved to be a complete gentleman, too much so.

Yet something niggled in my head that said the entire situation wasn't going to end well.

"Um, your shirt's in the dryer. Should be a few more minutes and then you don't have to hang around anymore." I sucked back the tears and jumped up from the table. "So, ah, want some rum and eggnog? 'Tis the season to drown stupidity and regret."

I refused to look him in the eyes and witness the awkward pity I knew would be swimming in them.

"I don't drink," he said.

"Of course not, because you're some kind of saint." I poured a glass of rum, forgoing the eggnog and extra calories. I needed it straight-lined and flooding my veins as soon as possible.

"No, I'm an angel," he murmured.

"Is that supposed to be funny?" I shot him a glare. "There's a time and place for sarcasm. This is not one of them. Besides, that's my job. You're supposed to be the hero, the knight-in-glaring-flannel." Rum sloshed up and over the side of my glass as I pointed at him. Alcohol fail. At that point, I couldn't even drink right. "This is not how things turn out in my dreams."

"How do things work out in your dreams?" He tilted his head as if he actually cared. The sincerity in his eyes almost did me in.

Why would he bother to care if he had no interest in me?

Unless this was all some kind of crazy setup by Grayson to get back at me for texting pictures of him basting Suzie's turkey to his mom. She didn't know how to text. She barely knew how to answer her phone, so it's not like she'd ever see them. I should have posted them on social media for everyone to see. But I couldn't get myself to do that, to humiliate him back like he humiliated me. I was such a failure. I couldn't even do revenge right.

I shook my head out of the thought and brushed past him. "You really don't want to know. Trust me."

He clutched the crook of my arm and brought me to a stop. "I really do."

"It doesn't matter."

He took a step, pressed his chest against my back, and whispered in my ear, "But it does to me."

His warm breath against my ear launched a disorienting shiver through me, and I lost control of myself. Like his whisper was some kind of truth serum. "You save me. Every time I do something stupid in one of my dreams, you save me. You bring me home and kiss me. Kiss me like I've never been kissed before. Make me come alive at your touch. You make love to me as if your life depended on it." Tears pooled in my eyes, burning as they fought to break through the barrier I'd struggled to hold on to. "You love me."

The words scorched my lips and sliced my heart as they left the sacred place in my mind, where things were perfect and there was no pain, no rejection, no emptiness, no regrets. Realizing they'd only ever be a dream hurt more than I thought. I was no longer anything but a shell. Not because some perfect man of my dreams didn't want me, but because neither did the scum of the Earth like Grayson. I belonged nowhere. I belonged to no one. Not that I needed a man to feel whole, but even my own mother rejected me. Even my job rejected me when the grant for my next excavation was denied. At every corner of my life stood a giant brick wall, and every day they closed in on me a little more.

His hands trembled against my shoulders and his heart thundered, drumming a frantic rhythm against my back the harder he pressed against me. "I wish with everything in my heart that I could. Trust me, you have no idea. In a human heartbeat, if things were different..."

A lightbulb glared in my brain, and I spun around. "Are you married?"

He shook his head, the blues of his eyes darkening.

"Gay?" I choked out.

"Well, yes, I like to think of myself as cheerful and jubilant—"

I cut him off with a glare, and he paused. I arched a brow, and it nearly reached my hairline. Sometimes he acted like he was out of place and time, and it was really odd.

He stared at me for a moment before his eyes widened. "Oh—Ohhh! I don't think so." He scratched his head. "I never thought about it, honestly. This is all new to me."

"I think you should probably leave," I choked out in a whisper as I raised the glass to my lips, struggling to hold on to it with trembling fingers.

"Eden, please don't." He cupped his hand over mine clinging to the glass, and with his other, he whisked the bottle away.

The way his voice lilted as he said my name forced my heart to skip. I didn't really want him to leave, but the pain and guilt of rejection burned in my soul. I couldn't take another round of it. Yet I listened, captivated by the struggle in his tone, thick with emotion like mine.

"It's not what you think."

"Isn't it? I just threw myself at you and got rejected. Like I need to sit here and stare at you, reminded of my humiliation. Merry Christmas to me. Strike three this year, guess I'm out." I ripped my hand from his and walked to the table.

In two strides of his long muscular legs, he managed to get in front of me and held out his hand. "Yes, you're out, and you need to get back in. That's why I'm here. Come walk with me."

"Outside? In the snow? It's twenty-eight degrees and snowing. It's Christmas Eve, and the only invite I have is to my pity party. I just want to stay inside and drink. By myself. It's what I'm good at. It's where my strength lies. I'm nothing but a screw-up and reject that should never have been born."

With a huff, he pried my fingers from the glass of rum and set it on the table. "You need to learn a few things. Let's go."

He yanked me out of the kitchen and through the living room to the front door. Theo was serious, and the look of anguish on his face warred with the fury in his eyes. They said he wasn't taking no for an answer. That look, the genuine concern, it made me think maybe Grayson hadn't sent him. Maybe he really was just a nice guy who had saved me at the tree lot and wanted to make sure I was okay.

"Dude, seriously, I'm in a tank top and fuzzy pajama pants. Can I at least get dressed before we go into the frozen tundra?" I stared at him still standing in only a towel. "And you don't even have clothes on!"

Shock replaced the intensity on his face. "Right. Clothes. Go put some jeans on and a jacket. I'll get my shirt and jeans from the dryer."

Rolling my eyes, I stomped to my room and said screw it to jeans. If he was making me go for a walk in the snow, it was going to be sweatpants and my frumpiest sweatshirt. I wasn't getting laid any time soon, so what did it matter what I wore? My days of looking cute for a guy were over.

I slid into my furry boots and grabbed my polar snow jacket with the ratty fake-fur hood I used only for shoveling in the dark. It looked horrendous, but it kept me warm. Theo walked in from the laundry room in his clean, now only slightly coffee-stained T-shirt, jeans that left nothing to the imagination, and his red-and-white flannel.

"Do you want a warmer coat? You'll freeze now that it's night-time." Why I bothered to care was beyond me.

"I'll be fine. Cold doesn't bother me."

Right, because he was part yeti.

He held out his hand, and I slapped my mitten-covered one against it. Clasping his fingers around it, he pulled me to his side and out the door.

Dusk settled in, swallowing the last light of day. Thick, snow-filled clouds hung in the sky, turning the waning sunset a pinkish-gray. A little breeze of chilly air bit the tip of my nose and forehead, the only parts of my body exposed to the elements outside of my wool scarf tripled-wrapped around my face.

"You look like an Eskimo." Theo laughed.

"I feel like that puffy marshmallow man, but at least I'm warm. I don't understand how you're not freezing in a thin flannel."

As the words left my lips, a shudder ransacked his body, and he shook his head. "Okay, so it's a little chillier than I thought it would be. We won't be gone too long. I just want to show you a few things."

He tightened his grip on my hand and pulled me along.

"Fine. What do you want to show me? Are we looking at holiday lights or something? There's a cool waterfall display around the corner."

"Maybe later. But right now, I need you to understand something." Around the block from my house, he jerked us to a stop and pointed at a dilapidated home with boarded windows, except for an octagon-shaped one in what I assumed was the attic, or converted attic, now someone's room. A bright-yellow star stood on the top of a small tree. "You see that house?"

I nodded. "Hard to miss. I can't believe anyone lives there. I thought it was condemned or something. I never see anyone there."

"Yesterday, you were in line at the Sack 'n Save, and an elderly woman stood in line in front of you trying to buy food but was twenty dollars short. You put your cart of groceries back, sans eggnog and rum, and paid for her entire bill. You went without, so she could have food. What you don't know is her next stop was going to be the pawn shop, to sell her vintage wedding ring to pay for her electric bill. The food you bought fed her grandchildren, and she used the grocery money to keep heat on in that old house. Her husband died, as well as her daughter. She cares for two young grandkids on her own, with no job because she can't work and only lives off social security. This morning, you paid for the wreath her grandson put on his mother's grave."

My mouth popped open, and sadness swallowed my heart. "Wait, that's them? I had no idea. Can I do something else? Do the kids have Christmas presents? What can I do?"

"You've already done what you were supposed to. You saved her life, as well as the lives of those kids. There are other things in store for them, so you don't have to worry. But you made a difference in her life." Theo squeezed my hand.

Tears welled in my eyes, and I wiped them away with my other hand so they wouldn't freeze like icicles to my cheeks. A thought popped into my head, and I tore away from Theo's grip and ran right up the stairs to the house, slipping and sliding over the icy steps along the way. Nearly breaking down the door, I pounded a balled, mitten-covered fist against the wood. Snow crunched in the distance behind me, and I knew Theo had run after me, but he stopped and waited on the sidewalk.

The weatherworn door creaked open, and behind it stood that same lady from the grocery store like he said. Salt-and-peppered hair sat high atop of her head in a messy bun, and wise, old gray eyes peeked out from behind her scratched glasses as she lowered them to the edge of her nose.

"Can I help—" She paused and placed a hand over her heart with a gasp. "It's you, from the store yesterday and the tree lot."

I nodded. "Do you have plans for tomorrow? I'd like to invite you over for dinner."

"But it's Christmas, child. Don't you have a family of your own to do dinner with?"

I shook my head. "Not really. It's pretty much just me. I'd like to have you and your grandkids over, say around three?"

Tears welled in her eyes, and she swiped at them with long, wrinkled fingers that trembled. "Can I bring a dish to share?"

"Normally, I'd say yes, since I'm the world's worst cook. But if you want to come over earlier, maybe you can give me some pointers instead. I'll supply the food. You supply the wisdom. Deal?"

A tear streaked her cheek as she nodded. "I'd like that. I'm sure the littles would, as well."

"I live just around the block. 2201 Maple." Happiness replaced the sadness engulfing my heart at the smile twitching on her lips.

She glanced over my shoulder to Theo on the sidewalk, and she gave a nod with an even brighter smile. "An angel out on Christmas Eve. I never thought I'd get to see it with my own eyes."

"Oh no, I'm no angel. Just trying to be neighborly." I shifted from foot to foot, trying to regain feeling in my frozen toes.

She smiled, tossed a wave to Theo, and slid back behind the creaky door.

I trudged down the steps off the porch, making my way back to Theo, and thumbed over my shoulder. "Do you know her? I guess that explains how you knew all that about her situation."

Theo didn't answer, just gripped my hand in tight-lipped silence. I tugged on it, demanding an answer. But he walked me another two blocks before speaking.

"That house there." He pointed to a modest two-story brick home a few houses down from where we stopped.

Snow clung to the roof in heavy drifts. Bright colored lights twinkled in the bay window at the front of the house. Behind the sheer curtain stood a tall tree, glowing blue and white lights hanging from its branches. A stout woman in her fifties peeked from behind the curtain as a car pulled into the driveway. The front door whipped open, and she stepped out onto the porch, wiping her hands on a white apron. A tall, lanky man got out of the car, followed by a beautiful redheaded woman. They paused, beaming a loving smile at each other as they locked hands and walked up the steps. The older woman looked down at their hands before throwing her arms around the man, her body convulsing in sobs.

"What's going on? Is everything okay?" Panic hit my heart, thinking someone might have died from the way the woman cried.

"It is, now. That's her son, and he just got engaged to his girlfriend behind him. His mom noticed the ring on her finger. She's happy."

I quirked a brow and shifted my hands to my hips covered underneath my bulky jacket. "How do you even know this?"

"Three years ago, you volunteered at a homeless shelter. You served about two hundred and fifty meals that day, but you sat down and ate with only one of them. A man named Donnie. Years before that day, he went off to college, but instead of getting an education, he found drugs. His parents tried to get him into rehab, but he refused. Eventually, they had to cut off his funding, hoping that if he was forced from that school, it would take him out of the reach of the drugs and bring him home. But he chose the streets instead, robbing people to get money to buy his next hit. He squatted in an abandoned building for six months, but on Christmas Eve that year, he was hungry and broken enough to go to a shelter for a meal. You talked with him that night. For hours, about nothing in particular, but you made a connection."

As I looked closer, that ashy-brown hair and lanky body struck my memory. "Oh, I do remember him. He stank to high heaven, and I remember holding my breath for much of the conversation. But I couldn't leave him. He was only a couple years younger than me, and it hurt my heart that someone my age was living on the streets. When I thought about homeless people, it was always like vets with PTSD or older people down on their luck with life. I didn't realize it could be anyone, even someone like me who just made really shitty choices. I thought maybe he wanted some company. I had no idea what to talk about, so I pretty much babbled."

"Well, he listened to you. You told him all about your life in college and how you were about to start your own excavation team for your first solo dig in Egypt. He was fascinated by your stories and the opportunities you had before you, and it hit him how much he wanted that too. That he had thrown his life away for drugs. You held his hand without even knowing it. You told him he could reach his dreams—he just had to want it more than drugs. That night, he showed up at his parent's house after not seeing them in over a year. That was the start of his recovery process. Now he's a social worker, trying to get kids off the street. He had to go through trials to find his way, but you were the link in his life that started a chain of events that got him where he is today."

"I hope he smells better. By the fact that she said yes to marrying him, I'm guessing he does."

Theo laughed, and it echoed through the quiet street. "I'm sure he does. He's had a couple of showers since then."

"How do you even know this? Are you some government caseworker?"

"I told you, I'm here to help you. I'm a friend. Trust me." Gripping my hand once more, he tugged me along. Another shiver ripped through him, and he shook his shoulders out. His reddened cheeks clashed with the bright blue in his eyes.

"We should go back. You look like you're freezing."

"I'm fine," he said, shaking his shoulders again. "Just a tad colder than I thought it would be."

"Do you want my mittens?" I took them off and handed them to him.

He grabbed them and slipped them back over my hands. "You need them more than I do. I'll be okay. Trust me."

"All this *trust me* stuff is really annoying. I hardly know anything about you." I tried to cross my arms, but my puffy jacket wasn't having it. "How about you do some sharing about you instead of me? Tell me how you know all this stuff about these people."

"Tonight isn't about me. It's about you. You need the discovery. You need to see things more clearly." He brushed my cheek with the back of his ice-cold hand. "You need to start believing."

"How am I supposed to trust you?"

He glanced at me with a smile as we continued on our journey. "The same way you do when you know deep in your heart something is real and something is right. Have I given you any reason not to?"

"You're beyond infuriating, you know that?" I groaned and shoved my hands in my pockets.

I stomped a foot, and it slid out from under me as we walked over a patch of ice not yet salted. My legs wobbled beneath me like a newborn deer, and I careened right into the back of Theo, knocking him into a snowbank. Face first.

"I'm so, so sorry," I squealed and struggled to roll off him in my puffy jacket that made it really difficult to move.

Theo pushed himself to his knees and slid his arms under my shoulders, hoisting me out of the snow that acted like quicksand, sucking us down. Unable to hold his grip and stand on the ice, he toppled back into the snow on top of me. His face hovered over mine, and if it weren't for my scarf, our lips would have met. I instantly regretted my fashion choices.

His gaze locked on to mine, and he not only stared into my eyes but deep into my soul. He glanced at the scarf covering my mouth, and I swore he sighed.

"Now, I'm the one who's sorry. It's a little icier out here than I thought," he said, easing back from my face.

"I'm not only filled with rum but also regret."

He held out his hand and pulled me up.

"One more stop, and I promise we can head back." He hooked my arm in his, now soaked from the heavy, wet snow. Maybe he did want me more than he let on. Or maybe he was getting colder and wanted the warmth of my jacket. More likely, he didn't trust me not to fall on the ice again.

We walked another block and a half before stopping in front of an apartment complex on the backside of my neighborhood. I'd driven by it on numerous occasions, but never thought anything of it.

He leaned in and whispered in my ear, "Third floor, there's a window with a blinking reindeer on it. Do you see it?"

I nodded, biting my lip as I held back a shiver threatening to explode over my body at the heat of his breath and sexiness of his voice in my ear.

"That belongs to a boy named Max. He loves race cars and

coloring, and every night he prays to God, thanking him for sending an angel to save his daddy."

I turned and looked at Theo. "What?"

"He means you." A smile lit his lips.

"What?" I said even louder.

"Three weeks ago, you bought coffee at the gas station after filling up your car. Inside, you bumped into a man who was paying for gas in a container. You thought maybe he ran out down the road. So you offered him help, simply asking him if he needed a ride somewhere, and you got to talking to him. While he wasn't looking, you bought him a donut and a coffee because you thought he was hungry."

My heart skipped as his words threw me back to that moment in time. *A thin man with sullen eyes and a receding hairline carried a plastic gas container to the counter. He hunched over in his tweed coat, and I thought maybe he was cold as he shook, paying for his gas.*

"He bought gas to go home and sit in his garage, with the car running."

My hand flew to my mouth, covering the gasp that followed.

"He suffers from depression, a disease that whispers a human's worst fears in their mind. It snowballs and crushes them under the weight of falsehoods, destroying their self-worth and confidence. It destroyed his marriage. It was about to destroy him. Until you talked to him."

All my thoughts spiraled from that man to Amanda. She, too, had suffered from depression, only I couldn't save her. I shook my head, unwilling to believe what he was saying. "How did I have anything to do with him not committing suicide?"

"You bought him a blueberry donut."

"That's ridiculous. How did my buying him a blueberry donut stop him?"

"His son's favorite food in the world is blueberries. You also hummed 'The Sun Will Come Out Tomorrow.'"

"I was talking about the weather. It was snowing and windy. I was just trying to make him laugh because he looked so cold and lonely."

"You made him smile. You made him stop and think. You pulled him, for a long enough moment, out of the blackness invading his mind and soul. You showed him compassion. You showed him he wasn't invisible. You reminded him he had a son to live for, both physically and metaphorically. Tomorrow is a new day. It may be cloudy today, but you have a new chance, a fresh start, a sunny day tomorrow."

Tremors riddled my legs, making them collapse beneath me. I fell to my knees. Tears crept from my eyes, inching their way over my frozen cheeks. "Why couldn't I save Amanda?"

Theo crouched beside me. "You did. Countless times. You just never realized it. You don't understand the impact you have on people. Without you, think about how different those three souls would be today, how Amanda would have been lost long ago without you. You're not meant to save everyone, and not everyone is meant to be saved. There is a time and purpose for everyone's lives. Some are here for a short time, others for far longer. It's not your job to understand it, but to live to the fullest while you have the time. You may not feel like you should have been born, but I'm pretty sure each one of them is grateful you were."

While the sadness and anger lifted from my heart, regret blindsided me. Regret for feeling like such a failure at life. Regret for wishing I hadn't been born. Regret for wearing my scarf. I should have taken more chances, done more things. All the things I was too scared to do in life could have been missed opportunities that could have helped someone else.

Something wet and cold hit my face, and another tickled my nose. I looked up, and snow drifted down from the heavens, falling in soft, slow waves like dancing fairies blowing around in a gentle breeze. I glanced at the twinkling lights on all the houses around me, and the shrill laughter of children echoed in my ears as they tossed snowballs at each other. It was like something out of a painting, or I was trapped in a snow globe.

Theo shivered as he pressed a hand to my shoulder. "Let's get you home."

I nodded, wiping my eyes as I let him assist me up. We walked the last two blocks back to my street, but the closer we got, the more his pace slowed. Tremors rattled my arm, and I thought maybe I was having a seizure. But when I glanced down at my hand clasped in Theo's, I found it wasn't my muscles shaking, it was his. All his limbs shook, this time not stopping. His teeth chattered so loud I worried he'd chip a tooth, and his cheeks were solid red like Santa's.

"Theo, you don't look so good. We have to get you in the house —you're freezing to death out here."

"D-Don't w-worry about m-me. I'm f-fine." His words barely left his mouth as he collapsed in my front yard.

"Theo!" I dropped to his side and tried to heave him out of the snowbank. Damn him for being so muscular and heavy.

His head lolled to one side as I slid my arms under his shoulders and dragged his body to my front door. The snow helped immensely, but I would still have a crook in my back. And his ass would be so sore in the morning from me yanking him up the stairs, but I had to do what I had to do to get him inside out of the cold.

After unlocking the door, I channeled my inner warrior princess and zombie-shuffled him across the house, leaning him against my shoulder. Somehow we stumbled to my bedroom without toppling in a heap. I thanked my guardian angel for the assist on that one. With a grunt that could rival a tennis pro, I dumped him toward the bed. Luckily, my aim was better than I planned, and he managed to end up on it instead of the floor. He needed out of those cold, wet clothes and into some warmth.

"Forgive me, but I'm going to have to strip you naked, Theo."

A moan rumbled from his lips as he rolled his head to the side, eyes fluttering but not quite opening.

I ripped off his soaking wet flannel and T-shirt, careful not to let his head bounce back on the headboard. The last thing he needed was a concussion on top of hypothermia. Staring at his half-naked body, I counted the abs on his washboard stomach. Good Lord, he was a sight to behold. My hands hovered above his waist, knowing I had to get him out of his pants as well.

First, I shucked off my coat and scarf, giving me time to procrastinate pulling down some stranger's pants in my bedroom. Even though something inside me told me he was more than some stranger. I'd dreamed of him. He knew me. He knew my life. Okay, so the weird-ass info he had on the minute details of my life screamed stalker, but my heart and soul told me not to be afraid of him. Nothing added up where Theo was concerned. One odd mystery after another, and he avoided my questions like a trained ninja. But right now, he needed me. He took care of me today, and now it was my turn to put my big-girl panties on while I took his off.

Blowing out a hard breath, I unzipped his jeans and worked them over his hips, forcing myself to keep focused on the task at hand while not glancing up at his package. That was hard. Really hard. Thankfully, he wasn't. I guess it would have been super awkward had he sported a woody while he was passed out. In the end, curiosity got the best of me, and my gaze raked over his body. Even flaccid, the man was more than impressive, straight out of some porn movie.

Ripping my gaze from his godlike anatomy, I hoisted him over so I could grab the blankets and put him under them. But my legs twisted in my comforter, and he rolled on top of me. In any other scenario, I'd have been elated to have a completely naked Thor-like man pressed against me. But I preferred my lovers to be semiconscious during sex.

I wiggled out from under him and rolled him onto my pillows, tucking all the blankets around him. Sweat beaded on my brow, and I collapsed next to him, relishing in my accomplishment.

"Eden," he murmured as he curled into the blankets, rolling back and forth.

"Shh, I'm right here," I whispered, brushing a lock of hair falling over his closed eyes.

"So cold," he whispered back.

"I know. We're back home now and you're under the covers, so hopefully you'll warm up soon." I ran my hand along his arm, trying to generate some heat against his skin.

He grabbed hold of my hand and pressed it against his chest. "So warm."

My heart revved and took off like a Formula One car through my chest. I knew what I had to do. I knew what I wanted to do. But getting myself to go through with it was a whole other story. He wasn't going to warm up fast enough on his own. He needed more heat. Body heat. *My* body heat.

Which meant I was about to get naked.

6

THEO

Numbness spread through my body like a venomous poison. I lost all feeling through my limbs as the cold penetrated my bones. I'd never felt such cold before. Of course, I'd never walked through the snow in corporeal form for two hours either, let alone the wet clothing that clung to my body like an ice casing by the time we made it to Eden's doorstep. The temperature dropped, and I got caught unaware, lost in my mission to save Eden's soul.

I wavered in and out of consciousness. Every time I closed my eyes, Kasbiel appeared. Pure warmth and light shone around him, a beacon calling me home. My soul longed to reach him, to free itself of this mortal body and go back home with my brothers and sisters. The goodness and serenity beckoned me, reminding me of who and what I was, my purpose. It settled in my soul with a joyful noise, blanketing me with the happiness I missed. I reached out with my light, only a breath away from his.

But my heart fought to pull myself out of it, focusing on Eden's voice as she talked to herself. I used it like a lifeline to ground me back on this plane. My mind replayed the memory of her warm, wet kiss on my lips, the softness of her touch, the wild burning sensation of hearing her whisper my name that sent my heart soaring. It replayed the memory of her sitting with the old woman at the hospital, all the people she'd helped. Her soul shone as bright as Kasbiel's, drawing me back to her. There was a radiance to her that even an angel like Kasbiel couldn't compete with because Kasbiel was created to be that way. Eden chose to be that way.

My lips failed to move long enough to say more than her name, and even that came out in more of a moan than a word. I knew we'd made it out of the snow and inside the house, but the rest of the events blurred as I fought to stay awake. Then something warm pressed against my arm, and nothing had ever felt so good. I grabbed it, clung to it, held it in place for fear it would stop.

As I mustered the last of my strength to open my eyes, more warmth covered my body. Heat permeated my skin, flowing through me to my very core. The numbness regressed as feeling returned to my limbs, and I wiggled my fingers and toes. What a wonder the appendages still were to me!

I blinked my eyes open, relishing the cocoon of healing surrounding me. A set of dark-brown eyes stared at me, wide and filled with hope.

"You're back," Eden whispered.

"I'm sorry for leaving," I choked out, though my voice sounded far raspier than before.

"You scared me. I thought I'd lost you." She brushed her hand along my cheek and smiled.

My lips curved into a smile of their own, enjoying her soft caress of my face. "Not yet."

"Are you warming up enough?" Her heated fingertips traced the length of my arm, over my shoulder and across my chest, launching a shiver through my body. Not a reaction of the cold, but of delight.

"Yes. But can I stay like this a little longer? It feels really good." A sigh lilted through my words as I soaked in the heat pouring off her skin and into mine. I blinked as I realized how much of her skin pressed against mine. "Eden, are you...am I...are we both naked?"

She bit her lip, and a rush of adrenaline coursed through my veins. I wanted to see her do it again, it was...sexy. The thrill it launched through my body made my head spin.

"It was all I could think of to warm you back up. You passed out, and I was afraid hypothermia had set in. Your clothes were soaked from the snow and ice. All the color drained from your face, and your lips looked like grapes. I panicked and remembered hearing skin-to-skin contact is a way to heat a body back to core temperature."

My heart hammered against my rib cage. The wondrous fact that I had a rib cage, or a heart, was not lost on me, but how they reacted like a normal human being fascinated and worried me. I'd never lain with another being before, let alone completely bare. But at the moment of realization, something set me on fire from the inside out. All I could think about was how close our bodies were, skin to skin, nothing between us.

"Did you...see everything?" The words fell out before I could stop them.

Biting her lip again, she gave a curt nod. Something twitched near my stomach, and I had a feeling it was my new penis. It seemed to like her answer and reacted as if it had a mind of its own. I swallowed hard, and air rushed faster through my lungs.

She twisted against me, and something rubbed along my chest. I glanced down at the top of her exposed breasts, the majority of them remaining covered under the blankets. I realized then it had been her nipple, and another twitch hit my penis, sending a wave of sweet euphoria through me.

I liked it. I liked the thought of it. I wanted more.

"I can go get dressed. I think you're sufficiently warmed up," she said, rolling away.

I immediately missed the warmth of her body against me, and I wrapped my arm around her, halting her, pulling her flush against my chest. "Don't leave. Not yet. I like this."

She dipped her head as a shy smile lit her lips, and a blush bloomed on her cheeks. Framed by her long dark hair, she was the most beautiful being I'd ever seen. I caressed the pink in her cheeks with my fingertip, dragging it down along her smile, tracing it, embedding it into my memory. Pursing her lips, she kissed my finger before sucking it into her mouth. I found it a strange action, but the minute she slid her tongue against my skin, my eyes fell closed, and the sensation launched another euphoric wave through me. I sucked in a gasping breath, and she released my finger. Everything inside me ached to touch more of her, to feel more of her, be closer to her in any way possible.

Humanly possible.

She looked into my eyes, but stared into my soul, as if she were the only thing keeping breath in my lungs and a beat in my heart. She trailed her fingertips along my chest, sparking a fire in their wake.

"I shouldn't be doing this." I wondered if the words made it out of my head as I took a chance and let my fingers travel along her skin as she did mine, forcing down the worry brewing in my gut that this was wrong, so very wrong. But my heart never felt more alive and more right.

"Why?" she whispered, followed by a soft moan as I reached the top of her breast.

"Because I won't want to stop. We are worlds apart. This part was never supposed to happen."

My heart hammered again as she pressed her palm against my chest. "Maybe this is exactly where you're supposed to be."

"Trust me, this wasn't in the plan."

"How do you know? Do you have an agenda direct from God or something?"

"Well, indirectly—there're others I report to."

She hitched back. "Oh no, you're a priest? Is that how you knew all that stuff about me? Did all those people go to confession or something?"

I held tight to her in my arms. "No, I'm not a priest."

She relaxed, exhaling a long sigh of relief, and resumed her exploration of my body, rushing a thrill through me. "Okay, then you have nothing to worry about."

Easier said than done. Had other angels fallen so far before? Perhaps that's why the rules were implemented to begin with. Still, my mind warred with my heart, and even more so with my body as the thought of our kiss popped back into my head. I ached like never before to reclaim her lips. She stole the breath from my lungs, and her mouth would be the only thing that could bring me life.

I cupped the back of her neck and tilted her head as I pressed my mouth to hers. This time, I was the one that begged for entrance. Her lips parted, and I slid my tongue along hers like we did before, sparking that same euphoric feeling.

Our soft, gentle kiss turned needy and aggressive as both of us wanted more. She dragged her nails down the back of my neck, and a moan rumbled through me of its own accord. Rock-hard nipples grazed my chest as she moved beside me, raising her leg to rest upon my hip.

The neediness and aching seemed like it would never end. The more I kissed her, the more I wanted. Instead of satisfying me, it created a longing, a thirst I couldn't quench with her lips. A need I couldn't fill with her tongue. A hunger I couldn't sate with her touch.

This was why we could never become human. This was the reason to never touch. My head pounded from the thoughts screaming in my mind that I needed to stop. Everything about this was so wrong, forbidden.

My penis grew heavy, throbbing and twitching as it pressed into her stomach. Embarrassment momentarily replaced the ache in my heart for more of her. But she slid her hand between our bodies and cupped her fingers around the shaft.

A groan of pleasure ripped from my chest, carrying her name with it. "Eden..."

My heart launched into an erratic rhythm, making me almost

dizzy. She continued pumping her hand along my member, and like in the shower, my hips followed the motion, rocking with her.

"I want to touch you, as you are doing to me. Can I touch you, Eden?" Words made no sense to me, but I knew in my heart I had to make sure this was what she really wanted. I needed her permission.

I silenced the nagging thoughts in my head with the promise that this would be only one time, that I would never again fall prey to the temptations of a human body. I only needed one time to know, to experience, to fill my memory of Eden. How could an angel go thousands of years without ever knowing human touch, emotions, a connection like no other beings had with each other?

Releasing my penis, she guided my hand between her legs. I traced the fingertips of my other hand along her lower lips, the one at the apex of her legs, until they pushed between the opening. I was ill-prepared for the sensation that followed as they slid inside her warmth. A silken liquid filled her core, and my fingers danced in it. I swirled around a fleshy nub, and Eden about came off the bed with a loud gasp.

"Did I hurt you?" I stilled, my fingers remaining inside her as panic ramped up my heart.

"No, Theo, no. That felt amazing. Do more of that. I love the way you touch me, explore me as if it's the first time you've made love. Never stop," she said, a moan punctuating her words as they trailed off.

I caressed the length of her opening, dragging more of the silky arousal with me until I circled the spot she said she loved me touching. Not wanting it to end, I took my time, flicking and drawing circles around it, swiping across it with long, slow strokes as I watched her facial expressions change. What initially looked like pain, transformed into pleasure as her body writhed beneath my touch. With closed eyes, her face radiated a beauty I'd never seen, almost glowing as her own euphoria swallowed her. Her moans elongated and filled the air around us with a song of passion.

I realized my heart sped just as hard and fast when I touched her as when she touched me. Passion filled me with every sound, and I longed to see what other noises I could get her to make. Pride swelled in my chest that I was the one making her feel this way. My simple touch brought her pleasure, and I loved that I got to feel her hidden places. That smile of hers I enjoyed so much rode her lips as she rode my fingers.

I usually left during her intimate moments with men, but never out of earshot, should she need me. I'd never seen her face so beautiful, I dare say close to angelic, as when I touched her.

"More," she breathed out as she rocked her hips against the palm of my hand.

As I sped my fingers, she wrapped her hand around my penis again, and I almost lost control. She pumped in rhythm as I worked on her. My concentration was torn between trying to make her feel good with my fingers and my own feelings washing over me. All thoughts left me as I succumbed to the sensations, freeing my mind.

"I need you, Theo," she whispered.

"You have me, Eden. Always and forever, yours," I gasped as she circled the tip of my penis with her finger, slipping along some kind of liquid. Had it come from me? I wasn't sure.

"No, I need you inside me. Now," she said louder, breathier, and with an urgency I hadn't heard from her before as she guided the head to her opening.

I stilled.

Sex.

Real sex.

I couldn't.

No.

But, oh, how I wanted to.

She rolled on top of me as I warred internally. I opened my eyes wide as she angled my fingers so they still pressed against her nub and eased her body down my shaft. I gasped. I groaned. I died in that moment, as everything exploded at once while she rose and fell, bouncing on top of me, eliciting moans that sent sparks of adrenaline back through my heart. That same euphoria bubbled up, this time swallowing me as she slid my penis in and out of her.

I was inside my own personal Eden.

She pressed her hand to mine still holding on to her core, and I realized I needed to rub her some more. I traced a finger over her— right above where our bodies met. Her head fell back as she moaned and shuddered. Her inner walls clenched around me, and my own back arched as something spiraled deep in my core, straight through me into her. A sensation took over my body, a mix of passion and euphoria, and a groan sprang from my lips as my body shuddered beneath hers.

I struggled to regain breath in my lungs. That overwhelming euphoric sensation hummed around me, an echo of what it was just moments ago, the insatiable hunger quelled. How could something this amazing, this powerful and spiritual be so wrong? Was it not made for two people connected to share and enjoy? Two people in love making love.

My heart sped at the thought. I'd loved all my charges, for without love I could not have saved them time after time.

There were many forms of love, and the Greeks expressed it best with their multiple variations of words for it. There was *philautia*, or self-love. Respecting and honoring yourself so that you could love others. There was *pragma*, or longstanding love. The love of duration and strength. *Agape* love, a selfless love, a love of others with nothing in return. *Philia*, or a friendship love. The love that encompassed loyalty and honor. *Ludus*, the light and playful kind of love found in flirting and dancing, a carefree love with little attachment but much joy. And *eros*, the sexual love. It represented passion and desire. That love frightened the Greeks most of all, who named it after the god of fertility, as those who fell prey to this fiery love often lost their minds.

Yet I could not put a name to the love I had for Eden. Most of my charges would have fallen simply under pragma and agape. I loved them all and did my duty to them through their lives.

But this time, I was *in* love. This time I shared each and every form of love the Greeks had, and many more they couldn't begin to put a word around. I now understood eros though, and how it was the most dangerous of all. The Greeks were right to fear it, for there was no way out when you let go. I lost myself, my thoughts, my way, all to have just one chance to be with Eden.

Pressing her palms along my chest, she leaned forward and claimed my lips, swirling her tongue over mine. We remained locked together, body, mind, and soul as she kissed me. And I kissed her right back. I clung desperately to the hope that I could remember every moment, relive them somehow in my head because I knew in my heart this would be only one time.

I didn't want to hurt her more when I inevitably had to. But the longer I stayed in her embrace, connected physically and mentally to her soul, the harder it would be on both of us when I would get ripped from her.

Eden was paradise, and I didn't want to leave.

7

EDEN

M<small>Y EYES FLUTTERED OPEN AS</small> I <small>HUGGED THE PILLOW BESIDE ME.</small> A delirious smile twitched on my lips as I recalled every single moment of making love with Theo. It had been perfect. More than perfect. It had been spiritual.

He had a gentleness to him, a shyness like he'd never had sex before. It was a huge, unexpected turn-on. But the way his fingers played my body like an instrument, surely the man was the furthest thing from a virgin a person could get. Sex with him took me to another plane of existence, another time. We connected differently. We sounded different. The entire event seemed heavenly.

Most of all, he cared. He cared how he moved. He cared how I moved. He cared how I felt and watched me with an intensity like his very existence depended upon my pleasure. I'd never been with someone who, especially while making love, cared more about me than themselves.

There were moments—moments that I looked into his eyes and gazed upon his soul, one very, very old. Love, goodness, and light filled him, made up his entire being. When we kissed, he all but glowed, like an aura of pure happiness radiated around him. And when we connected, having him inside me physically, he also entered me emotionally, penetrating my heart and mind. I'd never had that with anyone else, ever. It was like I could see eternity, full of only bliss and sheer joy. Words couldn't even begin to define what happened. We seared a place in each other's soul.

He was the one. I understood, now, why things fell apart in all my other relationships. I even forgave Grayson for being the lying, cheating bastard he was. My mind was never freer, nor my heart lighter than when I let go of my resentment, my anger, and sadness. Forgiveness was a powerful thing, not only for the perpetrator but also for the victim. I truly forgave him because everything had become so clear.

It was hard to see the entire forest when I was sinking in mud at the base of a tall redwood. But once lifted from the muck, I could see so much with all the clutter cleared away. Hindsight being twenty-twenty was true, of course, because we didn't know in that moment of destitution what was planned for us down the road.

His scent lingered on the pillow in my arms, such a mysterious smell of sunshine after rain, like new life in the spring as blooms open, and woodsy like the hottest burning flames in a campfire.

It hit me that he was gone. I sat up, clutching the covers against my chest. Why, I had no idea because it wasn't like we hadn't just been bare to each other in every way possible. Plus, he wasn't in the room.

How long had I fallen asleep for? I glanced at the clock and found it nearing ten at night.

I slid out from the bed and put on a new pair of fuzzy pants, covered in penguins wearing a mix of Christmas lights and wreaths, and a simple white T-shirt.

I looked toward the bathroom, but the lights were off and the door open. Sucking in a fearful breath, I made my way to the living room. Dim twinkling lights shone through the darkness of the hall-way, beckoning me closer. As I turned the corner, my heart skipped through my chest. Theo knelt in front of my tree, murmuring something I was pretty sure wasn't English, or even one of the six languages I knew. It sounded like some Gregorian chant. His fists hit the ground as he fell forward, head bowed, and I wasn't sure if it was intentional or if he was having a seizure.

The tiny lights twinkling off the tree reflected on his naked, tan body. His chest bounced, rising and falling as sobs ripped through him. He was crying. Naked. In front of my Christmas tree that I didn't remember even decorating. Earlier we had left in such a whirlwind, he never finished bringing the boxes down from the attic. And of course, he was barely conscious when we got home from the longest two-hour journey of my life in arctic temperatures.

He must have decorated the tree after we had sex. Who did that? And why was he crying? Was the sex that bad? Here I thought it was nothing short of magical, ethereal, and life-changing. I mean, there was nothing wrong with a man crying—in fact, I thought more men needed to let go of stereotypes and get in touch with their feelings, but not right after the most amazing sex of their lives on Christmas Eve.

I tiptoed through the living room and knelt beside him on the floor. Taking a chance, I slid my hand along his bare back and rubbed his warm skin to soothe him. His body hitched, as if he held his breath, and stilled.

"Are you all right?" I bit my lip, not sure if I really wanted an answer.

Blowing out a long breath, he pushed himself up from the floor and sat back on his knees. "My apologies, I thought you were sleeping."

"No need to apologize. I was just worried when I rolled over and you were gone."

He stared up, where my angel sat high atop the tree. "I have to tell you something."

Oh, crap. No good ever came from a conversation starting with those words, especially after sex. I forced down the acid sliding up my throat, prepping for the worst. He was married. He was really gay. He was part of some weird cult where I needed to be sacrificed after sex. Or possibly he was some kind of alien because that would explain all the weird shit that happened since he'd been around.

"Okay, you can tell me anything, Theo." I rubbed along his back once more, and his hard face softened into contentment, but just as quick, he closed his eyes and the brooding brow returned, as if he warred within himself about my touch.

"I'm not from here." He tucked his chin and bowed his head.

"Okay, that's not a big deal. If you need a place to crash, I'm not going to kick you into the street after having the best, most amazing sex of my entire life." Clearly, I didn't need rum or eggnog to say the most inane and embarrassing things.

He turned his head, still bowed, in my direction, and a sly grin cracked his sullen lips. "The most amazing sex of your entire life?"

My knees tingled, and I wasn't sure if it was from sheer humiliation or if my legs fell asleep from kneeling against my hardwood floor. I uncurled them from beneath me and crossed them, nodding at him as I accepted my fate. "Yeah. It was unlike anything I've ever felt before."

There, I said it. It was out there in the universe for him to use against me at any time. I was sure, like all men, it would go to his head, and he'd be all smug for the rest of the night, but...well, damn if he didn't earn the right.

He dipped his head low, again, away from my gaze. "Same for me."

A flutter ransacked my heart and threw it down a set of stairs, all the way to my stomach. Did mine ears deceive me? He admitted he felt the same. He surprised me at every turn.

"Really?" And of all the times to lose my words, this seemed like a great one.

He nodded and reached for my hand, brushing the back of it with his thumb. "Please, believe me when I say I've never had such an incredible experience in all my existence."

Joy danced in my heart. I knew it. I knew he was the one. I felt it with my body, mind, and soul as we lay connected together in a way that shattered me to pieces. Good pieces. Pieces of a hard shell that needed to be broken, shed, torn off in order for me to learn to live again, to know there was good in the world still and that I was worthy of it. He showed me just how worthy I was. In this one magical moment on Christmas Eve, I finally got my wish. His starting the conversation with the dreaded, *I need to tell you something*, might actually lead to the words my heart longed to hear… that he had feelings for me.

Okay, so we'd only known each other a grand total of twelve hours, but they were twelve of the most amazing hours of my entire life. Well, it didn't start out that way, since he met me with a tree in my face. But still, things took a turn for the better, with a weird roundabout in the middle where he knew all this crazy shit about my life, and while that part still niggled in my head, he didn't seem like some sociopath. There was so much familiarity about him, like maybe we were past soul mates reincarnated or something. He just fit me, and I him.

"My time here is short, Eden, and I could be taken away at any moment."

He turned toward me, and my concentration disintegrated as I stared at his chiseled chest that led to the most fantastic penis funnel I'd ever laid eyes on. It was like God himself molded this man and sent him to me.

He pressed a finger under my chin, directing my attention back to his face. Heat bloomed across my cheeks. "Did you hear what I said?"

I bit my lip and nodded. "Something about you having to go soon. Are you military?"

"In a sense, I'm part of an army, yes." He nodded. "That's a very good way to think about it."

Relief flowed in my veins. Military I could handle. It would suck if he got deployed or something, but that definitely explained his amazing body and life-saving skills, not to mention the freakishly keen knowledge, probably special access to government secrets. He most likely had to do a thorough investigation on me before getting involved, so I wouldn't blow his cover. Yeah, that had to be it.

"You don't have to leave right this moment, do you?" I tilted my head as I cupped my hand around his fingers.

"The sooner I do, the better off we'll all be. I can no longer hear my brethren. Their voices have been cut off from me. I fear I've been down here too long now." He glanced at his free hand, turning it back and forth, staring at it like some foreign object.

"Down here, what do you mean? We're in Jersey. Oh, are you Canadian? Are you a Mountie?" Excitement took my voice up a notch, as the thought of him in a Mountie uniform on a horse sent a thrill through me.

"No, I'm not Canadian," he said with a laugh.

"I like when you laugh." I cupped his cheek. "Your smile is brilliant and could light up a room."

"As does yours," he said, mimicking my motion as he cupped a hand on my cheek.

"Come back to bed, Theo. If you have to leave soon, let's make the most of our time." Dropping my hand from his face, I grazed his bare chest with my fingernail, eliciting a shiver from his body.

He curled his fingers around my hand, pulling it from his chest. "I really want to. But I promised myself only once. If I indulge any further, I may never be able to go home."

"What does that mean? Why do you speak in riddles? You're like some archaic text I'm trying to translate." Frustration laced my words, and they felt bitter as they left my lips.

"It means I need to tell you the truth."

"That would be freaking fantastic because I've been trying to get answers from you all day." I huffed and crossed my arms.

He rose from the floor and pulled me up by my hands, guiding me to the sofa to sit next to him. Scrubbing his hands along his face, he blew out a hard breath before turning to face me. "I'm not of this world."

I blinked and stared at him. *And here comes the crazy...*

"I'm…" He paused, and anguish filled his eyes.

"An alien?" I burst out.

He threw his head back and laughed so hard his body bounced the sofa. "No, I'm not an alien."

My heart slowed a bit, but my lips remained pressed to a thin line as my frustrations mounted. "So just spit it out then. Stop with the riddles and the pauses for dramatic effect. What could possibly be so b—"

Without letting me finish, he blurted out, "I'm an angel."

I quirked a brow. "You're acting like the devil torturing me. Will you just tell me the truth?"

"I just did."

My brow arched higher, and I hitched back. "No, you're still playing games. So stop it. Please don't ruin our wonderful night with lies."

"I'm not. I swear to you, I'm an angel." He clutched my hands between his own and pulled me closer, staring deep into my eyes. The truth in them shocked my heart, like he really believed his own words. Gone were the eyes I first saw, the ones that showed me wonders and took me to a place deep within his soul. Anguish and pain clouded the blue to a watery gray.

"You actually believe that, don't you?" Tremors sparked in my hands, and I didn't realize it until Theo pressed them flat between his own in an attempt to calm me down.

He tightened his grip and pulled my hands to his chest, laying them flat against his heart. "I do because it's the truth. No more lies. Well, I've never actually lied to you, as it's impossible for me to lie. I just may have omitted some portions of the truth in our conversations. But honestly, I've never lied to you, and I'm not lying now."

I shook my head, and fear pitched and rolled in my stomach. I knew he was too good to be true. Once again, I let my heart lead over my head. In the end, all I attracted were the worst of mankind. Part of me wondered if there wasn't some target on my back or a microchip implanted in me that acted like a homing beacon for the wayward and psychotic.

He pressed my hand tighter against his chest, and his heart thumped an erratic rhythm beneath my fingers. "Look deep inside your heart, Eden. You've always known."

"Look, Theo, or Theliel, whatever you call yourself, I have enough crazy for the both of us. I really don't need anymore. If your home planet is calling, perhaps you need to answer and grab a bus. I'll even cover cab fare to the station because at least the sex was out of this world. I'll give you that."

Panic hit my heart, jackhammering in my chest as he continued his intense stare, almost willing me beyond my control to look him in the eyes. Every inch of me wanted to flee, to look away and run to the bedroom and lock myself in. But something hooked me to his gaze instead, and it burned all the way to my soul.

"I'm *your* angel. Your guardian angel." He cupped my cheek, stroking in slow swipes along my skin.

"You're flesh and blood, naked on my sofa. How are you my guardian angel? My guardian angel is some woman in a white robe drinking copious amounts of heavenly wine after having to deal with me, and I don't blame her one bit. In fact, I'm hearing the sweet siren song of rum right now, so I think I'll go send her a toast." I wiggled free of his hold and tried to push my way off the sofa.

The doorbell rang, and my raging heart slowed. *See, I told him he wasn't my guardian angel. She just sent someone to intervene and save my life from this weirdo.*

Theo's expression turned as pale as a ghost, and he shot up from the sofa. "Don't answer the door."

"Why not? Afraid it's a man in a white coat sent to take you back to your planet or the insane asylum?" Anger burned in my gut, burying the fear that churned there. I raged inside that I had once again fallen for some stupid asshole's tricks.

I darted to the door and clamped my hand around the knob.

"Please, don't do this, Eden. I'm in love with you." He reached out a hand, palm face up, begging me to come back to him.

"Does an insane person even know what love is? Love isn't lies. Love isn't a game. Love isn't hurting someone for your own selfish desires." I twisted the knob and pulled open the door. "Love isn't declaring you're in love with someone you just met."

"But I've known you your whole life, Eden."

Something in his words hit me in the gut, his familiarity, his warmth and calming effect on me. But there was no way what he said could have been true, could it?

A man stood on the other side in jeans and a black leather jacket. His presence radiated a warmth that immediately calmed me, almost like the moment I first met Theo. Though darker than Theo, his skin had that faint glow to it, like he walked under his own personal ray of sunshine. He twirled a coin between his fingers, flipping it back and forth over his knuckles.

"Good evening, Miss Credere. My name is Kasbiel. I'm looking for a friend of mine named Theliel." He flicked his wrist, and the coin launched into the air. He caught it with the same hand he tossed it with while offering a handshake with the other.

Theo dashed to my side and yanked me from the door. "No, don't touch him!"

I jumped back, startled by Theo's outcry.

"Ah, there you are, Theliel. I've been sent to take you home. You're well past your time to return, dear boy." He lowered his brow, as if there lay some hidden meaning behind his words that Theo should understand.

I stood there, blinking, as I realized Theo was still naked and this Kasbiel person really didn't seem to notice or care.

"Take him home? Where?" I crossed my arms and jutted my hip to the side as I looked to Theo for an answer. Was he going to keep up this angel facade, or did home mean the loony bin he'd escaped from?

"To the angelic realm," Theo replied, though his answer wasn't to me—it was directed to this Kasbiel person.

"Oh, right. So...not heaven, but some realm where the angels hang out, naked, and what...play Yahtzee between saving people's lives?" I pursed my lips, staring at Theo, who stared at Kasbiel, who stood there with a stupid smile plastered on his lips like a Stepford wife.

"Home, Theliel. It's time to go home. This"—he fanned his arms around the room—"is not where you belong."

"What if I don't want to go? What if this *is* where I belong? I've waited centuries for this, for her. This is where I'm meant to be. I know it, Kasbiel. Something this right cannot be wrong. Listen to me," Theo pleaded, taking a step toward Kasbiel.

"If you come with me over here, Miss Credere, I'll see to it you won't be bothered by Theliel any longer. I'm so sorry for all the confusion. I'll take care of that for you if you just take my hand," Kasbiel said, ignoring Theo's pleas.

"No!" Theo pushed Kasbiel's hand away. "He's going to wipe your memories. Our memories. Don't let him touch you."

I glanced between the anguish on Theo's face and the smile on Kasbiel's, and decided on neither of them as I raced to the kitchen and grabbed my trusty bottle of spray bleach still on the floor from earlier.

"Stay away, both of you. I mean it. This freak show ends right now. Both of you, get the hell out of my house!" I aimed it back and forth between the two of them.

This is how it all ends, isn't it? I have the best sex of my life with some psycho I just met, and then he kills me with his friend on Christmas Eve. Everything in my life has spiraled to this ridiculous moment. Maybe I should let it happen. What more did I have to live for anyway? I wish I could have told my mom I still loved her, even if she stopped loving me.

Theo stepped forward and brushed a lock of hair behind my ear. "Eden, she still loves you. She's just as stubborn and prideful as you are. Where do you think you get it from?"

My eyes shot wide open as I processed the possibility that all he said could be true because the dude had literally read my mind. There was no way he could have guessed that was what I was thinking exactly in that moment.

He turned to Kasbiel. "Take me. But leave Eden be. Let her have one happy memory of us, so she doesn't fall back into that darkness. She has so much she's meant to do yet. I beg of you, don't make her go back to that place."

"Wait, what? No! Don't leave. I have so many questions." I lowered my arms holding the spray bleach. "How'd you do that? How'd you read my mind? Theo, is this all true?" Tears pooled in my eyes, and the tremble from my hands now hit my lips.

Theo opened his mouth to speak, but Kasbiel cut him off by holding up his hand. Theo raised his own hand, a soft hazy glow illuminating from his palm as he thrust it forward, and without even touching him, he sent Kasbiel flying across the room.

Did I really just witness that?

Okay, him reading my mind was one thing. Seeing him launch another man through my house was another. I blinked, shaking my head, replaying the incident over in my mind. Then I realized, I never heard Kasbiel hit anything. He should have theoretically landed in my Christmas tree.

I darted to the living room to look for him. "Theo, where did he go?"

"He'll be back. I may have just transported him to Siberia, or Antarctica, I can't be sure. It was a split decision." He winced for a moment before looking me in the eyes. "I wanted him gone long enough to tell you...I'm so sorry. I didn't mean for any of this to happen. I wanted to tell you from the start, but I couldn't. I never intended for it to get this far. I wanted to help you. Make you believe in yourself again. Show you how to love yourself. But something happened to me. I...I fell..."

I blinked as I processed this entire situation, trying to read between the words he couldn't say. It sounded like he was going to give up. "Wait, Theo, you're not going back with him now, are you?"

Sadness and defeat darkened his eyes. "I have to. Angels were never meant to be humans." He hung his head. "I must go back and accept the repercussions for my actions."

"Theo, don't leave me." I threw my arms around his shoulders. "I lo—" The words stuck in the back of my throat as I curled my fingers into the hair at the nape of his neck. Yet they wanted to burst out of me every second I held him in my arms.

It was crazy, absolutely crazy, to say to a man I'd known only for a day. But in reality, he had known me my whole life. Somehow, I knew him too. It explained all the unusual dreams I'd had of him. I knew him. I loved him. It all came barreling back to me in an instant. For no matter how bizarre it seemed, my heart knew it all to be true. It was why my heart trusted him from the moment I saw him.

I forced the words out, relinquishing doubt and believing in them as they left my tongue. "I'm in love with you. It's insane, but this feeling in my heart, I can't explain it. It's like...it's like I've known you all my life. In my dreams, and now here, really here in my arms. I've never felt so whole."

His body hitched and stilled as I clung to him, and he tightened his hold on me, curling his fingers into my flesh. Something hot and wet hit my shoulder, and I realized it was Theo's tears as he whispered against my ear, "I love you, too, Eden. I always have, and I always will. Believe that."

Theo clung to me tighter. I knew in that instant Kasbiel had returned and was standing behind me. I shook my head. "No, please, no."

A spine-tingling heat spiked the hairs on the back of my neck. I turned around and blocked Kasbiel from Theo. "Please, there has to be another way. I beg you."

"It is not *my* will that I do this for." Kasbiel looked me in the eyes, a glassy remorse filling them before he turned his attention to

Theo. "Theliel, you know this. It is not up to me to make that decision." Sadness filled his words, each one sounding heavy and full of
regret.

A single tear rolled down my cheek, and I clasped my hands
with Theo's. I wasn't giving up. He tightened his hand on mine as
he brushed the water from my cheek.

"There's got to be another way. Maybe I can go to the council,
talk to them. Ask them for a special dispensation? I don't know.
Kasbiel, please, help me out here," Theo begged.

Kasbiel shook his head. "I have my orders, as you did. You broke
them, and now I have to fix it."

Had Theo just read my mind earlier, we could have spent my
unused honeymoon tickets and been in Barbados by now, avoiding
this whole scenario. Of course, if this Kasbiel was an angel like
Theo was, he'd probably still find us there.

"I promise you, Miss Credere, I'm not going to hurt you. It'll all
be over in a moment." Kasbiel reached for me.

Theo lunged at Kasbiel, trying to push down his arm. But this
time, Kasbiel's palm was the one that glowed as he held Theo back.

"Eden," Theo choked out, palms flat against some kind of invisible force field or shield around Kasbiel as he closed in on me.

"No." I narrowed my eyes and raised the spray bleach again,
aiming right for those suspicious eyes as Kasbiel slid a single finger
along my forehead. A funny fizzle tickled my skin, like static
without the painful shock. Fog swirled in my mind as I struggled to
focus on Theo's face, concentrating on the agony in his eyes as I
watched him fade. "Theliel..." I cried softly. "No..."

Kasbiel lowered his arms, and Theo stumbled forward, gripping Kasbiel by the shoulder as he shoved him out of the way to get
to me.

Tears pooled in his eyes as he pressed his lips to my cheek in a
soft kiss and whispered, "*Pisteúō*."

The bottle of spray bleach dropped from my fingers as blackness surrounded me.

8

THEO

I DROPPED TO MY KNEES AND CRADLED EDEN IN MY ARMS. ANOTHER tear slid down my face, crashing upon her cheek as I clutched her to my chest. Her limp arms hung heavy at her sides, and her head lolled back.

Kasbiel looked down at me. "You know she only sleeps. The pain will be less for her if the memories are also stripped from her dreams."

Dreams. Eden mentioned earlier that evening that she had dreamed of me, many times before we ever even met. What did that mean?

"What if the memories aren't stripped from her dreams?" I asked without another thought. "Will they recur through her dreams?" Could that be why she had dreamed of me? Did we meet in person once before? Surely I would have remembered if she ever saw me corporeal. Though I couldn't recall ever being in human form and interacting with her in all my memories.

"Let her go, Theliel. The sooner you do, the less pain you shall have as well." Kasbiel rose and walked toward the tree, tilting his head to glance at the top. "Why do they always give us wings in their renditions? Not every angel is a seraphim." He shook his head with a sigh.

I stared at him, not with anger any longer, but with pity, for I had a feeling Kasbiel would be less apathetic about the situation if he had any frame of reference to love. "Have you ever loved, Kasbiel?"

He spun around and clasped his hands behind him. "Of course. I love everyone. Love is a part of our entire existence."

"No, I mean really loved. Been *in* love. Felt something more for one of your charges. Something so different and extraordinary, drawn to them."

He shrugged. "Not really. I loved and cared for all my charges. But I've never favored one above another."

"She's a unique human." I grazed her cheek with the back of my hand, relishing the sensation of her skin one last time.

"Every human is unique. There are no two alike, like snowflakes. Even those who are twins may look similar, but differ widely inside." Kasbiel crossed his arms.

"She was unique to me. I'd never had a charge that always put her needs second to others around her. She always took the time to help, to talk, to encourage others. People often took advantage of her, yet she never turned down someone in need."

"There are countless humans who lead such lives. This Eden is only one of many who are born with a servant's heart and heed the duty they're called to do."

"But she was my only one. I witnessed how she changed people's lives for the better. I witnessed how one human's light could change the world. She was hope. My hope."

"She can still do those things."

"I don't know. In the last month, she lost her fire, her light. Her soul darkened, and her spirit dampened." An ache welled in my soul as I thought back to the heaviness in her, the darkness that had been starting to swallow her.

Kasbiel dropped to a crouch in front of me. "You know all our charges go through trials. It's how they learn, and in turn teach others and use their tribulations to make change."

"But she lost her light along the way, lost her own hope. Hope that she would be loved after the rejection of her mother and her own fiancé. Hope that she made any difference in the world. Hope that there was more out there than just pain and sacrifice. I tried to give that hope back to her. That's all I wanted. But what happened was so much more. I gave her my hope. I gave her my love."

I pressed my lips to hers one last time as I carried her to her bed. After tucking her under the covers, and one last touch of her face, I met Kasbiel back in the living room.

"You sorrow in vain, brother." Kasbiel laid a hand on my shoulder. "Her new guardian will guide her, help her find her light again. Trust in that, Theliel." He extended his other hand. "Come, we must go now."

I hitched back, shaking my head. "What do you mean, new guardian? *I'm* her guardian."

"I'm afraid after this final incident you'll be removed from Ms. Credere and assigned a new charge."

"No. I'm not going back if I can't still be her guardian. At least in the shadows, I can still watch her, guide her, care for her. Please, don't take that away from me too." Desperation took hold of me, weighing down my heart at the thought of never seeing Eden again. I replayed his words over in my mind, stuck on something he'd said. "What do you mean *final* incident?"

"This is not for me to discuss. You can plead your case to the council. I'm only sent to retrieve you, not pass judgment."

I nodded, knowing I didn't have much choice and that Kasbiel would not be the one with the answers I needed. With a sigh, I closed my eyes and prepared my soul to release from its human form.

Nothing happened.

I opened my eyes and glanced around. Kasbiel disappeared, but I still stood in Eden's living room. Naked.

I closed my eyes again and willed my soul to leave the corporeal flesh surrounding it.

Again, nothing.

I looked at my hands and wiggled my fingers and toes.

"Kasbiel," I whispered.

Silence surrounded me, except for the faint sizzle of electricity humming through the wires of the Christmas lights.

"Kasbiel," I said, this time a little louder.

Kasbiel shimmered into view. "I thought you were right behind me. Quit stalling. The sooner you come and get it over with, the sooner you can move on."

"I can't." I held my hands up.

"What do you mean, you can't?" He quirked a brow, studying me.

"I mean, I can't morph. I tried. I'm stuck." Panic released a wave of adrenaline through me, like a thousand little jackhammers attacking my heart. "Did I stay human too long?"

"I don't know. I'm an angel, not omnipotent. Try conjuring something and see if all your powers are gone." Kasbiel folded his arms and pressed a finger to his chin as he assessed the situation.

"Like what?"

"Try clothes. I'm tired of looking at your new penis."

I rolled my eyes. "Are you suffering envy, Kasbiel?"

"I have no need to look upon the human anatomy. We were not given genitals, so what need would I have to gaze upon them? It's insufferable, just dangling there between your legs. And how it elongates and grows whenever you look at your human, it's like a wind sock. Why would I want one?"

I stifled a laugh. The more he defended his viewpoint, the more I wasn't sure if he was trying to convince me or himself. "Okay, let me try clothes."

I closed my eyes and visualized a pair of jeans and a white T-shirt. Popping one eye open, I glanced down to find myself still naked and well hung. Defeat and worry warred with each other in my soul. *What have I done?*

A bright-blue light blazed through the room, separating me from Kasbiel, and I hit the floor, repenting, for I knew all too well what that blue light meant. Phanuel, the archangel, was coming, and coming for me.

I prostrated myself, showing respect and allegiance to my brethren, and prayed that my punishment would be swift and redeeming.

"Dear Theliel, please, get up, brother," Phanuel said, clasping his hands in front of him.

Love glowed in his bright-blue eyes, but a shadow of sadness hid within their depths. Long, ginger locks of hair sat upon his shoulders, flowing and draping him like a majestic cowl.

"Phanuel, brother, it's good to see you." I hoped the worry in my heart didn't manifest in my voice. I wasn't worried about me, as I accepted my fate and knew there had to be punishment. But my worry stemmed from the possibility of losing Eden all together.

"It's good to"—his gaze dropped to my waist—"*see* you as well, Theliel," he said with a soft chuckle. "And there's apparently much more of you to see these days."

I shrugged and let out a sigh. "I tried to morph, but I'm somehow stuck in this human form."

"Yes, I'm aware. I'm here for that very reason."

I swallowed and nodded. We lower-tiered angels were rarely fortunate enough to gaze upon one of the elders. Phanuel was one of the four archangels, his very name meaning *the face of God*. It just so happened he was the angel of penance and repentance, which would be exactly why he was here.

"It appears you've lost your way, Theliel." He lowered his brow a bit. "There's been much discussion among the council, as well as with the One at the head of the table. We see what's in your heart and know of your struggles. While we're disappointed you succumbed to temptation, we also see your plight and love for this human, as each time it's happened, the same outcome occurs."

His long white-and-gold robes slid up and down his arm as he gestured with his hands. I almost lost myself in the trance of his movements, hypnotized by his aura and presence.

"So we are offering you a choice."

My ears sharpened at the words *each time it's happened*, and I snapped my attention to his glowing face. I cocked a brow. "What do you mean 'each time it's happened'?"

Phanuel's lips tugged to one side as he dipped his head and looked me in the eyes. "This isn't the first time you've gone corporeal with this charge."

My eyes widened. "What are you talking about? I've never corporealized in front of Eden before."

Kasbiel smirked as he stood next to Phanuel. "Try three times, brother."

I stared at Kasbiel in disbelief. "That's impossible. I have no such memories—" Kasbiel's words came rushing back to me. Earlier he said something about this being my final time. "Are you saying Eden and I have been together before? In love? Three times?"

Kasbiel glanced at Phanuel, and then they both looked to me. "Yes."

"But..." I shook my head and looked between both of them.

"Your memories were cleansed," Phanuel said. "You, of course, retained knowledge of Eden, your charge, but all memories of falling in love and corporealizing were removed. Yet somehow you continued to show yourself to her and fall in love. So this time, we're giving you a choice."

"A choice?" I asked, still trying to process the information. That must have been why Eden dreamed of me. We'd been together before. Neither of us remembered, but our souls did. They were drawn to each other, meant to be.

Phanuel nodded. "You have the choice to come back to the fold one final time, our wayward son. You will be given back your powers, but this time, you will be assigned a new charge. We can remove your memory again, if you wish, as it will make the transition away from your current charge easier on you. But you will be stripped of Eden completely, not just the times you went corporeal."

His words choked me, wedging a lump of emotions in my throat. Yes, of course I wanted my powers back and to once again be among the angels, my brethren. It was what I was created for, my purpose in this existence. I'd done so much good through the millennia and wished to continue to serve. But to be wiped clean of my memories of Eden, forever and completely, a piece of me that I'd never remember, how could I agree to that? How could I ever willingly forget her? My heart would never let me.

I raised my head and looked up at him. "What is the other option?"

Phanuel glanced at me, as if startled, pulled from his quiet talk with Kasbiel. "Hmm? Oh, yes, well, we could make you human. Permanently."

I blinked. *Did I hear him correctly?*

"Did you say I could be human, permanently?"

Phanuel nodded. "Well, not permanently as in immortal." His hands rose and fell as he gestured with the animation of an orchestra conductor. "You would live an ordinary human life. Which would mean you would give up being an angel forever. As we angels were never mortals, thus, if you become human, you can never be an angel again. So upon your death, you would be like any other human. Oh, that brings up the next item—you would also be subjected to a mortal death."

I ran a hand through my hair as I processed the information. I had a chance to be human. Have a real human life. My dream of being with Eden, making her my wife, possibly having children, grandchildren, it flooded my head with delight at the possibilities. In that moment, I knew. I knew in my heart, no matter how much my head wavered, that was what I wanted.

"Now, before you choose." Phanuel interrupted my thoughts spinning out of control. "One more thing...if you become human, you do so as a fresh start."

"What does that mean?" I quirked a brow. "I need to be birthed?"

"No, no." He chuckled. "What woman could push you out of her loins?"

"What, then?" I stared at him, longing for him to just spit it out and stop prolonging it. I wanted my new life to start as soon as possible.

"You will not continue *here*. You will be made human permanently on the Earth, but with no memories of being an angel or of Ms. Credere. You will basically have to start from scratch with your life from this moment on." Phanuel clasped his hands in front of him.

"What?" I gasped. "I couldn't possibly...how would I find her?"

Phanuel shrugged and looked at Kasbiel before focusing back on me. "You managed it three times before."

"But that was as an angel. You said it yourself—I retained knowledge of Eden. I knew her. I just didn't have the memories of me and her together. This would be no memories as a mortal. No powers. No help. No nothing."

No. How would I find Eden? How would she find me? She would have amnesia from Kasbiel's memory wipe, as would I. Neither of us would know the other even existed. I fell back on my butt on the cold floor and pressed the palms of my hands to my head. How could I choose?

"If you and Ms. Credere are in love and truly meant to be, you will find a way back to each other." He winked. "That's all I can say on the matter. These are the parameters of your penance. Now you must choose between them."

"So you're saying there's a chance we could make this work? We could find each other again?" Hope squeezed out the fear in my heart. All I needed was hope, to believe in a chance. I had to have faith.

"There's always a chance. There is only One who knows what will happen. Even we archangels aren't omnipotent, remember?" Phanuel smiled, but Kasbiel's eyes darkened as he looked between the two of us.

"I know it is not my place, Phanuel, as you are the one to dole out penance, but why would you allow him to fall from grace?" Kasbiel fanned his arm in my direction.

Phanuel placed a hand on his shoulder. "It is not a fall from Grace, but to Grace. For His mercy is great, and Grace is given to all who believe. The humans are loved no less than us. If there is a greater meaning for Theliel's life on Earth, then that is where he's meant to go. But we are given free will, so I am gifting him a choice."

"But won't all angels then wish to be human? Won't this set a precedent?" Kasbiel countered.

"Theliel is not the first, nor will he be the last, I'm sure. Not all angels seek to be human. Not all humans seek to be angels. Not all are destined for the same path, no matter their existence. Worry not, Kasbiel, for losing a brother. He will need his own guardian soon, should he choose humanity." A smile played on Phanuel's lips, close to resembling a smirk.

"What if he never finds Eden?" Kasbiel glanced at me, a strange glint in his eyes.

"I'll find her. I know it. My soul won't forget her. We'll find our way back to each other." While my words sounded sure, my mind teetered on the fence.

"Neither of you will have any memory of the other. You could be sent to Malaysia." Kasbiel crossed his arms. "There's a real possibility you may never see each other again. Is this really what you want, Theliel? A mere fraction of a chance to find your human? Is giving up your immortality, your brothers, your powers, and your existence worth this?" Kasbiel pleaded, not only with his words, but also with his eyes.

Knowing him as well as I did, I had a feeling that glint earlier was of sadness, and if angels could cry, it would have been a tear.

It filled my heart with joy and intense sorrow that my brother cared so much about me and my future to plead on my behalf. But Kasbiel had never known love, not in the way I now had. Not that I wished him to fall into temptation to do so, but I realized a part of him would remain empty without it.

"Kasbiel, if you'd ever known love like I have, you would understand that there is no question. I would give anything for a chance at a human life with Eden. If this is what I must do, I will. I know if I go back, with my memory wiped or not, something will ache in my soul, an emptiness will still be there without her. I may fall back into temptation again if I choose to stay an angel, just to try to fill that void, unaware of what it is that I'm trying to find."

Phanuel tapped his foot and whistled, looking around the room with a gleam in his eye and a smile on his lips. What he was so happy about, I had no clue. He caught me mid stare. Startled, he strode over to the tree. "Oh, look, an angel." He tilted his head. "Why do they always show wings? The seraphim are a tiny sect of angels, yet they get all the credit. Oh, well."

He walked over and placed a hand on Kasbiel with a reassuring smile. "All will be okay. We may not always get what we want. But we're always given what we need."

Kasbiel nodded in silence.

Phanuel turned to me. "Have you come to a final decision, Theliel?"

I swallowed hard as I looked toward Eden's bedroom and back at Phanuel and Kasbiel. "I have. I want to become human."

Phanuel smiled with a nod. "Peace be with you, brother."

"And also with you both." I closed my eyes with hope in my heart and a very naïve fantasy in my head.

Phanuel was right: we didn't always get what we wanted because more often than not, what we needed was a good, hard lesson to learn first.

9

EDEN

SUNSHINE BURST THROUGH MY BLINDS LIKE A BUGLE WAKE-UP CALL. Groaning, I reached for my phone to check the time. The numbers clicked over to noon, and I shot up in bed but immediately regretted that decision as my head throbbed with a horrible ache. I flopped backward. What did I have to drink last night?

I blew out a sigh and pressed my palms to my throbbing skull. A niggling feeling poked at me, like I was forgetting something, but between the brain pain and the fact I'd slept so late, I figured it would come to me later.

"Well, today's bad decisions aren't going to make themselves." With a yawn, I shuffled out of bed and into my living room.

I blinked, staring at the barren spot where my Christmas tree should be. Pushing the front window curtain aside, I glanced at the curb where the remnants of my old plastic tree sank into a snowbank, singed and black, just like my soul. Stupid Grayson, ruining one more facet of my life. He even tainted my love for Christmas, the bastard.

A weird déjà vu sensation hit me, and a picture flashed in my mind. Although blurry, it appeared to be me lying on the ground under a tree with branches smashed in my face. I shook my head and forced out a breath. I tried to focus on the vision, battling waves of dizziness. The more I tried to see it, the more nauseous I became, forcing me to give up for fear I'd end up passing out. In a huff, I folded my arms as I made my way to the kitchen to make some coffee.

A rap on the door startled me mid pour, and I jumped back, spilling hot coffee all over my white tank top. Why was I wearing a tank top in the middle of winter? Maybe I really did drink too much rum and eggnog yesterday.

Another flash hit, this time of a coffee stain, and for a split second, I swore I smelled peppermint mocha. I sniffed my shirt, but it only smelled like coffee and regret.

The rapping noise continued, and I staggered to the door. On the other side stood an elderly woman in a worn tweed coat with two cherub-looking children in their finest Sunday attire, until I glanced at their old, worn tennis shoes.

"Merry Christmas," the elderly woman said with a small smile. Behind it lay years of worry and sadness, showing clear in the lines curving around her quivering lips and the dark circles on her light-brown skin.

"Merry Christmas." I forced the words out of my mouth. "Can I help you?"

The woman tilted her head and several strands of her salt-and-pepper hair fell from the bun wound at the back of her head. "Are we too early? You mentioned last night to come over and we could go over some recipes you'd like to learn for Christmas dinner."

"What?" I blinked and shook my head. "I'm sorry, recipes?"

"Oh, if you need a few moments to freshen up, I can take the wee ones back to the house and wait." She guided the children off the porch.

"No, wait." I had no clue what she was talking about, but the disappointment was clear in her eyes. Maybe in some drunken state I'd told her to come over for dinner or something. The longer

I stared at her, the more her face lodged in my memory. "You're her, the woman from the grocery store."

She nodded with a smile. "That's me. These are the grandchildren you helped feed that day." The two children, one boy and one girl, bowed and curtsied as she tapped them on the shoulder. Long braids hung high from bright-red ponytail holders on the little girl, whose cheeks pinked in the cold. A shy smile twitched on the boy's lips as he fidgeted with a loose-hanging button on his tattered coat.

"They're beautiful. Please, come in. I just spilled coffee on myself." I fanned my hand to show her the lovely mess I'd made. "Give me a minute to clean up and we can get started."

"No worries, child," she said with a grin. "You take your time. We'll occupy ourselves with a story."

I shut the door behind them once they'd shaken off the snow and come in. "Forgive me, I'm Eden. Eden Credere." I extended a hand to her.

She shook it. "Thandie Branson, and these are my grandbabies, Janae and Jordan."

"Would you guys like some hot cocoa?" I bent over to look them in the eyes. "I've got marshmallows!"

Soft giggles floated around them as they looked at each other and then at their grandmother, who nodded her approval. Grins splitting their little faces, they nodded in return to me.

"Can I offer you something to drink, Miss Thandie?"

"If you have any coffee left, I wouldn't say no to a cup." A smile curled on her lips that reached her eyes.

"Great. I'll be right back." I dashed off to the kitchen to make their cocoa and coffee.

As I returned and passed out the drinks, they settled onto the sofa, nestled against their grandmother.

"Thank you kindly," she said before taking a sip of the steaming cup.

I nodded and took the moment to head to the bedroom and put on some clean clothes.

"Now, this is the story of an old lady who was blessed by two Christmas angels. She didn't know they were angels at the time because that's how angels work. You don't always know they're angels, you see. They go around blessing people through acts of kindness, and sometimes just by saying a few words of hope."

I jerked to a stop outside my door and cocked my head to peek back into the living room.

"That's what these two angels did. One man and one woman. The first angel, the woman, she didn't know it, but her simple act of kindness to a stranger allowed a whole family to eat and keep their heat on for Christmas."

"How, gramma?" the little girl asked, bouncing her legs off the edge of the sofa.

"Well, she paid for the woman's groceries one day at the store, so the old lady could use the money she had for some bills. Nothing's free in this world, my dear." She patted the little girl's knee. "Except a smile and a kind gesture. And this woman, this angel, she didn't ask for anything in return. She just did something out of the goodness of her heart, not knowing the old woman's story, nor asking to be paid back. So she had to be an angel."

"I like angels," the little boy said, holding tight to his cup. "I think Miss Eden's an angel because she bought me my Christmas wreath."

I quirked a brow and almost said something, but decided against revealing my eavesdropping. When did I buy him a wreath? I couldn't remember, but I knew in my heart it was me he was talking about.

"Do all angels have wings?" Janae asked.

"No. Most of them don't. Only the special angels called seraphim do," I blurted out as I stumbled around the corner, unable to understand why I said that, nor how I knew that bit of trivia. Perhaps I'd come across it somewhere in my research or excavations, but I couldn't for the life of me remember where.

"There's more than one kind of angel?" Jordan asked.

"Oh, yes," Thandie said, her voice notching up in excitement. "There are archangels, there are seraphim and cherubim, and there are guardian angels."

Something pitted hard in my stomach, and I wondered if the coffee would make a resurgence. "If you'll excuse me," I said as I darted out of the room, barely making it to the bathroom before the morning coffee evacuated like Houston in a hurricane. I definitely overdid the rum yesterday and feared Captain Morgan's revenge.

I scrubbed my teeth for a solid ten minutes and made my way back out to the living room to tell my guests we might have to postpone Christmas dinner. As I stepped into the room, I stared into the kitchen behind it and watched as Miss Thandie and her two sous chefs wandered about my kitchen like they owned the place. Miss Thandie ordered them about, stirring, measuring, scouring my cabinets for ingredients.

"I hope you don't mind, Miss Eden, but the littles were getting restless, so it was best to put them to work to get their energy out. They know their way around a kitchen pretty good, as I've had them training under me since they could walk. If you need some time to yourself, you go have a rest. We'll take care of dinner. It's the least we can do." Thandie's smile was brighter than the sun.

"Are you sure? I fear I made some poor choices yesterday to drown my Scrooge out and may have overdone it." I ran a hand through my hair, hoping there weren't coffee grounds in it.

"I see you got you a matching shirt like your fella's." She pointed to the stain on my shirt.

I quirked a brow. "Huh?"

"Speaking of, where is he at? I thought he might be here for dinner. You two didn't have a fight yesterday, did you? Is that what you were referring to?"

I shook my head. "My fella was too hungry for one woman and sought dinner elsewhere this past Thanksgiving. Plus Grayson didn't even like coffee. That should have been my first clue we weren't meant to be."

Her brows pinched together, and a worry wrinkle crinkled on her forehead. "Is that so? Then who was that man with you yesterday when you came by?"

I pulled her away from the innocent ears in the kitchen. "I don't know who you're referring to, but I don't even remember coming over yesterday. Everything's a little fuzzy for me right now. I remember you from the store, but nothing after that."

"I got a remedy for that. You know, my husband, Darius—may he rest in peace—used to be a drunkard before he got himself right with the Lord, and he had this concoction..."

I jerked back. "Hey, I'm not a drunkard!"

She tilted her head, and a smirk slid across her lips as wide as her eyes.

My shoulders slumped, and I huffed. "Okay, not often. It's just the last couple of months have been kind of rough on me."

She gave my back a little pat. "Your guardian angel working overtime?"

An awful feeling in the pit of my stomach roared to life and churned, knotting my insides into a bow. A pain ripped through my chest, and I swore I was having a heart attack or a nervous breakdown. Again.

"You all right, Miss Eden?" Worry draped her face.

"No. I wonder if I'll ever be all right again."

"Why not go freshen up and lie down for a while? It'll be at least another couple hours before dinner's ready. You've done for us —let us do something for you."

I nodded, unable to argue, mainly because I feared projectile vomiting all over their clothes. Barely making it to the bathroom, I collapsed in a heap on the floor, convulsing in sobs. The weirdest part—I didn't know why. Yes, I was still pissed at Grayson, and my job, and my mom, and all the other metric crapton of shit that had happened to me in the last couple of months, but that was just it...I was pissed. Angry, vengeful even. Not sad.

With my dad, I'd held in my grief, trying to be strong for the rest of my family, so when it hit me, it was like a tsunami. I'd have good days and bad days. With Amanda, I suffered guilt through my waves of tears. But this, whatever this was, was different. Why on earth was I bawling my eyes out like there was a hole inside me?

Grabbing a tissue off my nightstand, I blew my nose before collapsing back onto the bed.

Maybe it was the fact that it was Christmas, or that sweet old lady in my kitchen making dinner with her grandkids, who had nothing more than the clothes on their backs, and here I was lamenting about dating a cheating asshole.

Yet an emptiness hollowed out my soul. Something just felt off...missing. I knew it wasn't Grayson because just thinking his name made me want to stab something. Maybe missing the idea of him at the holidays? But still, I'd been single through many holidays and never felt like this.

I rolled over and tugged the covers up around me.

Maybe missing my mom? But even when I thought about her, aggravation filled my thoughts, not sadness, and frustration that she wrote me off so easily after all I'd done for her in my life. But in the end, I understood a little because she'd never been alone. Pops married her fresh out of high school. She reacted out of fear, not because she didn't love me. Yeah, I missed her. But also, this alone time would be good for her in the end. Time to teach her to rely on herself, and that she was strong enough to survive.

Plus, she hated Grayson, but I wouldn't heed her warnings. I was in *love*. Or at least, I loved the idea of being in love. I clung to it with an ironclad fist. And I thought she didn't want me to get married so I could live with her for the rest of my natural life. Clarity only came when you took off the blinders and stepped outside yourself. But still, that clarity didn't stop the ache in my soul or fill the void building like a swirling storm.

Maybe I would call her a bit later. I should. It was Christmas, after all.

I was pretty sure the black hole in my heart wasn't for my job.

Yes, I loved what I did, but there'd be other grants. There'd be other opportunities for excavations and research. It wasn't the end of my career, just a new direction I needed to seek out.

So after all that introspection, I still came up empty in my head and my heart. Eventually, I drifted off into a fitful sleep. Images came to me: a blond man who looked like a Norse hero in flannel, soft lips against mine, hands worshipping me. When I woke, they faded away, leaving me feeling empty and sad all over again.

I climbed in the shower and hoped the hot water would sear out whatever plagued me. But instead, it left me wondering, racking my brain. Especially when I thought back to Thandie's question about where my "fella" was. She mentioned I had come over to her house last night with some man, who apparently liked coffee enough to wear it like me.

Surely I hadn't drunk so much rum to completely black out and not remember a whole day in my life? But the harder I tried to remember yesterday, the more everything blurred.

As I toweled off and redressed, the smell of roasting turkey permeated every corner of my house. My stomach growled, and I made my way back to the kitchen to inspect the damage.

"You feeling better, Miss Eden?" Thandie smiled as she scampered about, transferring food from the stove and oven to the table.

"A little, thanks," I said, forcing the lie out.

"Good. Dinner's just about ready." She smiled and turned to get the kids seated at the table.

My phone buzzed in my pocket, and I nearly jumped out of my skin. I opened the email, and my mouth popped open as I read the words on the screen.

"Something the matter, Miss Eden?"

I shook my head. "No, actually. I'm just in shock. Something good just happened. I can't believe it."

She punched her hands to her hips. "Now, why wouldn't you believe that something good can happen to you?"

I shrugged. "If it weren't for bad luck, I'd have no luck at all.

That's pretty much my motto in life. Murphy's Law and his rebel cousin Mercury Retrograde rule my life."

Thandie relaxed her shoulders and smirked. "Now, that's no way to think about this life we're blessed with. You just got to be thankful for each day you have breath in your lungs. A new slate every morning to work on. Some hands you get dealt aren't as good as others. But everything happens for a purpose. You don't know how you will be needed to help someone out, or how someone else will show up to help you out."

Her words sounded familiar in my head, like someone said something like it to me once before. I sighed. "I guess."

"Well, come on now, share your good news," Thandie said, wiping her hands on her apron.

I smiled. "My grant, the one I lost the funding to months ago, it just got reapproved. I'm going back to Egypt!"

"Oh, how wonderful!" Thandie clapped her hands together.

"But who the heck sends an email on Christmas Day about grant funding?" I shook my head, rereading the words to make sure I wasn't being pranked.

"Well, it *is* Christmas. Miracles aren't out of the realm of possibility on a day like today."

"That's pretty much what this is. There's no other explanation for it. I don't have the words..."

"Then there're no words necessary but a thank-you to the man upstairs, and do your best to make this second chance worthwhile." She winked.

I nodded.

Thandie turned to head back into the kitchen, but stopped and glanced back at me over her shoulder. "Oh, do you have any whipped cream for the pumpkin pie?"

A picture flashed in my mind of a peppermint mocha with whipped cream flying through the air. No faces. No places. Just a cup of spilling coffee. I gripped the edge of the dining room table to steady myself.

Thandie walked over to me. "Miss Eden?"

The room blurred, and my legs wobbled beneath me. An ache throbbed in my wrist the longer I gripped the table, along with a sharp slice of pain shooting through the toes on my right foot.

Thandie placed the back of her hand on my forehead. "Maybe you need to go to the emergency room. You look white as a ghost."

My stomach churned at the words *emergency room*. The spilling coffee flashed in my head again, this time expanding a bit, and I realized it had spilled in an emergency room or waiting room of some sort, something to do with a chair.

I shook my head and blinked. "No, I'm okay. I just have a bit of a headache, and the room spins if I go too fast."

I tried to think of something to stop her questioning, because how could I possibly explain to some stranger how I couldn't remember anything about yesterday but fuzzy pictures spiraling in my brain at random moments, making me want to vomit?

She tilted her head. "You know what you need?"

I quirked a brow and had a funny feeling no matter how I answered that question she was going to tell me.

"Your momma." She nodded.

I snort-laughed. Did she just pull a yo momma joke on me, or was she serious? But she folded her arms, and her thin pursed lips said she wasn't joking.

"Not really. My momma and I aren't exactly on speaking terms right now."

"Exactly why you need her. Christmas is the perfect time to let bygones be bygones. A time for new beginnings, fresh starts, rebirths."

I stared at her like she was some kind of messenger from the man upstairs or something. Another jab of pain sliced its way through my head, and I tucked my chin to my chest with a wince.

"Uh-huh. Exactly. You're sick. You need your momma." Thandie came around and slid an arm around me. "You know, if I had my baby girl still with me, there's no place I'd rather be than with her.

Life's so short, sugar. You shouldn't waste the days you have with each other. I'd give anything to have my daughter back for just one more day. Fighting or not, you're still blood. You're still family. She's still your mother."

I forced out a hard huff.

"I'll even go with you and hold your hand." She smiled. "And with the littles," she said with a nod to her grandkids. "She won't yell at you in front of them." She tossed me a wink.

I rolled my eyes with a laugh and sighed. "Fine. You win."

"Well, just take it slow. You've got nowhere to be, so no rush, child. I'm here if you need me. I'm a friend."

That ache stabbed at my heart. A friend? I'd just met the woman, and while she was as sweet as the pumpkin pie she'd made, I didn't know her at all. Yet something about her made me trust her and her words. Her spirit provided comfort and temporarily soothed the ache in my soul.

Maybe a friend was what I was missing.

10

THEO

A WOMAN'S LOUD SHRIEK STARTLED ME AWAKE, AND I BLINKED OPEN my eyes.

"He's naked!" the voice squeaked again.

Women huddled around me, pointing and staring. Some staring a little too low and a little too long. I rolled over and plunged my face into something icy and wet.

Snow.

Tremors ransacked my body as the cold set in, and I realized I was lying in a snowbank and was indeed naked.

"Where am I?" I groaned and slammed a hand to my head as an ache like I'd never known assailed me.

A dark-skinned man in a brown Carhart jacket broke through the wall of gawking women and crouched next to me, tossing a blanket over my shivering body. "You're in a snowbank in a church parking lot in south Jersey."

"How did I get here?" The man eased me from the snowbank as I wobbled to a stance, clutching the warmth of the blanket around me.

"That's a mighty fine question, young man. Was hoping you knew the answer to that. Mrs. Sheffield"—he thumbed over his shoulder—"called in about a naked man in the snowbank about ten minutes ago." He extended his hand. "The name's Pete, and you are?"

The answer should have been easy, but for the life of me, I didn't know my name either. It hovered over the tip of my tongue, but never quite formulated into a word. His hand blurred before my eyes, and I took a step to keep myself right-side up as I clutched his palm. "I'm afraid I don't know. Everything's a little fuzzy, and my head hurts."

"Too much rum in the ol' eggnog last night, eh?" He chuckled and released my hand back to me.

Sharp pains pierced my head at the words *rum* and *eggnog*, and I pressed my palm to my forehead to try to ease the throbbing. "Perhaps. Though, I'm pretty sure I'm not a drinker. I can't recall having a drop of alcohol in my life."

"Well, maybe you had yourself an accident, though how you ended up naked is a boggler. Maybe you got mugged?" He scratched the scruffy gray hair covering his chin. The way the man said naked sounded more like "nekkid" and took me a moment to process.

I shrugged and tightened the blanket around me.

"Well, let's get you checked out at the hospital and then a warm meal in your belly. I was on my way to church when I heard old Sheffield screaming and figured I'd check it out."

"I'm sure I'm fine. I don't want to stop you from going to church." Another shiver attacked me, and I glanced around at the growing crowd of onlookers, as if I were searching for something or someone, perhaps a familiar face to help remember things.

"Don't worry about church. They've got several services today, being it's Christmas and all. Besides, Pastor Andy has enough wind in his sails for a two-hour sermon. I could get back in time for half of it." A chuckle rocked his belly.

I jerked back at the thought. "It's Christmas?"

He nodded. "Yes, sir. How long you figure you've been unconscious?"

"I...I don't know." Worry knotted my gut the more I thought about it.

Who am I? What happened to me?

"Well, let's get you patched up at the ER, find you something warmer than a blanket, and we'll figure out where to go from there." Pete guided me to his white truck, still running and warm. The heat permeating through his black leather seats unfroze my skin, allowing the shivers to ease their relentless attack. "I'm just a retired old man, so I ain't got much. But I volunteer at the homeless shelter around the holidays, helping pass out meals. If you're feeling up to it, I figured we might go down there after the hospital and get you something to eat and see if maybe someone recognizes you."

I nodded as Pete hopped in the driver's side and drove off, I assumed in the direction of the hospital, even though I didn't think I really needed to go. But since I couldn't remember my name, let alone where I lived, maybe I did have some kind of head trauma. At least it would be a good place to start.

"So you don't remember anything?" Pete asked, tossing a glance my way.

I shook my head and stared at the passing unfamiliar land-scape. "No," I mumbled.

"Do you think you're from around these parts? Or did someone just dump you off on the Jersey shore?"

I know he probably meant to help spark something in my head, but his questioning irritated me. More so, I got irritated at myself for not being able to remember anything. What did I do to myself? Was I in some kind of trouble?

"I don't know," I managed to say in a somewhat civil tone, trying to hide my growing frustration.

"Well, let's see what a doc has to say, make sure you're not hurt." Pete nodded, pulling into the ER parking lot.

Pete took it upon himself to act as my guardian, so to speak, and helped me check in with the triage nurse. I settled into the waiting area and closed my eyes, hoping something would come back to me. I must have fallen asleep, as Pete nudged me awake, and the scent of coffee inundated my nose.

"Figured you could use something hot while you waited." He passed me the cup.

"Thanks." I curled my hand around the warmth, and something calmed in my soul. Coffee seemed to be something familiar. Obviously, I liked it.

He handed me a pair of jeans and a T-shirt along with a red flannel jacket. "It's from Mrs. Sheffield. She said her grandson was about your size and stopped by to drop it off for ya while you were snoozing. It's Christmas, so the ER is backed up a bit. May be here awhile."

"Please, give her my thanks." I managed a smile and made my way to the bathroom to put the clothes on so I didn't scare anyone by walking around in only a blanket.

After dressing, I stared at the stranger in the mirror looking back at me. I didn't even recognize my own face. How would I recognize anything else? Longish waves of dark-blond hair fell just short of my shoulders, and days-old scruff covered my face. The worry clouding my blue eyes matched the worry sitting in my heart.

Who am I?

With a sigh, I took a sip of the coffee as the bathroom door opened and startled me. Coffee splashed out of the cup and down the front of the clean white shirt I just put on. I stared at the stain, and a picture flashed through my mind of a T-shirt stained with coffee.

Déjà vu? It felt like I'd been there before. I looked at Pete, peeking in the door.

"Oh, man, so sorry. I got worried you might have passed out

again or something, so I came to check on you. I'll see about getting you another shirt." He pointed to the stain.

I shook my head. "I'm okay, just had a weird déjà vu kind of thing happen, though."

"Oh?" He tilted his head with a smile. "Memory coming back to you?"

"No, unfortunately. But it feels like I've done this before."

"Done what? Lost your memory?"

"No, the shirt. Spilling coffee. I remembered coffee on a white T-shirt. After it happened, my head seared for a minute, and then a vision of me in a T-shirt getting splashed with coffee hit me."

Pursing his lips, he gave me a nod with a mix of worry and confusion on his face. "Well, I'm sorry about the spill, but at least it jogged a memory. I'm sure it'll all come back to you eventually. Give it some time."

I nodded and forced a smile. "I hope so."

After a series of x-rays and vials of blood, I waited in the exam room with a heavy heart. I glanced at the empty chair beside me. Pete waited in the lobby to give me some privacy with the doctors. A niggle inside my heart told me there should be someone in that chair beside me.

Pain brewed in my left temple before shooting across my forehead to the other side. Wincing, my eyes slammed shut as another picture flashed through my mind—the coffee spilling again, this time someone else was with me, someone stuck in a chair, flailing as the coffee flew through the air and splashed me. A quick glimpse at the legs said they belonged to a female covered in a pair of yoga pants. But there was no face to go with them.

I clutched a hand to my chest as the exam room curtain whisked to the side and a doctor came in. He smiled, and I fought the urge to throat punch him. Shaking myself from the thought, I closed my eyes and reopened them as I released a cleansing breath. Why would I want to punch some random doctor? Maybe I had anger management issues that got me into some kind of street fight, which would explain how I ended up passed out in a snowbank. Still, though, why I was naked remained a mystery.

"So you're my John Doe," the doctor said, extending a hand. "Dr. Rayce Carr."

I quirked a brow at the name.

"Yeah, I get that a lot," he said with a laugh. "Well, looks like there's no brain swelling or tumors, and no signs of a stroke. No contusions or signs of bodily injury or frostbite. All your blood work checked out fine. It is odd, though. Amnesia patients usually remember who they are. It's details around them or short-term memory loss that is more common. While popular in movies and books for a plot device, not remembering *anything* about yourself is rare."

I nodded with a sigh. "I've been having periodic flashes, quick images with no faces. So I hope something comes back to me."

"That's a good sign. Just be aware, some things may end up permanently lost, so any progress is good. Don't get upset if it all doesn't come back." He jotted down some notes before tearing off a sheet of paper. "Here's a script for some prescription strength ibuprofen. As the memories come back, you may suffer some headaches."

"Thanks," I said, taking the paper.

He turned around and pointed his pen at me. "You know, you do look familiar."

I glanced up, and a spark of hope hit my heart.

"Can't figure out from where, though." He tapped himself on the temple with the pen. "It's been a long double shift. Gets rough here around the holidays. Wish I could be more help."

"It's okay. I'm sure things will work out as they're supposed to." Frustration dampened the spark once more.

He left, and Pete came into the room. "Doc says you're ready to be released. Might do you some good to be among some folks on Christmas, see if something sparks another memory."

"Yeah, that sounds good." A rumble hit my belly at the thought of food, and I stumbled back at the feeling. For some reason, the sensation seemed foreign to me, unexpected.

"Seems to me your stomach agrees." A chuckle rippled through his words.

With a nod, I slid off the gurney and followed Pete out to the truck.

"We need a name for you, so we don't have to keep calling you John Doe," Pete said, pulling out of the hospital parking lot.

"I have no idea what to call myself. It seems weird to have to think about it."

How could I name myself? What if I lose who I really am forever?

"Well, you kind of look like a Ben or maybe a Christopher."

I quirked a brow. "I do?"

He shrugged.

I hated this. Hated everything about it. Why couldn't I just remember who I was? Pressing my head to the window, I watched the scenery, searching for something to spark another memory. We stopped at a red light, and I glanced at the building to my left, Theodore Roosevelt Public School.

"What about Theodore?" I tilted my head and looked at Pete.

"Sounds mighty stuffy. You're a young man. Probably need something akin to your generation. Maybe like Teddy."

I nodded. "Yeah, probably. Maybe I'll go with Teddy. It feels approachable, like I'm a good-sounding guy? Right?"

Pete laughed. "Worried about your reputation already, Teddy?"

A smirk teetered on my lips. "I guess if this is some kind of fresh start, I should try to make something of it."

"That's a good way to look at it. I think Teddy will work. Women will like that and probably call you Teddy Bear. Heck, half the town already saw your fur coat." He chuckled as he pulled into the parking lot of the shelter. "Oh, by the way, got you something a little warmer to wear than that coffee-stained T-shirt of yours."

I slid out of the stained shirt and into a white sweater that was clearly a size too small and barely fit over my arms, clinging to me like a second skin. Embarrassment heated my cheeks, and I blew out a hard breath. As the picture revisited my mind, I was glad I didn't remember anyone I saw in town, and it appeared that no one knew me. Other than the doctor, who said I looked familiar. While I might not have lived in this town, it was a clear possibility I'd at least been here before.

Another thought burned hot in my soul with a blackening dread working its way in, dampening the spark of my fresh new start. "What if I'm married? What if I have a bunch of kids somewhere, and I never see them again?"

Pete cracked a half smile and pointed to my hand. "There's no ring on your finger. Not even a tan line. So that probably means you're free and single."

It made sense, and a bit of relief flowed through me. Yet something toiled in my gut, a nervous flutter and niggle about the woman in the yoga pants in my vision. Who was she?

Pete stopped me and placed a firm hand on my shoulder. "I know it may seem a little scary, not knowing who you are or where you're from. But even if you did, you have to focus on the future and make the best of each day you've been given. Things happen for a reason, right? Maybe you just need to discover a new part of you. You may never remember who you were, but this is your chance to become who you need to be."

I nodded. "Wise words, Pete. Thank you."

"I've been around the block a time or two, son." He winked. "I know you haven't got much right now, but at least you've got a friend."

A comfort settled in my soul for the first time since I woke up in the snowbank. I now had someone to trust, a guide in this strange new world—a friend. Sometimes, that was all it took to bring back hope.

The word *friend* mulled around in my mind, and I whispered it, as if I'd said it to someone else recently.

We walked in a comfortable silence to a red-bricked building in the middle of town. Chaotic chatter mixed with the sound of pots and pans clanking, echoing into the rafters of the vaulted ceiling. Wisps of steam spiraled in the air as countless men, women, and even children scurried about the large dining hall carrying trays of hot food. The smell of pumpkin pie and ham floated around me, but the underlying stench of body order and urine still made me cringe.

I studied the faces in the crowd, many dirt-laden with sorrowful eyes. So many looked as lost as I felt. Years of struggles etched into the dark circles under their eyes, and worry lines of burden rippled on their brows. Clothes, some tattered, some torn, some with nothing more than a flannel shirt for warmth told the stories of their struggles. Some seemed here by chance. Others seemed here by choice, all coming together as one.

Emotion wedged in the back of my throat, and pain filled my heart. I stopped short, not knowing if I could continue on staring at them, walking through so much despair. But a few among them chose joy, and their smiles shone from the corners of the room, making the best of their situation, thankful for a hot meal and a warm room. Maybe a couple were friends, thankful they weren't alone. Maybe some were angels, keeping watch and sharing kind words of hope.

A jolt of pain struck my head, and I bent over, pressing my hand to my temple. Through a hiss, I closed my eyes and a flicker of random faces scrolled through my mind. Nothing made sense, just a mix of people changing through time, like an evolution, with varying clothes and hairstyles and faces.

Pete gripped my shoulders. "You okay, Teddy?"

"I think I had a flash of some memories. But it doesn't make sense. Just random people that changed over time. I don't know what it could possibly mean. So many people, I can't even count. Some happy, some sad. All changing, evolving. Maybe it was from a movie or something. I don't know." I rubbed my temple as the pain eased.

"No one says you have to make sense of it now. I'm sure pieces of the puzzle will eventually fit somewhere. You have to build the foundation before you can arrange all the parts that go inside it." He squeezed my shoulder and guided me through the room to the serving line. "If you'll excuse me, I see some folks who could use some help. Why don't you hold our place in line? I'll be right back."

Before I had a chance to even ask if I could be of help, the incoming crowd swallowed his body. I let out a sigh and turned around, facing the serving line still twenty people in front of me.

"Thank you, kind sir," a warm, rich female voice said, echoing above all the noise in the room.

It hit my ears and immediately struck my heart, sending it racing through my chest. I had to find out who it belonged to. As I weaved side to side, jumping up and down over heads and bodies, I still couldn't find the source.

I finally managed to find the top of Pete's gray, tweed newsboy cap. He stood in front of a woman at the door with a blue puffy coat and a red knit cap pulled over long, dark-brown hair that flowed in waves like a waterfall down her back. His body hid her face, and as I closed in on them, a sea of people coming into the serving line blocked my path.

"I'm afraid my friend Thandie and I made far too much to eat, so we wanted to share it with others. Merry Christmas." That melodic voice floated through the air once more and hit me straight in the heart.

"Pete," I yelled out between people coming at me like I was a toaster at a Black Friday sale.

The crowd closed in on me, blocking my view as the woman left the building. She turned the corner, and I still didn't catch a glimpse of her face. One thing I did notice though as I watched her disappear—she had on yoga pants.

I had to find her.

11

EDEN

NINE MONTHS LATER...

I never thought I'd miss the Jersey shore so much. Though, after spending the last six months in the Middle East, my skin glowed, mainly from being sand-blasted day and night. Rich people paid to do that kind of thing. I got a free facial while excavating a new dig site. But my skin also needed moisture, and there was nothing like coming back home to the salty sea air.

Today was all about the fresh. Fresh air, fresh start, fresh relationship with my mom.

Christmas Day, my friend Thandie convinced me to go see my mom. Since then, we'd all been getting together for dinner once a week. In March, I got Thandie and the kids out of their old rickety house and moved them into mine, since I was going to be out of the country on a historical dig. Thandie and my mom became besties, and she moved in to help her with the kids when Thandie started working at the local church as the choir director.

Over the months I'd been gone, Thandie saved up enough money to rent a nice two-bedroom apartment about fifteen minutes from me. I didn't see her as much these days, but we still tried to do dinner every couple of weeks.

Mom and I had several long talks before I left, a couple of them Thandie had to play referee for, but we were at least communicating. We agreed that when I got back from Egypt, she would continue to live in my house. The biggest issue, aside from her loathing of Grayson, was that she didn't want to be alone, and living in their old house, she was swallowed by the memories of my dad. Since I was no longer engaged, let alone even dating anyone, I figured life was too short to argue anymore.

Now that I had gotten back and Thandie had her own place, we decided to move the rest of Mom's stuff from her old house to storage and try to sell it. Her dream had always been to open a bakery, so I talked her into using the money she'd get from the sale to open a business. Mom was only in her late fifties, and Dad had left her enough money to live on without having to work. But over time, she'd gotten stir-crazy and needed something to occupy herself. She'd taken to making desserts for the homeless shelter and church in town, earning the title "that crazy baking lady."

The last of the warm nights of summer had come and gone, making way for the turning of the leaves and autumn's chill. I ran back into the house to grab the last of my mom's things and shoved them into my trunk. Something orange stuck out of one of the boxes, and I opened it to try to make it fit, but gasped as it hit me what it was. "You still have my Sally Sticky doll?"

Long, orange strands of yarn hung down for hair, dirtied over time. One eye was missing and only half remained of the other. The painted-on lips were cracked and chapped, but her smile was still as creepy as ever.

"I loved this thing. I can't believe you hung on to it."

"Well, I wasn't sure how long your invisible friend phase was going to last, so I figured I may need it." Mom slid into the passenger seat. "Can we swing by the shelter? I have to pick up some of my baking pans."

I buckled up and tossed the doll in the back seat. "What do you mean, my invisible friend phase?"

Momma rolled her dark-brown eyes and let her hands do most of the talking, sliding into her original thick New York accent. "Once that invisible boy came around, you chucked all your dolls. You don't remember him? You never did tell me his name, but you would go on and on about how this boy followed you around and held your hand at school, at church, at the playground. He was like your own personal superhero, saving you from all kinds of catastrophes in the universe. He must've been something pretty spectacular, because you never looked back at Sally Sticky again."

It dawned on me in that instant that the boy she reminded me about wasn't a boy at all. He was a man, with long blond hair and the bluest eyes I'd ever seen. My mom would have freaked her shit had she known her ten-year-old daughter had a man for an invisible friend. But he wasn't invisible to me. He was as real as she was sitting next to me. At least, in my mind I wanted him to be.

He had never left my side, like a bodyguard. Someone to talk to, someone to watch over me. He really was my friend, my best friend. It was never creepy or illicit, but I couldn't very well explain that to my mother. She would have taken me to a psychologist.

I slammed on the brake pedal, and my hands flew from the steering wheel to my head as a stabbing pain hit my brain. A flash of some man mouthing the words "I'm a friend" played over and over in my mind. His face blurred, but those lips, etched on a perfectly sculpted jaw, repeated the words on a loop in my mind.

"Eden Grace, what the hell is wrong with you?" My mother clung to her seat belt like a lifeline. "You could have gotten us killed!"

"I'm sorry, Ma. I'm sorry. A stabbing pain sliced through my head, and it hit me really hard. I could barely see." Panic hammered my heart as I watched a kid on a skateboard jump up on the sidewalk and whip me the finger. I mouthed *I'm sorry* one more time and blew out a hard breath.

"Maybe I should drive." My mother's stern eyes reprimanded me more than her words.

"I'm fine, the pain's fading." I put the car back in gear and made my way to the shelter down the street, pulling into the first available parking spot. "I think I'll just wait out here. I need to catch my breath."

She nodded and went inside.

The headache wasn't what distracted me though. It was the fact that the same invisible friend I'd had as a kid now manifested in my dreams. He was the same man I'd been dreaming about for years. They occurred in several variations, but in some facet he rescued me, we kissed and made love, and I'd wake up. Only his face would always fade from my memory minutes after I woke, no matter how hard I tried to remember him.

It all became so clear the moment Mom mentioned my invisible friend. They were one and the same. He'd never really left me, except he had, about nine months ago.

I realized I'd been sitting there with a smile plastered to my face as soon as my mom got back in the car and stared at me like I had two heads.

"What's going on?" Her brow quirked so high it almost kissed her hairline.

I arched my own brow in a sparring match. Coming from her gene pool, I could hold my own. "Nothing. What makes you think there's something going on?"

"You're smiling like the Joker. Every time you do that, a whole world of trouble rains down on you. Like the time you wrote *Cheating Asshole* all over Grayson's car while he was at work." Mom pursed her bright-red, lipstick-caked lips. Who was she getting all prettied-up for?

My shoulder hitched as I gasped. "Hey, I was doing the world a favor by letting all the innocent women in the tri-state area know what kind of person he was. It was an act of charity, not rage. Besides, I didn't etch it into his car with a key—it was in lipstick, a shade darker than what's painted over your lips right now. Speaking of, why did you get all dolled up? Two seconds ago, you didn't have any makeup on. Now you come out of the shelter looking like you were attacked by the MAC counter at Macy's."

Rolling her eyes, she threw on an indignant smile and faced away from me in a huff. "What? Just because I'm in my fifties doesn't mean I can't wear makeup anymore. You're making me go out in public, so why can't I look nice while I do it?"

I snorted as a smirk tugged at my lips. "You've got a crush on someone at the shelter."

She snapped her head back to face me and her eyes shot wide open, blinking as fast as a hummingbird. "I can't even believe you said that. I never! Your father has been in the ground barely a year. I'm not ready to find a replacement. Nor will I ever want to."

"There's nothing wrong with wanting to love again, Ma. Pops would want you to be happy. You're not replacing him. You're just trying to live again. He may be in Heaven now and you're still here, but it doesn't mean you have to be alone."

"I'm not alone." She whipped around in her seat and stared out the windshield. "I live with you."

"I don't mean alone, alone. I mean, you know, alone in your heart. Alone without a life partner. You're still plenty young. Why not live it up?"

She shook her head. "My days of living it up are long gone."

"Maybe it's time to go find them."

Her pursed red lips stuck out like a stop sign, and I fought back a giggle. Sometimes my mom could be so cute.

"You could work at the shelter, you know, kill two birds with one stone. Make a little money to supply your new MAC habit and grab the attention of a certain someone." Leaning in, I nudged her shoulder and wiggled my brow.

She huffed out a sigh and tossed me a side-eye. "They did ask me to come cook for them, and I already told them yes. It has nothing to do with your inane suspicions, so don't go thinking anymore about that. *Capisce*?"

"*Capisce*." I nodded, biting back a smile. "Oh, by the way. You forgot your pans."

"What?" She sat up and stared at me as I pointed out the window to the silver fox sauntering down the walkway, carrying her cake pans with a smile. She turned and clasped a hand to her chest as he approached the car.

I rolled down the window for her and didn't hold back my snicker this time. "He's cute, Ma."

She snarled at me before slapping on a bright smile as she turned to face the handsome gentleman sticking his head in the window. "Pete!"

So Pete's his name.

He looked familiar, and it dawned on me. I'd met him the day Thandie and I stopped in to deliver our extra food at Christmas. His dark-brown eyes twinkled behind black-rimmed glasses as he stared at my mom. Short salt-and-peppered hair hid beneath a newsie cap, and the coloring of his hair matched the goatee on his dark-brown face.

"Sorry, Mrs. Credere, but you forgot your pans inside. Didn't want you to get home and not have them. I sure could use more of your New York–style cheesecake." His sincere smile warmed my heart, and it tickled me to see them interact like a scene out of some holiday movie.

Plus, it would make my mom a whole lot less cranky to have someone else to talk to besides me. Thandie was her new bestie, but with the grandkids running around, she didn't always have the time to spend hours on the phone with my mom since she no longer lived under the same roof.

"Oh, Pete, you flatter me. I'll see what I can do." A blush colored her cheeks redder than the rouge already there.

My momma had herself crush. Well, at least one of us should be happy.

"You must be the lovely daughter she talks about." Pete grinned and gave a little wave.

I waved back, wondering what she had told him. Did she lament about all my poor life choices, or make something up about the daughter she always wanted but didn't get? "That would be me." While our relationship had improved since she'd moved in, it was by no means perfect.

"Well, I'll let you two ladies be on your way. I'll see you tomorrow, Mrs. Credere."

She crossed a hand over her heart. "Pete, please, it's Madeline."

"'Til tomorrow, Madeline," he said with a smile before he jogged back up the walkway to the building.

"Tomorrow, huh? Guess you'll be busy baking up a storm tonight." I smiled as I pulled away from the curb, loving every minute that I was right and could swim in the sea of uneasiness I knew was swallowing my mom.

"Cut the crap, Eden. He's just a friend." Her stark New York accent crisped each word.

"Of course. He's a *friend*." My heart fluttered at the word, and my invisible friend/man-of-my-dreams flashed in my mind. "We could all use one of those."

While my childhood mind clearly had imagined him, I wondered if there was an adult version of him alive in the world somewhere, some knight in shining armor come to save me from dying a shriveled old maid.

There had to be more in the world than just dirty, cheating bastards who couldn't control the snake in their pants. Somewhere out there was someone a woman could have meaningful conversations about life with, someone who wanted to explore all this world had to offer, together. I longed for my missing puzzle piece, that person I fit with perfectly, who, once I connected with them, I wouldn't know how I had functioned apart from them.

Of course, the way things worked in my life, my missing puzzle piece got dropped on the floor, eaten by a dog, and then shit out on the lawn. Or my puzzle piece was already a part in someone else's puzzle. Maybe I just had unreasonable standards, and there was no such man that existed.

Short of breaking into song with a horrible rendition of "Somewhere Out There," for now, I'd have to live vicariously through my mother. That, in and of itself, was a pretty disturbing thought.

Maybe someday my dream man would come to life.

12

THEO

LIFE HAD A FUNNY WAY OF TAKING CARE OF YOU WHEN YOU LEAST expected it. Maybe it wasn't life, but more like divine intervention. Or just plain luck.

Pete stuck by my side like a guardian angel. Without him, I was pretty sure I would have died in the snowbank, or at least gotten thrown out of town and probably not ended up where I was today. He even legally adopted me as his adult son, so I could have a legal last name—Saint—and I officially became Theodore "Teddy" Saint.

It didn't escape me that Saint Peter rescued me, and we periodically joked about it when we did dinner once a week at his place. He helped me secure an apartment and get a car. I'd been working for the homeless shelter in town as their handyman, and as needed, I helped serve meals. Some days I was an all-around floater kind of person.

But something inside me remained empty, like a part of me was missing. Well, a lot of me was missing, mainly my memories. While each day I gave my all to the work I'd been given, it felt a little meaningless, like I should be doing something more. A need inside me still hadn't been filled, a purpose, something worthwhile.

As I swept up the remnants of the day's lunch at the shelter, I noticed one of the regular patrons staring out the window. A large rip sliced up the back of his denim jacket, and loose strings of yarn hung down from his worn black knit hat.

I made my way over to his table. He never moved, not even a flinch. I tried my best not to stare, but the worry in his eyes drew me in.

"They'll forgive you, you know," I said, not making eye contact as I continued to sweep under his table.

He said nothing, but from the corner of my eye, I noticed his head tilt in my direction.

"Words are pretty powerful, but sometimes actions speak the loudest. Start with a hug. It warms the soul. It doesn't forgive, but it makes room for the words needed to heal." I stopped and gripped the top of the broom handle.

The stranger turned his head. "Do I know you?"

I shook my head. "No. But I know that look in your eyes. Even a bad past can be forgiven if you're truly sorry. But it won't happen on its own. Someone has to make the first move. They still love you, even if they hate the decisions you've made."

He jumped up from his seat and narrowed his eyes, inches from my face. "What makes you think you have any right to say shit to me? Huh? You don't know jack shit about me and my past. Spoutin' words like it's so fuckin' easy to just go home, hug my momma, and all will be right with the world. It don't work like that in real life. That's some fairy-tale bullshit, right there."

"Love is the most powerful thing in the world. It can both divide and make whole. Only you can decide which side of it to use."

"I don't need this bullshit." He brushed past me, slamming into my shoulder in his exodus.

I turned around and watched him walk out, but something compelled me to go after him, as if I knew there was more he had to hear, one more thing I had to say. "Peel back the layers. Ask yourself what you really want. What are you really afraid of?"

He jerked to a stop. The stranger turned around and stalked back to me, rising up in my face one more time. "I ain't afraid of shit. I'll prove it to you right here, right now, asshole."

Pete threw down his towel and took two steps toward me, but I waved him off.

"You're afraid she'll take you back." My heart thundered as the words left my lips, and I wasn't sure exactly where they came from, but it was weighing heavy on my heart to say.

The man stilled and hardened his jaw.

"You don't want her to, because she's the most precious thing in the world to you. If she takes you back, you have to admit to yourself you were wrong. And it's not her who can't forgive you for the decisions you've made, it's *you* who can't forgive your own self."

The stranger hitched back a shoulder as he clutched a fist, ready to strike a punch.

Pete took another step, but I shook my head.

"Avoiding her is avoiding the truth. But the truth hurts only for a moment, and you're letting that one moment steal away a lifetime with your family."

He dropped his arm as a pool of tears glassed over his eyes. He dipped his head, pinching his thumb and finger to swipe at them.

I clutched his shoulder and gave it a squeeze. The man fell forward and rested his forehead on my chest. "What do I even begin to say to her?"

I smiled. "Start with 'I love you.' Go from there. The words will come if you open your heart."

Pete smiled and crossed his arms. A flurry of women who worked at the shelter gathered around him, clasping hands to their mouths in shock.

The stranger lifted his head and swiped at one last tear slipping across his dirt-laden cheek. He held out his hand.

I gave it a shake and clutched it with my other hand. Joy soared in my heart. I'd never felt more happy, more complete, like I had fulfilled a purpose. "Let me know how it goes. I'm here if you ever need to talk."

He nodded and turned around, tossing a quick glance at the onlookers as he brushed a finger across his nose, dipped his head, and ran out the door.

"Teddy!" Pamela, one of the women, shouted.

"That was incredible!" another one named Karen cried out.

Pete walked over and slapped me on the back. "That was quite the step you took, son. Are you all right?"

I smiled. "I'm better than all right. I feel great." Though my heart still hammered in my chest, the adrenaline pumping through me and the warmth in my soul filled me with happiness.

"Weren't you scared?" Karen asked.

I shook my head. "No. He just needed someone to talk to is all."

"How did you know what to say?" Pamela asked.

I shrugged. "I don't even know. I knew that look in his eyes. I knew he was hurting, and I was drawn to him. Something in me ached to try to help him. I couldn't stop myself."

I wasn't exactly sure where the words came from, but I knew innately it was what he needed to hear. I couldn't explain it.

"That's mighty fine work, son." Pete smiled. "His name's Darryl. He's been coming here for nearly a year, and not a single person's ever talked to him. Oh, many have tried, but he intimidated most of them. Most folks just kind of leave him be. You're the first one to ever stand up to him, get him to talk. I think you have a gift, my boy."

I blinked. "I do?"

"I agree, Pete," Sandra, the head of the shelter, said as she walked out of her office. "I've seen you talk to a number of people around here. I can't tell you the amount of compliments I get each day from folks about you."

I glanced at the sea of faces staring at me like an animal in a zoo. "I don't know what you mean."

"I mean, you shouldn't be sweeping floors, Teddy." Sandra

wrapped an arm around my shoulder. "How would you feel about some training to be a counselor?"

The people from the church next door noticed my ability as well and called it a spiritual gift. They put me to work in a new capacity, and now I assisted the unemployed and destitute of both the church and the shelter, and I helped them get back on their feet.

In the months since I woke up naked in a snowbank on Christmas Day with no idea who or where I was, I managed to make something of this rebirth of mine, so to speak. I finally found a part of my purpose, a reason to get up each morning, a way to serve. My soul filled with a new spirit, and my heart soared, even if sometimes it did feel oddly half empty, as though something were still missing.

November...

While my memories still hadn't returned, glimpses from the past did come to me from time to time. At first it would be a word or a phrase that would trigger them, along with a searing pain I swore would eventually fry my brain. But even the pain faded over time, as did the desire to find out who I was, and I fell into step in the new life given to me.

The one thing that hadn't left my mind was the woman in the yoga pants. Every day I watched the crowds come into the shelter and church, scanning them, listening to them for a whisper of her voice again. It played in my head as clear as it did that Christmas morning, and it was what I fell asleep to at night.

I told Pete about her, that I swore I knew her from my past. He'd chuckle and slap me on the back and tell me I needed to try dating because he didn't know who she was either. But the thought of dating tied my stomach in knots. I was nearly a thirty-year-old man —at least as far as we could tell, since I couldn't remember my date of birth. When I took on Pete's surname, he suggested using Christmas, as it was my rebirth of sorts. Yet I couldn't remember ever going on a single date before.

Several women had approached me over the last year, showing interest in wanting to date or at least share their bed. The weird offers astounded me with what some of them were into, and I wondered if maybe I'd been in a coma for the last thousand years and missed some critical sexual awakening in the world. Some intrigued me. Most made me cringe. But not a single one got to me the way yoga-pants girl did in one brief second.

Part of me thought maybe I did need to go on a date, practice with someone, so if yoga girl ever did show back up, I wouldn't be a complete noob and not have a clue what to do. I'd hate to turn her off before ever turning her on. Yet something inside me could never go through with it. I even thought for a while I might be asexual with such a lack of desire for other women, or men for that matter, but every night that theory was proven wrong when I'd lie awake, replaying her voice in my head and an indelible ache coursed through me, a need, a want, a desire to find her, be with her, kiss her and hear her sweet voice as I made love to her. Which ended up giving me a woody and some callouses on my hands. At least I knew that part of me actually worked the way it was supposed to.

As the months went on and the days passed by without hearing her voice again, my hope faded. I threw myself into work in an effort to drown out her voice, the color of her hair, and the vision of her sexy legs in my mind.

"Mornin' Teddy," a sweet voice rang out behind me.

I spun around, carrying a load of dishes for Pete on my way to the kitchen. "Good morning, Miss Madeline. You're looking lovely as always." Her deep-brown eyes sparkled with delight, and a smile as wide as Texas brimmed on her bright-red lips.

"You're such a flirt. But I'm much too old. You should try my daughter. She's single and about your age." She winked and nudged me in the ribs with her elbow.

I forced a smile and shook my head. "I'm sure she's just as lovely as you are, but I have a feeling I'm meant for someone, and until I figure out who she is, I'm not really interested in being hooked up on blind dates."

She clasped a hand to my shoulder as we walked into the kitchen together. Large brown curls of hair bounced against her shoulders with each step. "How do you know it's not her you're meant for? If you never go on one of these dates, you could be missing out."

A laugh rumbled in my throat as I nodded. She had a point. But still, I kind of figured if it was meant to be, she'd come through that door like she did that Christmas day. It was part of the reason why I'd never left the shelter, fearing I'd somehow miss her. "Oh, I'm sure there's some truth to that statement, and when I'm ready to do so, you'll be the first one I come to."

"Well, don't blame me if my daughter gets swept up by some other man in the meantime." Madeline's laughter echoed off the stainless steel encompassing the kitchen.

"Duly noted." I tossed her back a wink. "Please give her my sincerest apologies. If I don't find my mystery girl soon, I'll invite her out for coffee."

"I know I'm her mother, so I'm pretty biased, but you never know, she could be the girl of your dreams." Madeline shrugged.

"I'm sure she's fantastic. But I just can't help this feeling I have about this mystery girl. I really think I'm married. Pete said I'm probably not because I don't have a ring, but somehow, I'm connected to her. Until I know for sure, I can't be with anyone else. I do hope you understand."

Madeline smiled. "That's very respectable, Teddy. And whoever she is, she's one lucky lady to have you. I hope you find her. But it's been almost a year now. If you were married, don't you think she'd be trying to find you as well?"

A heavy sigh sank my heart. "I know. I don't understand it. I keep hoping that it's because she doesn't know where I am."

"What about this yoga-pants girl?" Madeline tilted her head with a smile. "You think she's the one?"

I shrugged. "I'm not sure what I think anymore. I know I'm not from this town, so she could be somewhere else, anywhere in the world. I only know I felt a connection with her, just through her voice, that I haven't felt with anyone else in nearly a year. That has to mean something, right?"

"Then why are you still here at the shelter?"

"I figure this is where I was found. I was put here for a reason, and maybe she'll find me. Isn't it better when you're lost to stay in one place so both parties aren't looking and miss each other? If I've been here before, then she may know to come here. Maybe not the shelter, but the town. And Sheriff Conley said she's got my info in the system now, so if someone is looking for me, at least they have my picture, even if I had a different name."

"Have you gone into town and looked for her?"

I nodded. "Every day I search one new spot, the stores, post office, churches, gas stations. I haven't seen her. It's like she vanished."

"Well, the holidays are coming up again. Maybe you'll get your Christmas miracle." She smiled and took the desserts she brought out to the lunch serving line.

It would be a miracle if I ever found her. Maybe I was being stupid, holding out hope for some stranger I'd only gotten a glimpse of, assuming she was my possible wife or fiancée. Besides, her voice was cheerful and light. If she were married and had lost her husband, wouldn't there have been sadness in her tone? I hadn't even thought about it that way before now. I'd been putting my life on hold for what reason?

But every time I tried to tamp down yearning for her, it fired back up just as hot as before. I at least had to find her to figure out how we knew each other, even if it wasn't because we were married.

My head agreed with Madeline and told me I should try dating. But my heart fought me, and not a single person piqued my interest in ten months. So what good would it do to try to force it? That wouldn't be fair to the person or to me.

"Deep in thought, my boy?" A hand clamped on my shoulder, and I turned my head to find Pete with a rather roguish grin on his face.

"Aren't I always?" I smirked with a chuckle.

"Well, take a load off. Miss Madeline invited me over for Thanksgiving dinner next week." He playfully punched my shoulder. "I want you to come with me."

"So you finally got yourself a date with her!" The sly old fox had had an eye for Ms. Credere since the moment she walked in with one of her baked goods months ago. I was happy for him. She was probably about his age, midfifties or so, but one would never know it by looking at her, with her curvaceous figure and crisp attitude.

It warmed my heart every day, watching their flirtatious interactions like a soap opera. They were the talk of the shelter. Everyone knew they both had a thing for the other, but neither of them would make the first move. With her being a widow, Pete wanted to take things slow while Ms. Credere adjusted to the death of her husband. But it looked like maybe she was ready to move on and enjoy life, and a big family dinner was a good place to start. Pete looked over the moon with a glint in his eye and a smile that never left his lips as he glanced at her from afar.

I could relate, if I ever found yoga girl. I'd probably be smitten the same way.

"So you going to join us?" Pete stared me down.

I shrugged and loaded the dishes into the sink. "Probably not. It's your first date, so I don't want to intrude."

"You're my son now. You're my family. Holidays are all about family. I want you to come."

"I truly appreciate that, and please don't take this the wrong way. All you've ever been is good to me, like a real father. But I don't know where my family is, and I think it'll just make me sadder to watch everyone else acting like one when I'm still without mine. I know you don't think I'm married, but I can't shake this feeling about that girl. I haven't stopped thinking about her even one day. I have to find her, and until I do, I don't think I'll ever be whole."

"I know, Teddy. I understand. No one says you have to go out and find yourself a new one. But that's not what Thanksgiving is about. It's about giving thanks for life, about giving back to those who have given to you. It's about cherishing the moments before they pass you by. It's about letting go of regrets and taking chances so you don't have any more. It's about friends just as much as family. So please, come for a meal, some laughs, and some fellowship. You're not trying to replace your family but add to it."

His words hit me smack in the gut, and I nodded. He had such a way of phrasing things, looking at life that I just couldn't begin to see without his help. And they told me *I* was the one with the counseling gift. *He* should be doing it instead of playing handyman. Pete had missed his calling.

"Yeah, but if I go, Madeline will think I'm there for her daughter. She already tried to set me up with her today." Worry blanketed my brief moment of happiness at the thought of not being alone for the holidays.

"I'll talk to her. There will be no pushing, no expectations, no obligations."

I nodded. "I don't want to have to defend not wanting to date to one more person."

"No worries, my boy. Just come for the pie. I promise, it'll be worth it." He winked.

I was glad he had enough positivity for the both of us, because at that moment, I sure lacked my own. My hope dwindled each day, and a part of my soul darkened a little more as I clung to the only memory that kept me going.

You're out there. I know it. I'll find you.

13

EDEN

"You did what?" I shouted, a bit louder than I intended.

"I don't see what you're so worried about. It's just a dinner." Mom shrugged as she turned her back to me and strolled to the kitchen to finish preparing the stuffing.

I stomped after her, throwing my arms up in defeat. "I'm fine with you inviting your new boyfriend over, but you failed to reveal the little caveat about him bringing his very eligible bachelor of a son along with him." If my eyes had been lasers, she would have looked like a carved pumpkin.

She turned around, all smiles, and punched a hand to her hip. "Thandie and the grandkids are going out of town. Apparently, one of her long-lost cousins contacted her and invited her up to New York for Thanksgiving. So I figured it would just be the two of us with all this food, so why not invite some people over?"

"You couldn't have told me this a sooner?" I hardened my glare and folded my arms. I wasn't giving up on my seething rage before she gave up her melodramatic sainthood act.

"What, and miss this little diva show you're putting on right now?" She wiggled her finger in a figure eight toward me.

Rolling my eyes, I huffed and slammed my butt against the

counter behind me, holding back the shooting pain slicing its way up my spine upon impact. I wouldn't give her the satisfaction. "You're not setting me up with anyone. I mean it. You know what today is. Today of all days you decide to pull this kind of stunt?"

"Don't you think after a year it's time to move on from Grayson? By the way, did you hear he knocked that neighbor lady up and now he's stuck paying child support? Serves him right, if you ask me." She continued to strut around the dining room table, placing the good silver and china among the seats. "He's even cheating on *her* now too. Gloria told Sheila, who told Donna, who told me that some young dark-haired girl approached him at the Sack 'n Save, and he couldn't take his eyes off her and they left together. I knew he was trouble the minute you brought him home."

"It's the one-year anniversary of catching my fiancé cheating on me, and you're giving me the *Where Are They Now* special?" Okay, I gave my mom props—it did make me feel better to know he wasn't living happily ever after without me. But still, to just invite her new man and his son over to try to hook us both up was nothing if not a little creepy.

"You pull this at Christmas, and I'll make you go live with Thandie and the kids." I gave her the double-eyed finger stare as I marched toward my bedroom to get something on other than a tank top and yoga pants, but she wouldn't hear the end of it. Guilt trips were long and expensive in our family, and I was packing her a bag for an extended trip.

What did you wear to *unimpress* a guy? I wanted it clear and unmistakable that I was not interested. Maybe I should have left my yoga pants on.

"Make sure you dress nice. This is Pete, ya know, and his poor son that has amnesia." Mom's voice echoed off the walls in every room of the house.

I poked my head out of the room. "Oh, the one that they found naked in a snowbank last Christmas?"

"Yes. You don't have to date him, but you should be nice and make yourself presentable. He's a decent guy, unlike that piece of garbage, Grayson. You need to work on your choice of men. Like Teddy, the poor soul's been pining over a woman he can't even remember. That's love, right there. A man dedicated to one woman."

I really needed to rethink my mom living with me. I barely handled it for eighteen years before I ran as fast as I could to the opposite end of the earth for college. Doing it again twelve years later sucked even worse.

"So you want me to date some guy who's clearly not over an ex'? Yes, he's a definite step up from Grayson. This is going to go swimmingly." I slammed my bedroom door and threw myself on the bed. I might be nearly thirty, but she treated me like I was still sixteen.

I decided the best revenge would be to dress as inappropriately as possible, hoping to make my mom cringe all through dinner. They said the most beautiful makeup for a woman was passion, but cosmetics were so much easier to buy, so I slathered on the war paint like I was headed to a goth club.

Throwing myself back on the bed, I slithered my way into a tight pair of black leather pants. You'd think they'd reveal every last imperfection, but they were so tight, they sucked everything into place and held it there better than spandex, and it made my ass look incredible.

Of course, sitting would be a little on the uncomfortable side, but I had high hopes they'd leave before we even served the sweet potatoes after my mom shunned me for my wardrobe choices in front of them. Then I could curl up in my yoga pants and eat pumpkin pie right out of the dish.

Sucking in a breath, I worked my way into a tight, sweetheart-neckline top that acted like a corset, minus the armpit-poking boning in the sides. Scalloped, off-the-shoulder sleeves hugged my biceps and framed my breasts nicely. Lots of boob on display to make my mother launch into seven Hail Marys to repent for me.

I nodded and twisted side to side, inspecting my work. As I

studied my reflection, I was grateful that the mirror only revealed my appearance, and not the resentment settling like winter in my soul.

Out of nowhere something tickled me, like tiny little legs crawling along my skin. A scream bubbled up from the depths of my lungs, erupting in a wail that could have shattered windows as I spun around, swatting at myself in a wild spastic dance. I darted out of my bedroom to the kitchen to get my mom to do a spider check on my body, until I realized it was just my hair brushing my now bare shoulder.

A sigh of relief flowed through me. "I legit just did a week's worth of cardio because a spider fell on my shoulder. And by spider, I mean my hair." I brushed the mass of tangled locks out of my eyes as I looked at the horror on my mother's face, realizing we weren't alone. Turning my head to the living room, I found Pete and God's gift to lady bits standing with wide eyes, staring at me.

The remaining air in my lungs wedged in my throat when my gaze locked onto his bright-blue eyes. My heart roller-coastered through my insides as I took in his face, his hair, and his big, bright smile as he laughed at my antics. He'd walked right out of my dreams and into my living room. He was here...my invisible friend...the man of and from my dreams—blond hair, blue eyes, the body of a linebacker, and the most amazing smile I'd ever seen on another human being. I threw a hand across my gaping mouth, unable to rip my gaze away from him. He looked just as shocked to see me as surprise and wonder filled those big baby blues of his.

"Really, Eden?" My mom's shrill voice broke the deafening silence around me. "Please excuse my daughter. I don't know what's come over her. And what the heck are you wearing?"

I glanced down, and regret toiled in my gut. Shit.

"I...I..." Words jumbled on my tongue, and I couldn't get a single one out.

"It's okay," Pete said with a brimming smile as he stepped

forward, slipping his coat off. "We're a little early, so it's our fault. Can we help with anything?"

Mom took his coat, and a smile curled at the edge of her lips. "No, you gentlemen just have a seat, and we'll get the food to the table. Eden?" She snapped her voice in my direction, and I jerked to attention like a reprimanded soldier.

"Yes?" I whispered, still looking at the man a foot away from me, who wore the same puzzled stare I probably had.

"Come help take the food to the table."

I nodded and backed away from the guy. He stepped forward, raising a hand as if he were about to say something, and in a panic, I dashed to the corner of the kitchen and clung to the doorframe leading to the garage.

"Are you sure there's nothing we can help with, Madeline?" Pete said from the edge of the kitchen. "You prepared this wonderful feast. The least we can do is help serve it."

"Not in this house. You're a guest. You just relax and enjoy." Mom's proud smile beamed, and I watched their interaction with a smile of my own, temporarily forgetting about Hotty McHotpants, who I left in a stupor in the living room.

Mom closed in on me, and even in the dark corner of the room, her eyes blazed like fire. "What are you doing? Are you trying to ruin this dinner for me on purpose?"

"No." I shook my head like a scared toddler. "Well, maybe a little. Okay, at first, I wanted to. I just don't want to be pushed into something I don't want to do."

"This isn't for you. This is for me. Stop thinking the world revolves around you or owes you something. You've lost yourself, Eden, and it scares me."

"Mom..." My lips trembled as I choked the word out.

Her tone shifted, and for the first time in nearly a year, she turned back into the mom I used to know. "I love you. I only want to see you happy. I know Grayson hurt you. But if you don't open yourself back up to the possibly of love, you'll be stuck in this cycle of self-destruction. I had to learn to do it, and I was with your father for thirty-five years. So I know you can. You don't have to date someone of my choosing, but you do have to choose someone worthy of you. I know you know it in your soul that you didn't really love Grayson, did you?"

Her words hit me like a punch in the gut. She was right. Absolutely right.

"No," I whispered, and the realization shook me to my core. I'd been trying to convince myself of a lie for so long, I actually believed it.

"You settled because he fit into your lifestyle, your schedule, your ideals of what love should be. But maybe you need someone unconventional, someone who challenges you and doesn't make sense, but will love you with every part of himself." She placed a hand on my shoulder and pulled me into a hug, a real hug. I hadn't had a genuine hug from my mother in a really long time. Not even at Pop's funeral. It felt good. It felt like healing.

"I love you," she whispered into my hair as she pressed a kiss to the top of my head. "This is a time of giving thanks. Let's be thankful we still have each other and that we have a chance to still make something of the life we've been given."

I nodded, laying my cheek against her chest, and let a tear slide down my nose. "Love you, Momma."

"Okay, let's get this dinner served before everything gets cold." She wiped her hands on her apron and turned around to grab a dish from the stove.

The guys made their way to the table as we finished putting the last of the food on it.

"Let's do some proper introductions now. Pete, Teddy, this is my daughter, Eden." She fanned her arm between the guys and me.

I nodded and gave a little wave, avoiding Teddy's intense gaze. It didn't feel awkward, but more like I wanted to bathe in it. I wanted to get him alone and ask him a bazillion questions, and the more I thought about it, the more my heart raced. But he'd think I was some kind of psycho, telling him he looked just like the guy I'd been dreaming about for years. How did you even begin a conversation like that?

As I reached for my chair, Teddy dashed next to me, grabbed it, and pulled it out for me. "May I?" he asked, and my heart sputtered, skipping beats at the sound of his voice. So familiar. So calming. So warm. It made me dizzy, and I was thankful he slid the chair behind me and caught me as I fell into the seat.

A smile spread across my lips like a giddy schoolgirl. "Thanks."

"My pleasure," he said in that baritone voice, sending a warmth through me that tingled all the way to my toes. I could sit and listen to that man read me the dictionary.

I side-eyed him as he side-eyed me, and we both looked away with more smiles all through dinner. Straight out of some cheesy chick flick, but I indulged because it felt good, genuine.

Something happened through that dinner, softening my soul. Maybe it was just the ambiance of a classic Thanksgiving dinner. Maybe it was the wine. Maybe it was the tryptophan in the turkey, but our hands touched as I passed him the pumpkin pie, and we both locked gazes with goofy smiles.

"What do you say we take all these leftovers to the shelter, Madeline?" Pete said as he helped her clear the table.

"That's a splendid idea." She winked.

I had a feeling I knew what was coming. They were purposely leaving so Teddy and I could have some *alone time*. Seemed Mom wasn't the only one plotting and scheming this evening. Or he wanted to get my mom alone in a car and make out with her, and while I was happy for her, that idea made me cringe. She was my mother, after all. I clung to the first theory.

"Eden, why don't you put on some coffee? Pete and I will be back in a little while." Mom slipped on her coat, and Pete escorted her to the car with the food.

Nodding, I walked to the coffeepot. "So you like coffee, Teddy?"

"Love it," he said, suddenly right next to me, and I startled a bit. "Can I help?"

He took the filters from my hand, and our fingers touched, sending a jolt of adrenaline coursing through me. In a gasp, I stepped back and let out a breath.

"Are you okay?" He placed a hand on my bare shoulder, and it forced my eyes closed as heat permeated my skin, seeping through to my bones, sending a rush throughout my body.

I shook my head and chanced looking him in the eyes. They caught me, held me, swallowed me within their depths. "I don't know. This is going to sound really weird, but have we met before?"

Tremors rocked his hand, and he yanked it from my shoulder. Worry clouded his eyes, turning them a bit gray. He braced himself on the counter with his hands behind his back as he dipped his head. "I can't remember."

Guilt stabbed at my heart. What a shitty thing to say to the guy who had amnesia. "I'm so sorry. I didn't mean it like that."

A gorgeous smile graced his lips when he raised his head. I ached with everything in me to kiss them. "It's okay. I'm getting used to it. You do seem familiar. Your voice, I recognized it immediately tonight. You came into the shelter last Christmas with food, didn't you?"

I blinked and thought back with a nod. "Yeah, Thandie and I brought our leftovers in. You were there?"

"I couldn't see you. I was in line to get food. But I heard your voice." He looked away, almost ashamed. "It kind of stuck with me."

I arched a brow. "Is that a good thing or a bad thing?"

He chuckled and locked eyes with me again. "A very good thing. It's a really lovely voice. And I knew it had to belong to a really lovely woman."

Heat rose along my neck and splattered over my cheeks, which I was sure made for a fantastic blush that probably showed right through all the makeup I had on. "Just don't ask me to sing. I only sound good in the shower where no one else can hear me."

We both lurched forward and pressed a hand to our heads. Pain sliced through my brain, and I thought for sure someone carved it like a turkey. A picture hit my mind of me waiting for someone taking a shower in my bathroom. I stood behind a door cracked open with a ridiculous smile on my face. I thought the painful headache-inducing flashes were a result of too much rum and eggnog last Christmas. I hadn't had one in so long, I nearly forgot about them.

I looked at Teddy, who seemed to be in as much pain as I was. Did he have one, too?

14

THEO

FIRE BLAZED THROUGH MY HEAD LIKE A BOLT OF LIGHTNING. THE harder I pressed my hands to my head, the more it sliced through me. I exhaled a harsh breath as a vision sparked in my mind—*I was in a shower, talking to someone who stood outside the door waiting for me.* All that pain for just one second of a memory?

I shook my head and looked at Eden, the same pained grimace coloring her face.

"You okay?" I choked out.

She nodded. "I think so. You?"

I shrugged. "I think so."

"I wonder if it was something we ate." She turned back to the coffeepot, though her fingers shook like she'd already drank her weight in espresso.

"I hadn't thought of that." I wondered, though, if she had a vision or if it was just me. I didn't want to come off as some weirdo before I had the chance to make a decent impression.

I stood before the very woman I'd been searching nearly a year for. That voice I longed to hear one more time belonged to the most beautiful woman I'd ever seen. Long chestnut hair caressed her shoulders, and dark, soulful brown eyes captivated me every time I chanced a glance in her direction. But whether or not she was yoga-pants girl from my memory, I didn't know. And the only way I'd find out was if I talked to her.

But how did one start off a conversation like that? She'd think I was some psycho, claiming she was somehow connected to my past. A part of me didn't even want to know now, since she didn't imme-diately remember me upon sight. Clearly, if we were a part of each other's lives in the past, she should have recognized me. My heart sank a bit deeper in my chest at the thought. Finding her was a little less fulfilling than I'd imagined. I really had it set in my mind that she was the one, the key to my past, to who I was and all my memories, to what happened to me.

If she wasn't connected to my past, who was she to me? Why had she sparked such an intense reaction in me? Did it mean I could still be with someone else? The thought that once gave me some hope sat heavy in my chest each time I looked at Eden. She was stunning, and so sweet. Not to mention funny. I still laughed every time I pictured her swatting herself at the hair spider. I enjoyed being around her, and all we'd done was have dinner. Just her voice sent a wave of exhilaration through me. Now, looking at her, that spark of desire coursed through me like a wildfire. No other woman had that effect on me in nearly a year. That had to mean something.

She handed me a cup of coffee. Our hands met, and as she jerked back to let go, I clung to her. "So I look familiar to you?"

"Wha-What?" Worry darkened her eyes, and fear tightened my stomach in knots at her reaction. I didn't know what to make of it.

"You asked if we had met before. I thought...I don't know what I was thinking." I released her hand and stepped back, shoving my hand through my hair.

"I admit, you look like someone, but it's stupid. I mean, it doesn't matter, because he had longer hair than you." She glanced down, as if she was afraid to look into my eyes.

"Really?" A flicker of hope returned to my heart. "I cut my hair.

When I woke up in the snowbank, I had long hair, down to my shoulders. The social worker at the shelter thought it would be a good idea to shorten it to get a job."

Her head shot up, and a tear streamed down her cheek. Why would she be crying? An ache welled in my heart to see her shedding tears, and I wanted nothing more than to wipe them away. Without thinking, I brushed my thumb against her soft cheek, catching the tear.

"This is too much," she choked out and ran to the living room, collapsing in a heap on the sofa.

A part of me wondered if maybe I looked like an ex of hers or someone who might have passed away. Or what if he hurt her and left her.

Another wave of pain shot through my head, and I slammed the palm of my hand to my temple. What the hell was happening? I hadn't had a painful headache like that since weeks after I woke up in that snowbank. Now I'd had two within minutes.

I forced back the pain and walked to the living room, not even waiting to see what memory or vision appeared this time. And none did. Just the pain. Maybe I was dying? But all the tests the ER did months ago checked out fine. So why all of a sudden did the headaches come back with a vengeance?

"Do you need to lie down?" Her voice soothed the ache in my head.

She reached a hand to me, and I clasped on to it as she pulled me to the sofa next to her.

I rubbed my temple. "I don't know what's going on. Perhaps we did have too much wine."

"I'm sorry I ran out of the kitchen. You just remind me so much of someone. Sort of. But it's impossible." The soft yellow lights in the living room draped her face in a glowing halo. A myriad of emotions colored her deep-brown eyes a lighter shade, like honey. While she was beautiful on the outside, it was her inner beauty shining through that truly captured me. She was like a living work of art I could look at for hours.

"Why is it impossible? Maybe it's me. Maybe it's the key to my past." I sat forward, hope dancing like a damn parade in my heart.

"That's not possible, because he doesn't exist."

I quirked a brow. "What do you mean he doesn't exist? Did he die?"

She shook her head, and more tears careened over her delicate cheeks. "No. Because he was made up. He existed only in my dreams. My imagination."

"You've dreamed of me?" I gasped, and another red-hot poker of pain jammed into my skull, this time with a round of *déjà vu*, like I'd been in this moment before. I cringed and dropped my head into my hands.

Eden slid over on the sofa, pressing her fingertips to my temples as she rubbed in slow circles. I raised my head at her gentle touch, and we locked eyes. Her hands stopped as we both sat there, breathless, staring at one another. I cupped one of her hands and held it to my face. Air caught in my throat. An ache welled in my heart, begging me to kiss her.

She tilted her head, and we lingered, hovering over each other's lips. I leaned forward, ready to capture her mouth with my own. My stomach tumbled with the flutter of a thousand butterfly wings, launching a stream of desire coursing through my veins. A breath away from her lips, the door opened, startling us, and we shot back to opposite ends of the sofa.

We both sat with heaving chests, gasping for air, tossing glances at the other like a couple of teenagers caught making out by their parents, which for all intents and purposes we had been. Thankfully, this house had a foyer from which they couldn't see the front door.

"You kids get a chance to talk and get to know each other?" Madeline asked as Pete helped her out of her coat.

Eden jumped from the sofa and crossed her arms. "Um, a little."

"Perhaps we should go. It's getting late," Pete said, twirling a coin of some kind in his fingers, bouncing it back and forth over his knuckles.

I walked toward Pete, watching him with narrowed eyes. I could have sworn I'd seen someone do that before. It was almost hypnotic. I spotted Eden's sad face from the corner of my eye, and it shifted my focus. It looked like she didn't want me to go. I didn't want to go either, but I had to get out of there. While Eden's voice matched my yoga girl from Christmas Day, her memories did not. If we had any kind of past together, why wouldn't she remember me? Which meant I could still have a family or someone out there somewhere, and I'd nearly kissed her. I ached to do it. But I couldn't let anything happen until I knew for sure I was free. Or one of these brain-frying memory headaches produced a face instead of a pair of pants.

"Yeah, I guess we should be getting on," I said, glancing back at Eden, who nodded and folded her arms.

She cleared her throat. "Yeah, big shopping day tomorrow."

Pete took Madeline's hand in his own and brought it to his lips for a kiss. "Thank you for a wonderful evening, fantastic food, and even better company."

Madeline blushed. "Pete, you flatter me. Keep going though, don't stop."

Pete let out a hearty laugh. "Well, if you're not doing anything tomorrow night, I'd love to take you out for dinner."

"I'd like that, thank you." Madeline leaned in and brushed a kiss along his cheek.

"'Til tomorrow then," Pete said with a smile.

At least the evening ended a success for him. He deserved to find some happiness of his own after always helping others. I swallowed hard, unsure of how to end the evening on my end with Eden. But she did it for me as she stepped up and extended her hand. I slid mine along hers, about to pull it to my lips as Pete did, but she shook it instead. Awkward.

"Nice to meet you, Teddy. I hope you find your lost memories." She dropped my hand, tucking her arms back around her torso.

I nodded. "Nice to meet you, too, Eden. Thanks for the coffee."

She smiled and nodded. Nothing hurt my heart more than to leave her standing there. I didn't want to go. I wanted to run back, sweep her into my arms, and dip her into a kiss. Maybe I should have. Maybe a kiss would have told me what I needed to know. But the moment had passed, and her mom and Pete were back.

"Teddy, are you available to help me put up the Christmas tree at the shelter tomorrow?" Madeline's voice broke into my thoughts.

"Um, no. I'm sorry. I do counseling at the church on Fridays." I glanced between Madeline and Eden.

"Eden, honey, can you come help me put the tree up tomorrow then?"

Eden and I stared at each other as if we were both unaware there was anyone else in the room. She had to have been feeling the same. The draw to the other was unmistakable. But I was so torn on what to do. My heart shouted at me to ask her out. My head wouldn't let go of the possibility there might be someone else.

"Huh?" she stuttered, shaking her head from our trance. "Uh, yeah, I guess so."

A smile lit my lips. At least I knew where she'd be tomorrow, and I could see her again. I decided I would pop in on her at the shelter and at least ask her out for coffee. I made my way toward Pete and gave Madeline a gentle hug, thanking her for the evening. I shut the door behind me. But where God closed a door, he opened a window, or so the saying went, right?

I glanced through the window, hoping for one last look at her. She caught me, or I caught her, or we caught each other in one last stare. She might not know who I was, might not be a part of my past, but she was definitely something.

⋰⊙⋱

Eden

I snapped the curtains shut as soon as he saw me looking at him. Dammit. Could I have been more of a stalker? But my heart hurt watching him leave, and I couldn't figure out why. Well, yeah, he looked like the spitting image of the man I'd been dreaming about since forever. Aside from that freakish similarity, I didn't have a clue about him. Not to mention he didn't have a clue about his past. What if he had been a serial killer or something?

I was so stupid, thinking we were about to kiss. The way he jumped off the sofa and tried to leave the minute my mom and Pete got back made me rethink things. Maybe I imagined the attraction. Maybe what I thought was going to be a kiss was something completely different. But never in my life had my heart hammered so hard in that almost-kiss moment. It was the kind of feeling one lived for, the kind only described in books or movies, where the whole world stopped, the air thinned, and they were breathless and aching, just inches from the other person's lips.

I knew now what my mom said about Grayson was true. It was true about all my other relationships. Because never once had I experienced that kind of moment with another person on this planet. Never once had I longed to connect with another human being like I did with Teddy. And I'd known him, what, all of a couple of hours? How did I explain that? Insta-love wasn't a thing. It was a plot device in cheesy movies and books.

Yet my heart sank even further when he said he wouldn't be working at the shelter tomorrow. Maybe I could swing by the church and see him? That would be wearing desperation like a wig, though, and I thought better of it.

Nevertheless, in just a few moments without him in the room, an emptiness hollowed out my heart, like a part of me was now missing. Which was so completely impossible. It was like the feeling I had on Chris—I clasped a hand to my chest at the thought. I hadn't felt this empty since Christmas.

Thandie's words came barreling back to me. She had asked me where my fella was, told me some man had come with me to her house on Christmas Eve. I couldn't remember going to her house, let alone with anyone else. I thought she was medicated, or maybe needed some. But that Christmas Eve had been a little fuzzy for me. I chalked it up to too much rum and eggnog. All I remembered was anger and burning down my tree, and then nothing, which I blamed on a drunken stupor and thought maybe I'd just passed out.

No. I refused to even connect the two. I mean, really? Some man I'd dreamed of manifested and spent Christmas Eve with me, then appeared in a snowbank on Christmas a year ago with no memory and had been trying to find me? That was too farfetched for even my imagination. I sliced and diced that theory as quick as it snapped into my head. Besides, what was the probability that both he and I had some form of amnesia? The poor guy couldn't remember anything. That wasn't my case—I just couldn't remember half a day. Mine was alcohol induced. His was...well, no one really knew, possibly an injury or something.

"Eden," my mom shouted, and I jumped, nearly taking out a ceramic turkey on the coffee table.

"What?" I shouted back, not meaning to, but more out of shock.

"I've been calling your name for the last five minutes. What's wrong?" She stepped into the living room and crossed her arms.

"I'm sorry, I didn't hear you. I was lost in thought."

"I see that. Was Teddy in any of them?" The sly tone to her voice didn't go unnoticed by me, and I narrowed my stare. "Isn't he handsome?"

Handsome didn't begin to cover it. It was like he'd been created by the finger of God, and I couldn't imagine what he'd look like sans clothes. That wasn't true—I imagined it a lot, but I extinguished the thought as I caught the smirk of my mother and suddenly felt the need for a shower.

"He's not bad," I said to amuse her.

"Mmm-hmm," she murmured as she turned on her heel and headed for her room.

I stomped after her. "No. You get back here. You don't get to grill me without the return favor of asking about you and Pete."

"Parent's prerogative. Sorry!" she sang from down the hall and closed her door.

"Ugh!" I folded my arms and pressed my back to the wall.

"Good night, darling. I love you."

"Love you, too," I mumbled and made my way back to the living room and flopped onto the sofa.

Leaning my head to the side, I clutched a pillow to my stomach. Teddy's scent lingered on the fabric, and it sent a flutter to my heart as I inhaled. It comforted me.

My thoughts drifted back to my invisible friend as a kid, with his long blond hair and bright-blue eyes. Or maybe that was just how I wanted to picture him. The longer I tried to remember what I always said he looked like, the harder it was to picture. Mainly, I remembered what he used to do, like hold my hand when I was scared, give me a hug when I was sad, catch me when I fell, lift me up when I couldn't reach. He watched over me, comforted me. But I don't remember smelling him, or touching him, or hearing him. I remembered a sense of him near me.

When he came to me in my dreams as I got older, I saw him a lot clearer. I swore it was Teddy's face, but maybe I just wanted it to be, so my memories merged the two. The more I thought about it, the more I doubted myself. It angered me as I tried harder to remember the last dream I had, just the night before, but it vanished like a speck of dust in the windstorm howling through my brain. A tear streamed down my cheek. I didn't even know why, out of frustration, anger, sadness...I couldn't figure it out.

All I knew was my heart felt full when Teddy was here, and

when he left, it was like he took it with him. I had to see him again. I had to question him. But ask him what? He couldn't remember jack. My head told me I was crazy. Yet they said your heart would know when it found its other half, its missing piece, its split-apart. What if that was us? Then again, what if I just *wanted* it to be us because my mom now had someone in her life and I was still single?

I played the what-if game until I drifted off to sleep and Teddy's face appeared behind my closed eyelids.

15

THEO

I walked through the doors of the church with a bit of a pep in my step for the first time. Regardless of how things went down last night, a renewed sense of hope pulsed through me. I might not have gotten all my answers, but that overwhelming feeling being lost and forgotten didn't cling to the back of my head. Despite putting on a "brave" face each day as people encouraged me about this being some kind of fresh start, I never stopped longing to find a piece of my past, if nothing else but for closure.

I set my bag down in the church office and grabbed a cup of coffee.

"Mornin', Teddy," Harriet, the church office assistant, said as her nails clicked away on her keyboard.

"Morning, Miss Harriet. You're looking lovely as always." I smiled at her as she glanced up from her computer. In her early sixties with almost-white hair—a tint of strawberry blond from her younger days peeking through—she had smiling eyes and one of those *never met a stranger* kind of personalities.

"Such a charmer." She winked. "You've already got someone waiting in your office."

I nodded. It seemed a bit early for someone to be there already.

It was barely eight o'clock in the morning. A tingle hit my heart that it might be Eden, and a smile burst on my lips. "Thanks. I'm heading in now."

I made my way into the little office they'd set aside for me with a desk and chair. A small window faced the church parking lot to the east, allowing the bright morning sun to filter in, which I loved. The warmth from the rays kissed my skin and filled me with purpose, reminding me each day held a new chance at doing something to help someone else.

This morning I walked in to find a woman sitting in the chair with her back to me. Long brown hair fell down her back in waves, and I startled for a moment because I thought it really was Eden. But she turned, and it wasn't her. As she stood, a loose red-and-white flannel draped around her tight white T-shirt. Panic hit my heart as I glanced down to find her wearing black yoga pants. My coffee slipped from my fingers and crashed to the floor.

She dashed over to clean it up, and I couldn't even help her. I stood there, staring at her like she was a two-headed alien. I dropped to a crouch and we locked eyes, and she smiled. But nothing happened. My heart and soul remained a blank slate.

"I'm sorry," I managed to say after clearing the wedge of air from my throat.

She rose, her petite frame coming only to my shoulders. "I didn't mean to startle you. Miss Harriet said I could wait for you here."

"It's okay. I thought you may have been someone I knew." I walked to my desk and slid into the chair as she sat across from me.

"But I am. You don't recognize me, Theodore?" She leaned across the desk, batting her lashes so fast they probably could have taken flight.

Swallowing hard, I shook my head. "I'm sorry. It's really vague. I mean, the outfit you're wearing seems familiar somehow, but not your face. In my memories, I can never see faces."

Her smile fell, and she sat back, curling her hands in her lap. "Oh."

"So you're saying we know each other?"

A smile tugged at the corners of her pursed lips as she nodded. "Theodore, I'm your fiancée."

I coughed and lunged forward. Something rock-hard pitted in my stomach. "Excuse me?" I choked out.

Adrenaline surged through me, but instead of making me run toward her, it made me want to run away, fast. Everything I wanted to know sat in front of me, and I had the exact opposite reaction I thought I'd have. I pictured it so differently, like we'd instantly recognize each other, run to one another and embrace. Everything would come spiraling back to me as we kissed. Maybe I'd been watching too many holiday romance movies.

She bit her lip and scooted to the edge of the chair. "My name is Tera. You really don't recognize me?"

My heart hurt. I wanted to be able to say yes, but I couldn't. I couldn't lie to her. "I'm so sorry."

"I somehow hoped you'd instantly remember, and everything could go back to normal. I've searched for you for so long." Her eyes glassed over, and another prick of regret hit my heart.

"You have? Can you tell me what happened?" I figured the best way to handle the situation would be to ask the questions I needed answers for and take it from there.

"I can try. But I don't really know. You didn't come home one day. No explanation. You didn't answer your phone. You just vanished. We'd had a fight, and you left. I thought it was to let off some steam, but you never came back." Sadness filled her green eyes.

Green. I didn't think they'd be green. I thought they'd be brown, like Eden's.

"What did we fight about?"

"Money, like usual. We were perfect, but you were being too

hard on yourself because we had a baby on the way, and you were upset because we couldn't afford a kid."

I gasped, and my stomach knotted. "I have a kid?"

She lowered her head. "I ended up miscarrying. Doctors said it was probably the stress of you disappearing."

Guilt ransacked my heart as tremors shook my body. It was worse than I ever imagined. "I'm...I'm so sorry. I...I don't even have words."

She sniffed and wiped her eyes. "I'm just so glad I finally found you."

"But how? Where are we from? How'd you end up here? How did I end up here? We're not from here, are we?" So many questions formulated in my mind, and they all spit uncontrollably out of my mouth.

"No. We're from New York. I don't know how you ended up here exactly. I just traced clues. Asked around, showed your picture, and the trail ended here."

A thought hit me. "You have a picture? Can I see it?"

She nodded and pulled it from her pocket. Folded in half, a line crinkled down the center between Tera and a man that looked similar to me—proposing. Something struck me as off about the picture, but I couldn't pinpoint it because I had zero frame of reference. We looked happy. She looked at me with adoration in her eyes, and I looked at her with the same. The couple in the picture looked like they were in love.

But as I watched the woman sitting in front of me in tears, I felt nothing for her. Sadness, yes. Maybe even pity, or empathy perhaps, as I could relate to the last year of the unknown and loneliness. Yet my heart didn't feel anything remotely close to love. I had more feeling in my heart when I heard Eden's voice without even seeing her face than for the woman sitting across from me claiming to be my fiancée.

"I guess it looks like me." It was a complete jerk thing to say. But nothing about this felt right at all. "I'm so sorry, Tera. I wish I could remember. But I don't. I want to believe you. I want my memories to return. I've wanted it for so long, trust me. And I thought the moment I'd meet someone from my past, it would all come barreling back to me. But it's not."

She nodded, and more tears soaked her cheeks. "I wonder what happened to you. Some kind of head injury or accident?"

I shrugged. "The doctors all said I'm healthy as a horse. There were no signs of injury. It's a complete mystery."

She bit her lip and nodded. "Well, maybe if we..." She paused and shook her head. "Never mind."

"No, go ahead. Maybe if we what?"

She twisted and tilted her head toward her shoulder as if she were a shy teenager asking a boy out. "What if we kissed? Like we used to. Perhaps it would jog your memory?"

My heart hammered, and fear churned my stomach. Not that she wasn't gorgeous—she was. But I had zero feelings for her and couldn't just kiss a stranger.

"Please don't take this wrong—you're a beautiful woman. But if you see it from my point of view, I don't recognize you. You're telling me I'm your fiancé, but I can't remember. It would feel awkward to kiss you. Does that make sense?"

She nodded. "I know. It was dumb."

This poor woman poured her heart out to me, claiming I was her long-lost fiancé, and wanted some way to help me remember. Maybe a kiss would do it? I swallowed hard, but the more I thought about it, the more it did make sense to try. Perhaps I could get it out of my head and know for sure.

What if we did kiss and it unlocked everything? But then I thought back to my almost kiss with Eden last night, and this situation felt so completely opposite. I burned as if I were on fire when I was within moments of kissing Eden. With Tera, I looked at a stranger, as did my heart. While she held the puzzle pieces, none of them felt like they fit.

"It wasn't dumb, and you might have a point. It might spark something." I couldn't believe I was even considering it.

A smile broke on her lips as she brushed away the tears. "Really?"

I blew out a breath. It was just a kiss. One kiss. One effort to try to remember. It might or might not prove her story, but what could it hurt? I wasn't any closer to answers than I was before she walked into my office.

I walked around to her chair. She stood and faced me, her back against the edge of the desk. Staring into her watery green eyes, nothing but hesitation filled me.

She slid her hands along my waist. "I used to call you Theo."

The name toiled in my head. Theo. Something about that felt right and comforted my soul. That was the first thing she said that made any kind of sense. "That actually feels kind of familiar."

An almost seductive smile curled along her lips. "Finally."

The warmth left me the longer she smiled, like an iciness lay behind her eyes, a coldness in her touch, and that brief moment of familiarity vanished. But I needed to know for sure.

I had no idea where to put my hands. Should they be on her waist? On her shoulders? Should I cup her cheeks? Every concept seemed awkward and unromantic. I finally placed my hands along her arms and leaned in. Her peppermint breath hit my lips, and another spark of familiarity washed over me. Peppermint. The smell sent that same warmth to my soul. Maybe she really was who she claimed?

We leaned in farther, and her eyes darkened to pools of emeralds, not full of love, but lust. My heart warred with my head that this was wrong, and my body tensed as regret twisted in my gut. But it was too late. She brushed her lips against me, and her tongue pushed into my mouth, searching for mine. She clung to me, trying to deepen the kiss as she moaned, and I jerked back. It was the most uncomfortable and awkward feeling of my life.

"I'm sorry. It's just not working," I said, and glanced toward something moving out the window behind her.

A wave of panic hit me as I caught sight of Eden in the parking lot, looking right into my window as I held Tera in my arms. We locked eyes, and she threw a hand to her mouth and ran toward the shelter. Regret turned to a burning sense of shame and horror.

I looked down at Tera, who stood with a wide smile and darkness in her eyes. Anger welled up in my veins, and I pushed her away. "You're not my fiancée, are you?"

"What? Yes, I am!" She clasped a hand to her chest.

"Then why doesn't this feel right?"

She reached for me, her hand shaking. "Because you don't remember."

"Well, the kiss didn't help me. So I'm very sorry, Tera. But I...I can't." I walked to the window and stared at the empty parking lot, searching for Eden.

"Theo, please. Give us a chance. I can help you remember." She begged, but not with sorrow or despair of love lost, but with anger and resentment. "You left me when I needed you most. We lost a child. A future wedding. A life together. That means nothing to you?"

The name Theo still resonated in my soul, but it felt wrong coming from her lips. That was the only thing that made any sense. I didn't understand. Her words were laced with aggression and meant to inflict pain and guilt. And it worked. She clearly knew which buttons to push. But how could I trust her when my heart and head both said this was all wrong?

"I really wish I could tell you the kiss meant something to me, that it brought a memory back. Yes, I feel sorry you lost a child, possibly my child. Yes, I feel sorry you lost a fiancé. But was it me? I just don't know, Tera. I need time. This is a lot of information to process." I collapsed in my chair.

Tera walked around the desk and knelt before me, taking my hand in hers. Her cold fingers pressed harder against my skin. "We can start over. We can build a new life together. We've got a fresh start now. I've found you. We don't have to do this alone anymore."

I stared at her frigid touch, so unlike Eden's warm and soothing hand. "I have a fresh start. Here in Jersey. I've had nearly a year to build my new life. I wondered for so long about my past, but I have to be truthful. None of this feels right. I know in my gut that when I find my past, I'll feel something. Anything."

"Really? My kiss meant nothing to you?" Fire now burned in her eyes, drying her tears. "You expect me to leave here without you? I came all this way after searching." She climbed onto my lap, draping her arms along my shoulders as she pressed her lips to my ear. "Let me kiss you again. I know I can refresh your memory."

I pulled her arms away from my neck and pushed her off my lap, jumping from the chair. "What are you doing? This is crazy!"

"I'm sorry. I just miss you. I miss us." She dropped her head as a sob burst from her lips, and she grabbed her purse. "So you're just going to throw away everything we had without even giving it a chance?"

I closed my eyes and curled my hand into a fist. Her words buried my heart under guilt. Before I could stop myself, I succumbed to the weight of it. "Why don't we start with dinner? Can we take it slow and see what happens? I can't promise you I'm the man you once knew and were engaged to, but I can at least give you dinner."

She swiped at her eyes, brushing away the mascara-laden streaks coloring her cheeks. "Dinner is good. I'm at the motel across from the post office. Pick me up at seven?"

I swallowed hard and nodded. I could manage dinner. Then at least I would have given it a shot and could let it go if we didn't make a connection. "Sure."

She leaned up on her tiptoes and placed a kiss on my cheek. "'Til later, my sweet Theo."

I nodded as I watched her leave my office with a swagger in her hips, and I studied her movements. She might have been wearing yoga pants, but she wasn't my yoga girl. The body was all wrong. While my memory was filled with no faces, I knew the curves of her hips, the softness of her skin. The way they fit Tera wasn't right.

That wasn't to say Tera couldn't be my fiancée, because I had nothing solid to prove Eden was. I just knew I was still meant to figure out what piece of the puzzle she was.

In the meantime, I had to go talk to Eden and try to explain what she saw. I didn't know why I felt the need to. It wasn't like Eden and I were dating. We'd only met for the first time last night. But everything inside me ached, riddled with guilt over her seeing the kiss between Tera and me. I needed her to understand. I needed to explain.

But would she care? Had I possibly read her running off wrong? That part hit me the hardest, thinking she'd have no reaction to it. I wanted her to. I wanted her to be jealous and throw her arms around me and kiss me, to claim me for her own, to have her tell me it was her, that she was my yoga girl, my love, my missing past. But for the life of me, I couldn't figure out why. Why did my body, mind, and soul seem to want Eden, when Tera was the one claiming to be my fiancée?

I sat back in my chair and stared out the window, harboring my misgivings in silence. Closing my eyes, I whispered a prayer, one carrying Eden's name off my lips and to the heavens.

16

EDEN

I FANNED AWAY THE TEARS WELLING IN MY EYES AS I STARED IN THE bathroom mirror. *Dammit, why didn't I put on waterproof mascara today?* Sucking up my pride, I marched out of the bathroom, chucked my hat and coat in the shelter office, and searched out my mother to put up the stupid tree so I could go home and eat a carton of Ben & Jerry's. I was so stupid, always falling for the wrong guys, just like my mom said.

I thought Teddy would be different. We had some kind of magnetic connection. That zing, that sizzle of electricity that flooded someone's veins when they met The One, or supposedly The One. Everything about him felt so right. Or maybe I just wanted it to because he fit the idea of my perfect man, the man from my dreams. Perhaps it was more my imagination still at work than any kind of personal connection.

But no, I found my answer with a slap of reality and a side of *you should have known better* when I saw him kissing someone else instead of me. The more I thought about it, the more I thanked God we didn't actually kiss last night. I'd be even more of a schmuck for falling for his charm and Norse godlike looks.

"Oh, good, you're here," my mother said from behind me.

I spun around and nodded. "What do you need help with?"

She pointed to the tree in the corner of the dining hall. "Can you string the lights and put the star on top for me? I can't climb that ladder like I used to. I'll take care of all the stuff on the bottom. Thank you, sweetie."

With a sigh, I strolled toward the tree, but a little girl swinging her legs on one of the chairs at a table caught my eye. She sat alone with tearstained cheeks. My heart cried out to her. I wandered over and sat down next to her.

"You know. You're not alone. I was just crying in the bathroom." I pointed to my own cheeks where the tears had streaked lines through my makeup.

A small smile broke on her lips. "Why were you crying? Did you lose someone, too?"

I sighed with a nod. "Yeah, I kind of did."

"Do you think we'll ever find them?" She leaned in to hug me.

I shrugged as I hugged her back. "Maybe. Who did you lose?"

She swiped at her cheeks. "My doggy, Bert. Momma and me had to leave Daddy really fast because he got angry again, so we couldn't take Bert with us. I miss him so much."

My heart lurched into my throat. This poor kid ran away with her mom from some kind of domestic abuse situation, and here I was pining over some dude I met last night kissing someone else. Where the hell were my priorities?

"You know what? I'm sure God will take care of Bert while you're gone. In the meantime, I have someone who needs taking care of. Would you be willing to watch him for me?"

She sniffed and nodded as she bit her lower lip.

"I'll be right back." The shelter always kept a stash of stuffed animals in the back for kids who came in scared. I dug through the pile until I found a brown shaggy puppy.

I wandered back out and found Teddy sitting in my seat talking to the little girl. He tickled her, and a giggle floated through the unusually empty dining hall. The smile on her face lit up the room.

He reached into his bag, pulled out a white-and-brown stuffed dog, and gave it to her. She clutched it to her heart and hugged it tight, swaying side to side. I pursed my lips and tossed the brown shaggy dog over my shoulder. Ugh, of course he had to be amazing with kids. The jerk.

I huffed and watched as she thanked him and gave him another hug before I walked over. "Well, it looks like you've found someone to keep you company now until you get Bert back. I'm so glad, too, because my dog was, um...sleeping. So it all worked out."

She smiled and held up her new stuffed puppy for me to look at and Teddy stared at me, such depth and sincerity in his eyes. "I'm sorry, were you and Shelly talking? I just saw her here all alone while her mom was talking to Pete about a place to stay."

"It's okay. I've got work to do anyway. It was nice meeting you, Shelly. You take care of that doggy, okay?"

She nodded, looking up at Teddy like he'd hung the moon. I knew how she felt.

I glanced at Teddy, and my heart sank. The worst feeling I could have ever imagined was standing next to the person who meant the world to me, knowing I meant nothing to them. I forced a smile and all but ran over to the tree. Footsteps followed, and I knew Teddy was behind me. I spun around, and we bumped chests. He clutched me by the upper arms, and we locked gazes.

"I'm sorry." His grip on my arms softened, but he didn't let go.

"It's okay. I'm just glad she's not feeling sad anymore."

"No. Not about Shelly, about Tera."

I arched a brow. "Who's Tera?"

He swallowed, and his Adam's apple bounced in his throat. "The woman you saw me kiss."

I pursed my lips and nodded. "Right. That." There was no denying it. He saw me as I saw him. Because, of course, that was my luck. Well, at least the elephant was on the table and we could just move our separate ways, no awkward run-ins at the shelter or church.

"It's not what you think."

"What exactly do you think I think?"

He narrowed his eyes. "I don't know. What do you think?"

I shook my head. "Why does it matter what I think? It wasn't me you were kissing. Why don't you ask Tera what she thinks? I'm sure she thought it was swell to be kissing you."

He jerked back, and a smirk ghosted his lips. "Why would you say that?"

I threw my hands up. "Does it matter? Why are we having this ridiculously weird conversation right now? I don't care who you want to kiss."

"You don't?" His brows pinched, and the twinkle in his eyes faded.

"Should I?"

He paused, twisting his hands around the strap of his shoulder bag. We stared at each other for a wordless minute before I couldn't take it anymore and took a step to walk away.

He grabbed my hand and tugged me to a stop. "What if I want to kiss *you*?"

My heart beat a rhythm I could have probably danced to. "Do you?"

"Yes."

I hitched a shoulder. "No."

"Why?"

"You were just kissing Tera!" I pointed to the church next door.

He arched a brow. "Do you know her?"

"No, do you? I guess I hope you do. You were kissing her."

"But I don't."

"What do you mean you don't? You kissed her!"

"She said she was my fiancée."

I blinked, taken aback at his words. "Oh, that's much better. So Tera's your long-lost fiancée, and you want to kiss *me*?" I brushed past him, grabbing the box of decorations, and stomped to the tree.

Thoughts jumbled in my head, fighting with each other to

make it out of my mouth. They said the art of conversation was to say the right thing at the right time but also to leave unsaid the wrong thing at the most tempting moment. Right then, I had a lot of wrong things to say in that tempting moment.

He stomped right after me. "She thought it might jog my memory."

"Did it?" I whipped around.

"No."

"So why do you want to kiss *me*? To see if it jogs your memory?"

"Maybe." He bowed his head. "I hope it does." He looked up and took a step closer. "Because I really want to kiss you."

"So you're just going to go around town kissing women until one of them magically brings back your memory, trying on lips like a Cinderella shoe?" I turned and slammed the box down, praying the resulting clank wasn't anything breaking. "Better invest in some ChapStick, buddy."

"No. It's not like that." He waved his hands like he was coming out of a seizure. "Come on, Eden, hear me out. Please."

I turned and found him grinning ear to ear. "Why are you smiling? Is this funny to you?"

"A little." He shrugged. "You're upset."

I threw my hands up. "Of course I'm upset. This is absurd."

He smiled even brighter, grabbed my hands, and clasped them together between his own, laying them against his heart. "Because that means you care. Can you feel my heart? Can you feel how fast it beats for you? It started that rhythm the moment I heard your voice nearly a year ago, and it started again last night when I saw your face. I didn't feel that with Tera, even after a kiss."

Short breaths of air puffed in and out of my chest as his heart beat as fast as mine beneath my fingertips. Damn, he was charming. "You're good. Very good. No wonder Tera wanted to suck face with you."

"But I didn't with her. I toiled over it, and none of it felt right. I don't remember her at all. I looked at her, and I was as blank inside as the day I woke up in the snow. I look at you, and my heart races and I get all tingly. I wanted to kiss you last night."

I swallowed hard as he pressed his hand tighter over mine, which now shook like leaves in the wind against his warm chest. "It doesn't matter. What if she really is your fiancée? What if you have a family out there somewhere?"

He dropped my hands and pulled out a picture from his pocket. "She gave me this. It sort of looks like me. But I don't feel it. I feel nothing at her words, her voice, her face, this picture. That means more to me than what she claims. So I wonder if she's lying, but why would someone lie about something like this? It's not like I have money or am famous. There's no reason for her to lie."

"Have you looked at yourself in the mirror? You're gorgeous. Half the women in town want to sleep with you, and you're incredibly sweet and helpful, not to mention great with kids." I studied the picture. Something did look off about it, but I couldn't quite place it. Maybe he was right. What if she were lying, and this was some doctored photo?

"You think I'm gorgeous?"

My head snapped up after I realized what I'd said. The words just came out of my mouth as I looked at the picture without thinking. I 'didn't think I'd said them out loud. A stunned, gaping smile blazed over his lips.

For a moment, I wanted to smack him upside the head and then kiss that smile right off his face. Instead, I shoved the picture back into his hand. "It doesn't matter what I think. I'm not the one posing as your fiancée. Think about it, how would she have gotten a picture of you?"

He released a heavy sigh and stuck it back into his pocket. "I don't know."

I nodded and turned back to the box, rummaging through the decorations just so he wouldn't use my hands against me again. They longed to touch him, to soak in his warmth, relish the beat of his heart beneath their fingertips. They betrayed me.

"We're having dinner tonight."

"We are?" I quirked a brow. Not how I liked to be asked out, but there was something to be said for a man who knew what he wanted and took it. A part of me liked that take-charge kind of guy.

"No, me and Tera."

And my heart sank faster than the *Titanic*. "How nice. Don't order wine, you know you get headaches. She'll probably want to cure it with sex." I stormed off to the tree and climbed the ladder, yanking a ream of multicolored lights with me.

"I'm not going to have sex with her," he shouted, and then looked around and changed to a whisper. "It's just dinner. To ask her some questions. Maybe get some real answers."

I leaned into the tree and tossed the lights around the branches, not caring where they ended up. I wanted this done and over with so I could get the hell out of there and away from Teddy.

"Well, I hope you get the answers you seek."

"Me too." His voice faded, and I glanced over my shoulder as he walked away.

I stepped off the rung of the ladder, but my shoe slipped, and I reached for the only thing in front of me to try to stop from falling backward, which was the stupid tree. Instead of stopping me, it forced me down faster as the tree came down with me. As I realized what was happening, a scream burst from my lips.

Something caught me, breaking my fall. A warm hand cupped the back of my neck, and another held the small of my back, suspending me from the ground.

"Eden, are you okay?" a deep, rich voice asked. Teddy's voice.

"No. I'm far from okay. I just fell off a ladder, and there's a tree on my face. But thanks to you, I don't think I hurt anything but my pride, if that's what you're asking."

He chuckled, and I bounced in his hold. "Hang on, I've got you. Pete's going to pull the tree off. Don't move."

"Yeah, not going anywhere," I mumbled.

The tree whisked away from my face, and I glanced up at Teddy.

Our eyes locked, and one of those mind-searing headaches hit me. A pair of eyes so crystal blue stared at me, and the scent of pine lingered in my nose. The only problem, this tree was a fake. So where did the pine come from? Those eyes flashing in my mind matched Teddy's, and an overwhelming sense of *déjà vu* rushed me.

"Did you just..." I forced the words out of my mouth.

He grimaced. "Yeah, I got another headache."

I nodded as he eased me up and pulled me closer to his chest. I turned around to face him. "Was there..." How could I ask if he saw me in some kind of memory or vision? That would be beyond awkward, especially after the conversation we just had. Not to mention he was about to have dinner with his supposed fiancée.

What if I really was someone from his past? Perhaps some side piece he had, and his fiancée found out and hit him with a frying pan, and that was how he lost his memories. But how could I not remember, then, either? Nothing made sense.

"I had a memory come back. Like *déjà vu*. I'd helped someone in a similar situation before. I only saw a tree, and I held someone in my arms, like you. I think I rescued someone."

My heart raced to the point where I got dizzy. "Maybe it was m—"

He cut me off as he stared at the tree. "Maybe it was Tera?"

All the air whooshed from my lungs at the sound of her name. Yeah, maybe it was Tera.

17

THEO

I KNOCKED ON THE MOTEL ROOM DOOR, TRYING TO STOP THE WORRY swimming in my stomach. Tera opened it, wearing only a towel, and I immediately focused my attention on the ground.

"I must be early. I'm sorry. I'll just wait out here." I shoved my hands in my jeans and turned my back to her.

"You don't have to be afraid to look at me. We're engaged, Theo. You've seen me naked. A lot. Maybe if you explored my body, it might help you remember?" She walked into the motel room, leaving the door open. "You used to like to look at me. You used to like to do things to me."

I glanced over my shoulder. "I thought we were going to do dinner."

"Let's order in. Pizza and beer, just like the old days. See where the night takes us. You may not remember the past, but we can start rebuilding our future." She slid her hand into mine and led me into the room.

I shook my head, trying not to let my frustration get the better of me. As much as I could, I tried to look at it from her point of view. She'd just found her lost fiancé and wanted to pick up where they left off. But since I couldn't remember my feelings for her, I couldn't be what she wanted in that moment. "I don't think that's a good idea. I'm okay with dinner, but that's all I can give you right now."

She tightened her hand around mine. "Always the gentleman. You haven't changed in that regard."

My mouth dried as her towel slid lower, revealing the tops of her breasts. She was certainly beautiful. But if I just wanted sex, I could have done that a long time ago with other women. That wasn't what I was looking for.

"You should get dressed," I said, clearing my throat.

"I'm sorry. I didn't mean to make you uncomfortable. Give me a minute." She placed a kiss on my cheek and disappeared into the bathroom.

I sat on the edge of the bed, but all my thoughts drifted back to Eden. My headache this afternoon didn't reveal much other than I had rescued someone in the past. It could have been Tera. It could have been Eden for all I knew. But if it was Eden, why didn't she say something? I took the chance that it was Tera, hoping that tonight I might get the answers I needed.

She came out in a tank top and a pair of underwear, and I darted my gaze to the floor again.

"Sorry, forgot my jeans." She giggled as she walked in front of me and bent over to get into her suitcase.

I shot up from the bed and turned around. She certainly tried damned hard to tempt me. It would be nice to remember the touch of a woman. It had been nearly a year since I'd even kissed anyone, aside from Tera yesterday, let alone gone further. At least, that I could remember. That part scared me a bit, since I had absolutely nothing beyond Christmas of last year. I could very well have been a virgin for all I knew, as I couldn't even remember ever having sex. But surely as a nearly thirty-year-old man I would have, especially if Tera was my fiancée and did indeed get pregnant with my child.

"I've got some more pictures for you to look at." She zipped her jeans and walked over to me staring out the window.

"You do?"

I turned to her. She led me back to the bed and sat down on the edge of it, her a little closer to me than I was comfortable with.

She nodded. "A few. I didn't want to overwhelm you with too much, like baby albums and stuff."

She handed me a picture of us at a beach, turned to the side, looking at each other. And another of us at Christmas, where apparently, I proposed to her. The picture showed me on one knee, with a ring box and her hand over her mouth. I couldn't clearly see either of our faces in the picture, as my back was to the camera, and her head was dipped down with half her face covered by her hands.

"I'm sorry." I shook my head. "Still nothing."

She ran a hand through the back of my hair. "You cut your hair. I miss it long."

I nodded. "I thought short would be more professional when I was looking for a job and a place to live."

"I've missed you," she whispered, and a tear careened over her cheek.

My heart broke for her that none of the pictures brought back anything. But I couldn't fake what wasn't there. It wouldn't be fair to either of us. I brushed the tear from her cheek. "I don't know where to go from here, Tera."

"Well, we don't have to go backward. But what about forward? Do you think we could start over? Maybe date again? Get to know each other?" The hope in her voice made my heart cringe.

I hung my head. The decent guy in me wanted to give in to her hope and say yes. That maybe some quality time together would jog my memory. But a reserved part of me held back from giving her that. Something inside me kept telling me that it was all wrong. I wasn't even remotely attracted to her.

I shrugged with a sigh. "I don't know."

"Is there someone else?" she choked out. "Have you already replaced me?"

Eden's face popped into my head, making my heart race. I

closed my eyes, because the answer was crystal clear, yes. I could only give her my silence, because how could I replace something I didn't even remember having?

"I see."

The guilt ate me alive as I looked into her watery green eyes. And before I knew it, I gave into it. "I suppose we could try. Maybe have a real date or two. I can't promise anything. But can we agree that if it's not working, we can just be friends?"

"Friends?" She laughed and choked as she swiped at a tear. "Yeah, friends. Real easy when you don't remember anything and I remember everything. How do you go back to just being friends with the love of your life?"

"I know I must sound like an ass, but I'm trying, Tera. I really am. But I can't force something that's not there. It's not fair to you or me."

"I know. I always feared it might end up this way." She pushed my hair behind my ear before trailing her finger along my cheek. She leaned closer, and as she brushed her lips against mine, I shot up from the bed.

"I've got to go. I'll come back tomorrow. I...I just need some time tonight. I'm sorry."

I ran out the door and hopped in my truck. A jerk thing to do, but I couldn't be there with her anymore. The urge to find Eden stirred inside me, but I tamped it down. I didn't need to confuse myself even more by giving in to my desire to see her when I still had to figure out the situation with Tera.

I pulled into the parking lot of the church and pressed my head to my arms folded on the steering wheel. Someone rapped on my window, startling me from the spiraling thoughts in my head. I turned to find Pete standing outside my truck.

I rolled down the window. "Hey, Pete, what's up?"

"Was about to ask you the same thing. Something troubling you?" He quirked a brow.

I shrugged and tapped my finger on the steering wheel.

"Need an ear?" He pointed to the passenger seat, and I nodded, unlocking the door for him to get in. He slid into the seat and rubbed his hands together. "What's troubling you, son?"

I tilted my head back against the headrest and closed my eyes. "I'm just really confused. A couple days ago, I had been so sure about what would help me remember my past. You know how I told you all about yoga-pants girl? I knew that if I just found her, I'd have all my answers."

"What changed?" Pete turned in his seat, resting one arm on the long bench seat between us.

"Eden." I drummed my thumbs against the steering wheel, trying to calm the nervous energy coursing through me.

A smile brimmed on his lips. "Ah, you finally found someone you took a liking to?"

I shrugged again. "I don't even know how to put it into words. She was the voice I'd been searching for, but I don't know if she's t the key to my past. There's definitely something there, I can feel it. There's a connection, a spark. Nothing I've ever felt for anyone else."

"So what's the problem?" He tilted his head.

I swallowed hard. "Today, a woman came to see me at the church." Exhaling a long breath, I turned to face the one person who'd been like a father to me, a guide, a guardian, hoping maybe he could help me cut through the fog in my head, because it wasn't happening on my own. "Pete, she said she was my fiancée. Even showed me a picture." I reached into my pocket and handed it to him.

He opened the folded picture and nodded before handing it back to me. "Do you think that's you in the picture?"

"I don't know. I can't remember! She gave me all this information about my name, told me it's Theodore and that she called me Theo. Why did I pick Theodore as my legal name that day I woke up? When she said she used to call me Theo, it felt right." I glanced down at my lap, curling my fingers into a ball. "The problem is, *she* doesn't. Nothing about her feels right."

He folded his arms. "That's quite a dilemma. But anyone could have gone down to the courthouse and found out your name. And anyone could have doctored a photo these days. Not saying that's what she did, now, but that's not a whole lot of solid proof."

"I know. But when I saw her tears, I felt so awful. What if I am, and I just told my fiancée I don't remember her? That has to be the worst kind of rejection and pain. She told me she was pregnant when I disappeared, and that in the stress of me disappearing, she lost the baby. I feel horrible." I slammed my hands on the steering wheel and dropped my head against them, clinging to it like a lifeline.

"Well, what does your head tell you?"

I stared at my lap. "To at least give her a chance before writing her off. I'd never forgive myself if it turned out to be true and I didn't at least try."

"What does your heart tell you?"

My stomach tumbled with unease. "That I'd at least feel *something* toward the woman who I had a past with. I may not remember her, but something inside me would innately know her, some kind of inkling or attraction."

"And you don't have any of that with this woman?"

I shook my head and looked back up at Pete. "Not a single bit. I feel more for Eden in the few hours we spent with them over Thanksgiving than I did all day with Tera."

"So what about Eden? Do you think it could be her?" He stared at me with an intensity I'd never seen on his face before.

"I don't know. In all the memories that I've had, I never see a face. All I know is, since the day I woke up in the snow, no one's been able to make me feel anything until Eden. That has to mean something, right?" I pleaded to him with my eyes, wanting him to agree and tell me to run to Eden and kiss her and find out. I needed reassurance that just going with my gut was the right thing to do over logic and something that didn't feel right.

"What's stopping you from going to Eden?"

"If it's Eden, why doesn't she remember me either? And why did Tera show up exactly when I was about to try to make something happen with Eden? I had a grand plan to ask her out, take her to dinner, go for a walk holding hands, and tell her how I felt, hoping that it would lead to a kiss and it would unlock everything for me. But on the very day I was going to do it, someone claiming to be my fiancée shows up after a year and stops me, like some kind of divine intervention, and now I'm rethinking everything because I'm trying to do the right thing."

Pete nodded and let out a long breath. "That *is* a lot to worry about. But you know, the one thing I do when I feel worry coming on?"

I shook my head.

"I pray. Now, I don't mean to be taking you to church, but you mentioned divine intervention." He pointed upward to the heavens. "When we worry, it means we're trying to do something on our own. If you have the man upstairs doing it for you, then you have nothing to be worried about, right?"

I gave a half nod, not really sure what he was getting at. "Yeah, I guess so."

"Let me put it to you this way. There's an invisible war going on all around us. We don't usually get to see it, but trust me, it's there. He's got an army, fighting with us and for us. It's a battle of the angels."

My ears perked up at the word *angels*, and something in my heart flickered. "What do you mean?"

"Well, you know, the devil himself was once an angel." He pulled out a gold coin and spun it between his thumb and forefinger.

I nodded and stared at the coin as an image flashed in my head too quick for me to even register what it was, but it centered on the coin.

"This here is the archangel Michael, driving Satan out of heaven." He handed me the coin, and another picture hit my mind of it rolling along someone's knuckles, just how Pete did it the other night.

"When he fell, one-third of all the angels followed him, and they work under his reign here on earth, the devil's playground. Some may call them demons, but they were still created beings, once angels. So there're good angels and bad angels. And those bad ones like to wreak havoc, especially on something dear to His heart. They get in there, and when they see something that will show the power of love, they want to ruin it and cause pain, sadness, and torment."

I swallowed hard and shook my head. "What does that have to do with me?"

"The most powerful thing we have in this world is love. You said so yourself once. So when something meant to be is about to happen, that's when the battle of the angels heats up, because the bad angels will go all out to try to stop it from happening. Sometimes it's accidents. Sometimes it's temptation. Sometimes it's a natural disaster. Don't always call a hurricane or earthquake an act of God." He winked.

"So what are you trying to say? I feel like this is all some kind of riddle."

"I'm telling you, what you need to do is trust. Have faith." Pete smiled. "Believe."

"In God?"

He raised his hands. "In everything. Believe in angels. Believe in love." He tapped a finger on my chest. "Most of all, believe in your heart. The most difficult thing is making the decision. The rest is merely tenacity."

He made it sound so easy, as if that's all it took to find the truth, and everything would magically right itself. How could I possibly believe what he was saying? It all sounded like fairy tales and bedtime stories. All I had to go on was the tangible things in front of me, and I was supposed to just give it all up and play make-believe? It didn't make sense. Though, nothing did since the day I woke up in that snowbank.

"You know, the difference in tenacity and obstinacy is one comes from a strong will and the other from a strong won't. Think about that as you ponder what makes sense and what doesn't in that head of yours." Something buzzed in Pete's jacket. "Oh, that would be Miss Madeline. We learned how to text!" he said, giddy as a schoolboy. He turned to me and put a hand on my shoulder. "You'll do the right thing because deep down, you already know the answer. Like I said, you just have to believe it. Reason and faith are both banks of the same river."

That's what it felt like, like I'd waded down the middle of a long and winding river, trying to find my way out. Oddly enough, I had the tenacity to believe Eden was some part of my past. Yet I stood obstinate that Tera wasn't my fiancée. Even with the proof she laid out before me, was it really that easy to ignore and go on faith that my gut said Eden over Tera? The hardest thing to hide was something that wasn't there.

And my feelings weren't there for Tera.

18

EDEN

Two days before Christmas, and this year felt as gloomy as last year. I threw myself into my work to try to get my mind off the fact I hadn't seen Teddy in days. Every time I stopped in at the shelter to pick up my mom, he wasn't there. Not that I was looking, but I didn't happen to see his truck at the church either. As much as I was dying to ask Pete what happened to him, there was a big part of me that knew it would be better to just forget him all together, because I probably didn't want to know the answer, especially if it involved Tera.

I'd never met her, and I probably would need to repent for the thought, but I wished she would never have turned up. I wondered if she knew that in Greek her name came from *teras*, which meant monster. Sometimes speaking other languages didn't help me as much as I thought it would. It led to me seeking deeper meaning behind things, and that usually only made me angry. Like in this instance, where the monster stole my almost-would-be boyfriend, if we'd actually gotten to kiss that night at Thanksgiving.

The fact I was still so upset about some guy I wasn't even going out with when the monster came and swept the rug out from under me boggled my mind. Yet everywhere I went, every thought of the day somehow revolved around Teddy. Even my dreams intensified to the point where very little clothing was involved, and he had me singing the song of his people through the most magnificent orgasms of my life. I'd find myself drifting off, lost in thought about "what ifs" at random points in the day without realizing it. He completely invaded every part of me, and no matter how hard I tried to put it behind me, I couldn't. Like something kept me from forgetting about him. Just when I'd think I'd get through the day without thinking about him, someone would mention his name or say something that made me think about him—like coffee of all things.

I stared at the pictures of the archaic tablets I'd excavated from my last dig, trying to translate the ancient Greek for my files. But I always got stuck on the same word, well, half a word, as the tablet had a crack in the corner where the word was. As I studied the picture, it made me think about the picture Teddy showed me he got from Tera. It dawned on me why it looked so familiar.

I took off down the hall and grabbed one of the old bridal magazines still taking up valuable real estate in my room. Flipping frantically through the pages, I slammed my hand down on a picture of a very different man proposing to a someone who wasn't Tera with the same background as the picture Theo showed me. She did photoshop it! Maybe there was a logical explanation for it. What that was though, I had no idea. Should I tell him?

He deserved to get his past back, his memories and life, but not from a lying piece of garbage like Tera. Who even was she, and why would she make it all up? As much as I would have liked to have been the one, I couldn't have been, no matter how much he looked like the mystery man of my dreams. What kind of past would that have been for him? *Yeah, I'm the key to your past—you lived as my guardian angel for years until one day you came to me in a dream, and we made love and lived happily ever after.* A declaration like that, and Tera the monster looked better and better as an option.

I wandered back out to the kitchen and collapsed on the table in front of me, folding my arms and resting my head on them. My phone buzzed next to my ear. The more I tried to ignore it, the more it rattled until it bounced against me from the vibrations.

With a groan, I lifted my head and glanced at the message on the screen. Mom needed a ride home from the shelter, as Pete had to work on a project at the church and couldn't drive her. He'd become her taxi cab over the last several weeks, and gladly so, as it gave them plenty of time to spend with each other. I thought for sure there'd be a wedding by Christmas. Guess it was a good thing I never threw away the wedding magazines.

I texted Mom back and let her know I'd be there in a few minutes as I grabbed my coat and headed to pick her up.

My heart hurt, hanging heavy in my chest as I opened the doors to the shelter, knowing I wouldn't see him. Who knew when I'd get another chance to talk to him, and how would I broach the subject of Tera doctoring the photo? How did you even begin to start that conversation? *Gee, I was pining over you at my kitchen table when I suddenly remembered why your picture looked so familiar. So I ran to my bedroom where I still have boxes of wedding magazines I couldn't bring myself to throw away and found the exact same picture.* Yeah, because that wasn't crazy. Whatever happened between him and Tera, I would still have liked to remain friends. His smile undid me, always sending warmth to my soul and filling me with happiness, with hope. He was a special kind of person, and anyone who ever encountered him said the same. No wonder he'd become a counselor.

I glanced around the building, scanning the thinning late-night crowd for any sign of him, and of course he wasn't there. Releasing a sigh, I made my way to the office to look for my mom. I knocked on the door before letting myself in.

"Eden?"

I jumped back at the voice, finding Teddy sitting at the desk inside. "Teddy?"

He shot up from the chair and walked to me. "It's good to see you."

"Um, yeah, good to see you too." I scratched my head and forced back the flutter bouncing in my stomach. "Where've you been?" I couldn't stop the words from flying out of my mouth. Could I sound any more like a desperate stalker?

"I spent the last couple of days with Tera." He shoved his hands in his pockets and leaned against the desk behind him. "We've been trying to jog my memory by going to different places."

Of course, the monster. I nodded and bit my lip, ruminating on how to tell him about the photo. "Oh, I see. Any luck?"

He shook his head. "No."

"Sorry to hear that." *Not really.* A little bit of hope danced inside me. Before I could stop, the words flew out of my mouth. "She photoshopped that picture."

He arched a brow and looked at me.

"Here," I said, handing him the page I ripped out of the magazine, leaving out the part of where I found it.

He stared at it and blinked. "Where did you get this?"

"From a magazine. Look, maybe it's a coincidence, but I thought you should know." Regret made a sudden appearance and tightened my stomach into knots.

He let out a deep sigh and nodded. "I'll definitely ask her about it and see what she has to say. But why would someone go to such lengths to fake a story about me?"

"You're a great guy, Teddy. Guys like you are few and far between. Maybe she's lonely or maybe she's just plain evil. I don't want to hurt you or ruin anything between you and her, if she really is your fiancée. But I'd want to know if it were me."

He curled his lips into a smile, and his eyes brightened a bit. "I appreciate that. You're a good friend, Eden."

My heart sank a little further in my chest. Friend. Rolling that word around in my head shot tingles up and down my spine out of nowhere. I forced them back and settled on the fact that that was all I'd ever be to him. I thought now that he knew the picture was fake, maybe I'd have a chance with him. I would have started my own PI firm and investigated Tera into the ground, if I thought it might help. But there was a fine line between being a good friend and stalking, and if I had any chance of remaining friends with Teddy when it was all said and done, I had better not cross it. He had to be the one to make the choice to know who he was getting involved with. It was time to move on.

"Well, I was just looking for my mom. She said she needed a ride home." I looked back down the hall toward the kitchen, but no sign of her.

"I think she's next door with Pete. She said she'd be back in a minute. Do you want to have a seat and wait?" He fanned his arm to the chair.

I shook my head. "I'm good. Been sitting at home all day." Wow, that sounded like I'd been pining away for him with absolutely no life. While that was the truth, he didn't need to know it. "I mean, with my texts. Studying the pictures of the artifacts from my dig in the spring. You know, translating texts." I made a fist and swung my arm. "All fun. All the time."

"Oh? You speak other languages? Which ones?" He tilted his head as if he were actually fascinated.

"Archaic ones, mostly. Ancient Greek, Aramaic, Hebrew, Latin, a little bit of Farsi. Obviously English, sometimes a little bit of Yoda." Oh, yeah, real cute. Could I be any geekier?

"That's really cool. I know ancient Greek, Hebrew, and Latin as well, it turns out."

"You do?" I arched a brow and stepped closer.

"Yeah, found that out while I was working at the church and dug out some old books from their archives. I just somehow knew what they said. It was really weird. So we figure whatever I did in my past, I knew several languages."

"That's fascinating," I said in a gasp of excitement. "I mean, that just shows I'm not the only geek around here." I playfully patted him on the upper arm and cleared my throat.

He chuckled. "We have a lot in common."

I nodded and crossed my arms, fanning myself. "Is it warm in here?"

Everything burned hot, hotter than the fire of a thousand suns, and I needed to take my coat off. I slid it from my shoulders and tossed it to the chair.

"You okay?" He rushed over to me and cupped my cheek with his hand. "You're awful warm."

"Trust me, there's nothing you can do for that." Well, there was, but in order to quench my desire for him, he'd have to *not* have a fiancée.

He stared at me, and the longer he did, his eyes darkened, becoming richer, bluer, like swirling deep seas. It pulled the breath from my lungs, and the air around me thinned. Dizziness hit me, and my legs wobbled. He slid an arm around my waist and held on to me.

"Eden?" he whispered.

"Uh-huh?" I whispered back an octave higher.

He leaned. I leaned. His head tilted. My head tilted. Our gazes locked. He tightened his arm around my waist. I laid my hand against his chest, curling my fingers into his blue oxford shirt. His warm breath tickled my lips. We both glanced at each other's mouths, moving closer together. He brushed his lips against mine, soft, gentle, tentative, and tender. Leaning in, we pressed together a little more, inching closer. Seconds became minutes. Minutes became hours. Hours became days. Time stood still as our lips opened to each other. His air became my air. My air became his.

We moved our mouths in a slow dance. Our tongues met like two old lovers uniting, becoming one. Our lips twisted like a choreographed sequence, knowing just what to do to fit together perfectly. My heart stopped, skipping two, three, four beats, restarting as it caught up with his beating beneath my fingertips.

He curled his fingers against my cheek and a moan rumbled in his throat, waking us from the trance. Our eyes popped open as we broke the kiss, breathless.

It was the most magnificent moment of my life. As I looked at him, picture after picture flashed through my mind. Him by my side as a child. Him holding my hand. Him watching me from afar. Him watching me close by. Him at the park, the hospital when I was sick, the day I graduated high school, the day my father died, his arms around me as I stared into Amanda's casket. How? It didn't make sense. How could he have been there when I was little? How could he have been there when I was grown? He looked the same. The exact same. Well, with longer hair.

It was no longer a figment of my imagination or a dream. He. Was. There.

I gasped and touched my kiss-swollen lips with a trembling hand. "What are you?"

He took a hard swallow and choked out, "What?"

"I...I don't understand." Tears welled in my eyes. "It's not possible. Is it?"

"Eden, I'm so sorry. I didn't mean to make you cry. Did I suck that bad?" Worry streaked through his eyes, watering them to a dull gray.

A laugh bubbled in my throat. "What? No!" I threw up my hands in defense. "It didn't suck. It was the most amazing kiss of my life."

"Okay, good, because I thought so too." A beautiful blush rouged his stark cheekbones. "That's what I always imagined a kiss would be like. That was like tasting heaven." He slid a hand along my cheek with a smile.

"There you are!" My mom's voice cut through the fog in my head, and I startled, jumping closer to Teddy.

He caught me in his arms, curling his fingers into my sides as he clung to me. That movement felt so familiar, so comforting.

"Oh, did I interrupt something? I can come back."

"No. I mean, I don't know." I hitched back, pulling out from his embrace. "I mean...I don't..." I shook my head as I looked into his eyes, and it all spiraled back to me, every moment we made love in my dreams. His movements, his kisses, his fingers curving into my flesh. "I can't...I've got to go." I grabbed my coat and my mom and ran out of the shelter so fast it would have made my old track coach proud. I had to get away, get out and clear my head of the insane images filling them after that kiss.

I barely made sure my mom was buckled before I peeled out of the parking lot and drove in circles around the town, not wanting to go home. Because if I did, and Teddy was there looking for me, I didn't know what I'd do. I'd just kissed a man that might or might not be engaged. A possibly engaged man I was pretty sure was either a ghost, a time traveler, or a complete figment of my imagination.

"What is wrong with you, Eden?" My mom clasped a hand to her chest.

"I think I'm trapped in a vampire romance novel." My mind filed through image after image of Teddy in every facet of my life, like a stalker or a bodyguard. I wasn't sure. Maybe he was some kind of alien?

"Eden." My mom's voice slipped into a weird growl.

"I don't know, Ma! I need to think." The leg not on the gas pedal bounced like it was on crack as I sat nearly on top of the steering wheel.

"Can we please think at home? You're driving like a maniac, and someone's going to get hurt. Please, I just got my sex life back. I'd like to live to see sixty."

I snapped my head in her direction. "Ewww, Mom! Really? Really!"

"What? I'm your mom, I'm not dead."

At the stoplight, I slammed my head on the steering wheel and continued to bounce it until the gross image of my mom and Pete naked left my brain. At least that temporarily trumped the fact I just kissed an engaged immortal being of some sort.

"We can't go home. Let's go to Thandie's. We haven't seen her in a while. It'll be nice to see the kids, won't it?" I nodded with a cheesy smile.

"What's going on, Eden Grace?"

We pulled into the driveway at the house, and I thrust my head back against the headrest. "I kissed Teddy. Or he kissed me. Whatever, we kissed!"

She gasped and clapped like a fangirl. "That's fantastic."

I rolled my head forward, arching a brow. "Did you win some kind of bet?"

"Yes." She giggled. "Pete now has to do that thing we saw in that video."

"What?" The sheer horror of that statement would surely send me to additional years of therapy once I finished counseling for kissing an engaged time-traveling alien, vampire, god, werewolf, warlock, or whatever.

"Get your mind out of the gutter. He's got to do this hot pepper challenge." She shook her head and rolled her eyes. "Really, Eden Grace, what is up with you?"

Relief rushed through me in waves as I climbed out of the car and broke into laughter, falling in a snowbank as a fit of giggles hit me. I had truly crossed over the psychiatric bridge of no return.

My mom stood over me with her hands on her hips. "Are you on drugs?"

My eyes popped wide open. "What? No!"

"So what is with this weird behavior? Why did you run out on Teddy, then, if you kissed him? Don't you like each other?" She held out a hand and pulled me up from the snow.

"Yes, I like him. I don't go around kissing people I don't like, unlike Mr. Teddy over there," I said and stomped my way into the house.

"What are you talking about?"

"I'm talking about the fact that he's engaged and he kissed me."

"You don't think that Tera woman is really his fiancée, do you?"

I shrugged and flopped onto the couch. "He seems to think so."

"So why did he kiss *you* then?" She sat beside me and gave my arm a little bump.

I threw my hands up. "That's what I'd like to know! I mean, one minute we're talking about all the archaic languages we know, and the next we're drawn together like magnets, unable to stop the pull. And boom, we're locking lips in the most magnificent kiss of my life. I'm so confused, not to mention the fact that he's spent the last several days gallivanting around God knows where, doing God knows what to try to jog his memory, including kissing. So maybe he wanted to see if I was his fiancée, too? Apparently, that's how you tell these days, by going around kissing frogs 'til you get a prince, or in this case, a princess."

"Teddy's not that kind of person. I'm sure he kissed you because he wanted to. He's trying to figure out what's real and what isn't. He's gone so long now not knowing anything, and this woman showed up out of nowhere and threw a wrench into everything. He's just got to sort through it."

"So I'm supposed to be some side piece until he decides if he wants to have a go at it with his fiancée or move on with me?"

Mom tilted her head. "What did the kiss tell you?"

"It told me we're meant to be. I'd never felt as whole as I was during that kiss." An ache drowned my soul, a longing for that feeling to come back, a need to be connected as one.

"Then you have your answer. It'll all work out how it's supposed to." She patted my knee and stood from the sofa.

"What am I supposed to do in the meantime? Watch him go around with Tera, pretend to be happy for him while pining for him from afar?" Not that that would be much different from what I'd done for the last couple of weeks.

A smile lit her lips from end to end. "You need to believe."

"Believe what?"

"In love."

"Uh, I'm not sure we're in love. We just had our first kiss fifteen minutes ago. Not to mention the fact that he still could very well be engaged. So how can I believe we're supposed to be together?"

"Because believing is powerful. When you believe in something, it drives you, gives you purpose, provides direction. When you believe something, you give it your all. It's your passion and force."

"That doesn't change the fact that Tera's still in the picture. No matter how much I believe we're supposed to be together, it's not going to change that."

"You'd be surprised." She winked.

"What's that supposed to mean?"

"When you fight for what you believe in, truth prevails. Seek truth. But you can't find truth until you believe in it." She kissed the top of my head. "Believe."

I forced out a hard sigh and watched her close her bedroom door. I was left in a whirlwind of mixed feelings and vague dread.

What did I believe? Did I believe the random images in my mind that showed some guy that looked exactly like Teddy had been a part of my life since birth? That somehow the guy who should have been my mom's age looked no older than thirty and was in love with me even though he couldn't remember a damn thing about himself? That some stranger who woke up naked in a snowbank a year ago was somehow my soul mate?

Tears streamed down my face from out of nowhere. I swiped at my cheeks to brush them away, but they only fell harder. Whether it was frustration leaking out of my eyeballs, or the realization that as those images showed me that love also filled my heart. All kinds of love for Teddy, from friendship, to loyalty, to romantic. All the forms of love the Greeks used to talk about. They had many words to express love in their language because they believed they couldn't put one word on something that had so many facets. And the one thing that encompassed every single kind of love was the image of Teddy.

I clutched the throw pillow that once had his scent, where we had almost kissed, now faded over the weeks that had passed. My chest convulsed as sobs ripped through me, and I had no idea why. But it felt good to release it, like it had been pent up for much longer than a month. Maybe I cried for a missed chance that night on Thanksgiving. Maybe I cried out of anger that someone else was about to get my happily ever after.

Yes, a part of me grieved for something missing.

But the bigger part of me already knew the answer and refused to accept it. Perhaps I cried not over something lost, but something found.

19

THEO

I COLLAPSED IN THE CHAIR AS I WATCHED MY PAST RUN AWAY FROM ME like she'd seen a ghost. That kiss brought with it a host of memories, flooding my entire being. Memories not only of images, but of touches, feelings, joy, and heartbreak. I saw myself watching her as a child, guarding her, protecting her, shielding her. I saw myself smiling at her birth, holding her hand through her first steps, hugging her through tears, standing watch as she grew into the person she was today. It didn't make sense. It was like we grew up together, were best friends. The problem was, I never changed. But she did. She grew up. I stayed the same.

As she became an adult, I watched her with new eyes. Eyes full of longing and a different kind of love. Wonder and desire filled *those* eyes as they looked upon her with a more encompassing love.

I glanced at my hands, turning them over, back and forth. She even said it with her own words—what was I? Did she see the same? She must have seen something to prompt her to ask that question. And that was a very good question, one I had no idea how to answer, because I had the very same one. What was I?

A delirious excitement burst through me, rattling my hands with tremors as I stared at them. That kiss unlocked something, but I had no idea what it meant. She was definitely the key, yet she tore off as if I frightened her. That wasn't love in her eyes, but fear.

I couldn't blame her. If she now had visions like I'd been getting, it probably freaked her out. As much as I didn't want to cause her more pain, I had to talk to her. If not for me, for her. We had to try to understand what was happening, for each of us to find peace.

Do I go after her now? Do I let her process what happened? Do I give her time to come to me when she's ready?

I touched a shaking hand to my lips and closed my eyes. *That* was what a kiss was supposed to feel like. It was nothing like my kiss with Tera. Kissing Eden was like a door to a different time, a different place. She took me to a different world, where we fused as one, like two missing pieces of one being. I no longer felt lost, alone, or confused. I felt whole. The emptiness in my soul filled with her goodness, her light, as if she were as much a part of me as my right hand.

She just made sense. My heart hammered thinking about her as if she were still there.

A knock at the door pulled me from my thoughts, and hope sparked in my heart that it was Eden. But instead, the face that peeked around the doorframe belonged to Tera. My heart sank to my stomach like a rock.

"Hey," she whispered.

"Hi," I managed to choke out, unsure of what to even say to her at this point. But I had to find out about the picture and if what Eden said was true. I handed her the magazine page. "Can you explain this?"

She narrowed her eyes, and what I thought was a growl escaped. She cleared her throat, and a smile graced her lips. "I'm not sure what you mean?"

"This is the same photo you showed me in my office the first time you met me, claiming to be my fiancée. But this is a picture from a magazine with two totally different people in it. Did you doctor the photo?"

She paused and looked over my shoulder, as if searching for something before answering me. "Theo, baby, this was at a photo op station outside the hotel we stayed at when you proposed. So of course there would be other people using it. You wanted to get a picture of your proposal to me, so we asked someone to take our picture and reenacted the moment. Don't you remember?"

"Clearly, I don't." I couldn't hide the agitation in my voice. I was really hoping she would admit it was all a lie and I could just move on and run after Eden.

I tried to calm myself. Was it possible I wanted her story to be false so bad that I couldn't see it any other way? Her explanation was plausible. Still, it felt so awkward. I didn't know what to believe anymore.

"So I was wondering if you had plans for tomorrow night. It's Christmas Eve, and we always had this tradition of going for a walk around the neighborhood and looking at Christmas lights, and then we'd run home after being out in the cold and warm ourselves up by...well, we could just start with the walk and see what happens." She inched her way into the office, clasping her hands in front of her like a shy child.

I swallowed hard and tried to think of something to tell her without hurting her feelings. Maybe we *were* engaged, perhaps at one point in time, or we might have shared some kind of past or link, but it was clear I also did with Eden, and since she was the only part I remembered, I had to run after it.

But then a horrible thought hit me, and I wondered if I couldn't remember Tera because I didn't really want to. What if I cheated on her with Eden? What if it was all true, but they were both part of my past? Bile singed my throat, and my stomach roiled with unease.

"Um, that sounds nice," I said, trying to figure out how to either tell her what happened or if it would be ridiculous to just point-blank ask her if we had relationship problems other than money. In the midst of my hesitation to finish my sentence, in her constantly overeager way, she accepted it as a yes to her invitation.

"Great, why don't we meet at six? Maybe do dinner at your place or something?" She grinned and stepped closer.

"Did I cheat on you?" The words came out before I could stop and filter them.

Her eyes widened before tears welled in her eyes. "Did you remember something?"

"I don't know, that's why I'm asking."

She paused before nodding. "You told me it was a onetime thing and that you didn't really love her, that you loved me. We were on the road to healing, fixing our relationship and starting over when you disappeared."

Another inkling of suspicion worked through me. "So we didn't have a fight about money that night, it was about her? This other woman?"

She hesitated as if trying to find the right words. "Well, we did fight about money because of the baby. But yes, part of it had to do with her. You left to go tell her it was over, only you never came back."

Guilt struck me like a red-hot poker. Was I that much of an asshole? Could I have really been one of those guys? I didn't want to accept it, but the pain in Tera's eyes ripped me to shreds. Maybe I did cheat on her with Eden. Maybe I couldn't remember my life with Tera because I always wanted it to be Eden.

"I'm so sorry," was all I could say.

She closed the space between us and knelt before me as I sat glued to the chair, grasping at the pain riddling my chest, the pain that I was a cheater, a horrible person. I couldn't remember my fiancée, but I could remember the woman I cheated on her with. It hit me like a hammer, rendering me to dust.

She curled into my arms, and her tears soaked my shirt. "I forgive you. Thank you for giving us another chance."

As if I couldn't feel any worse, my soul crushed under the weight of her forgiveness. The words Pete said days earlier rushed back to me. Believe. I had to believe Tera was my fiancée, and maybe it would all rush back to me.

I closed my eyes, hugged Tera tighter, rubbing her back to comfort her. She pushed away from my chest and inched her way to my lips. But the anticipation of the kiss was nothing like between Eden and me. I didn't want it. I tried to pretend it was Eden's face, anything to get me to feel something for Tera, to believe I was what she said. As she crushed her lips against mine, my heart became even emptier, hollow and brittle, a tainted version of what it should have been in that moment.

Someone cleared their throat, and instead of breaking the kiss, Tera deepened it, twisting our tongues together as she let out a moan. I pushed her back, pulling my lips from hers. "Tera, stop. Someone's here."

"Oh," she said, covering her mouth with a hand as she slowly glanced over her shoulder and narrowed her eyes at Pete standing behind her. It happened so fast that everything blurred, but I swore she hissed at him.

Pete glared at her, but his face softened as his gaze met mine. "You ready, Teddy? We've got some meals to deliver to some home-bound church folk."

I nodded and helped Tera stand as I eased out of the chair.

She clung to my waist, unwilling to let go. "So tomorrow then?"

Pete shook his head as he folded his arms, leaning against the doorframe. It almost looked like he was disgusted, not with me, but with Tera.

"Are you worried about something, Pete?" Tera asked, a snide tone sliding through her words, and I looked down at her as she tightened her hold on me.

"Never." Pete smiled, as calm as the day was long. "I was telling Teddy just the other day about not having to worry. When you believe, the truth will always reveal itself." He pulled out his gold coin and flipped it back and forth over his knuckles before flicking his wrist, launching it into the air and catching it with the same hand. Taking a step closer, he held the coin up to Tera's eyes, as if showing her the image of what was on the other side.

The two stared each other down. Pete's smile got wider, and Tera's arms got tighter.

"Okay, I should probably head out." I pried myself out of her embrace and nodded to Pete.

As I reached for Tera's purse to hand back to her, a piece of paper floated to the floor. I picked it up. "Who's Grayson, and why do you have his phone number?"

She blinked, cleared her throat, and snatched the paper from my hand. "He was just helping me look for you is all."

Pete practically beamed as he tossed a wave at Tera and clutched a hand to my shoulder, guiding me out of the building, leaving her standing in the office in a stupor. I eyed him like I saw him again for the first time.

"You know her?" I asked as I slid into the truck and he climbed in the passenger seat.

"Tera?" He shook his head. "Not personally, no. But I have come across many like her in my time."

"What do you mean?" Frustration laced my words, as much as I tried not to sound ungrateful for all he'd done for me. But if he had information he was holding back, it would be a stabbing betrayal.

"I thought, perhaps, after our talk the other day, you would have come to your own conclusion on your situation."

"What? You mean your soliloquy on not worrying and believing? Maybe if you didn't talk in riddles and metaphors, I'd have understood it a little more." The words fired off my tongue like a rocket, aiming to bring pain, a stab to hurt him for toying with me. Immediately after the words left my mouth, I regretted them.

He sighed. "She's already influenced you, boy. Temptation leeches in, sinking deeper until it's controlling you without you even realizing it."

"I haven't fallen for any temptation. We haven't slept together, if that's what you're getting at." I stared at the shelter, expecting Tera to come walking out after us, and I had the urge to get the heck out of the parking lot before she did. But she never came out.

"Temptation doesn't always mean sex. She's tempting you with what you want most."

Sitting in the car, away from Tera, it was like I could see more clearly, think without a guilty fog. I looked at Pete, who sat with a soft smile on his face.

I stared into his calming topaz eyes that held a starlike twinkle I hadn't noticed before. "What am I?"

His smile brimmed wider. "You're in love is what you are."

I shook my head. "No. Me. Who am I? What part does Eden play?"

"That, my boy, is what you must believe in. I can't tell you. Not that I don't want to, but it's not something I can do. It has to be done from inside you. This is your truth to discover. I'm just a friend here to help guide you in the right direction."

I pondered it for a moment and realized my breathing had sped up as all the days leading up to that point crisscrossed in my mind. "So you think Tera's not really who she says she is?"

He held his hands up in a half shrug and nodded to the side. "The closer we get to truth, the harder the lies fight to keep it hidden."

"What does that mean?" I threw my hands up, just short of yelling.

He stared me in the eyes, not with anger, but with determination. "It means you need to put on your armor and go to battle. Fight for what is right. Nothing worth anything ever comes easy. Your heart already knows what the answers are. Stop listening to the lies trying to bury it. I didn't think you'd be this stubborn."

"You're like my own personal Morgan Freeman. It's really annoying sometimes." I pulled out of the parking lot, and his laughter filled the cab of the truck.

"Oh, Teddy, I have faith in you. It's time you had some in your-self. It's just that easy."

Easy. Sure. What did I have faith in? That I was a cheating asshole fiancé to Tera? Or that somehow Eden and I were meant to be together? Tera did get freaked out a bit by the paper with the name Grayson on it. Not to mention her trying to swallow my face with her lips this afternoon still made me feel nauseous. It was nothing like my perfect kiss with Eden. In my gut, I knew Tera wasn't being straight with me, but the fact that she had an answer for everything always made me come to a grinding halt when I wanted to make my choice to be with Eden.

One way to find out would be to talk to Eden and ask her what she meant when she asked what I was. A part of me was scared to know the answer and thought maybe believing I was Tera's fiancé was the easier path, even though it felt wrong. But if faith and belief were what I needed to get my answers, I had to believe it all had to do with Eden. I just hoped she believed it as well.

20

EDEN

I CURLED MY HAND AROUND A MUG FULL OF EGGNOG, SANS RUM. I really wanted the rum, especially after the last couple of days, but I promised myself I would do my best to actually remember this Christmas Eve. Not that I really knew why, since it was shaping up to be another lonely one. I stared at the angel topping the tree, suddenly tilting to the side, falling from its perch. Well, maybe the angel was drunk for me. "I feel you, angel. I feel you."

"You sure you don't want to come caroling with Pete and me at the church?" my mom asked, tucking her hand inside a glove as Pete helped her into her coat.

"No. I'm good here with my eggnog." I held up my cup and forced a smile. My mom deserved a fun Christmas Eve with the new love of her life. I'd only be a third wheel, channeling my inner Eeyore.

"Oh, just a moment, I forgot my purse." Mom gasped and scurried back into her bedroom like she was on fire.

Pete whistled as he rocked up to his tiptoes and back with a smile, rolling a gold coin in his hand.

I tilted my head, studying the shiny object in his fingers. "Hey, is that a touch piece?" I pointed to the coin-like object. I hadn't seen one in so long. "They're pretty rare. You know, royalty used to use those back in the fifteenth century to supposedly cure the sick with the 'Royal Touch.'" I snort-laughed. "Oh, those crazy, wacky, arrogant royals."

He smiled. "Actually, it's an angel coin."

"Wait, that's impossible." I studied his coin closer, noticing it was one solid piece. "Angel coins were the precursor to touch coins, and they were pierced in the center. Yours is intact. I think someone scammed you, Pete."

"Ah, not all of them were. There're a few intact specimens floating around. Have to know where to look for them." He smirked. "I've got a few friends in high places. Oh, and for the record," he said, leaning in as if he were about to whisper, "the tradition of touch pieces actually goes back to first-century ancient Rome, when Emperor Vespasian gave coins to the sick at a ceremony known as 'the touching.'" He glanced at me from the corner of his eye as he rolled the coin over his knuckles before he flicked his wrist, tossing it in the air to me.

Startled, I caught it and stared at the image of the archangel Michael slaying a dragon, which many thought symbolized Satan. An image flashed in my head of a gold coin rolling over someone's knuckles. I blinked, trying to focus on where I'd seen someone do that before.

"They were also given to folks for good luck, as well as healing." Pete smiled and let out a long sigh, pulling me from my musings. "Tonight's a special night, you know."

"Yeah?" I pursed my lips.

He nodded and looked at the tree. "There's just something magical about Christmas Eve. It's a time when hope is restored. When we open our hearts and minds to the possibility that anything can happen. From a man in a red suit bringing exactly what a child wished for, to the hope of a nation's deliverance of a king."

I snorted. "So is Santa going to deliver me something special?"

He chuckled and placed a hand on my back. "Well, maybe not Santa, but tonight, I pray there will be a deliverance. Perhaps not one you expect, but one that you need."

I quirked a brow. "When did you become such an optimistic philosopher?"

A sly grin tugged at the corners of his mouth. "Oh, I've always been an old softy."

"What do you know that I don't?" I narrowed my eyes.

"Call it a feeling." He shrugged. "Oh, here comes your lovely mother. Excuse me." He took a step toward my mom coming down the hall, but halted and leaned back, handing me a small, wrapped box. "Merry Christmas."

"Merry Christmas." I stared at the box with a guilt-ridden smile, as I had failed to get him anything. I wondered with a flash of guilt if the drugstore was still open.

He pulled me into a hug, placed a kiss on my head, and grabbed my mother's hand.

Mom gave me a look. "Last chance," she said.

"Go have fun, you crazy kids. Love you."

Mom blew me a kiss and closed the door behind them.

I let out a sigh and put my eggnog on the table to open the present from Pete. Pulling at the red velvet bow, I slipped it off the box and lifted the top. An ornament sat on a bed of ruffled gold tissue paper. Bright, polished silver letters spelled out the word *BELIEVE,* and a red ribbon hung from an eyelet at the top. A tear slid down my cheek as I held it in my hand and stared at the word, tracing each letter with my fingertip. I sniffed and walked over to the tree. I hung it on the one barren branch in the middle.

A loud knock startled me, and I wondered if Mom maybe forgot her keys. As I opened the door, my heart sped to find Teddy on the other side. Layers of blond hair fell over his eyes, a bit disheveled, but every bit rugged and handsome.

"Merry Christmas," he said, shoving his hands in his pockets.

"Merry Christmas," I managed to say back to him over the wedge of emotion in my throat.

I didn't think I'd see him again after I ran out on our kiss yesterday. Fear still held me in its grip, wondering what it all meant, and instead of facing it head on and finding out, I cowered behind my tears and tried to ignore it.

"Can we talk?" He locked eyes with me, and my heart fluttered so fast I lost my breath.

I nodded and stepped aside, allowing him in.

"Do you want some eggnog?" I glanced over my shoulder as he took off his coat. His white long-sleeved sweater hugged his biceps, and it took everything in me to tear my gaze away. When I did, it shifted to his muscular thighs threatening to rip the seams of his jeans. How did he even get them on?

"No, thank you." He rubbed his hands together and let out a long sigh. It didn't sound good, and I buckled up for what I was sure was going to be an emotional ride. "About yesterday." He paused, looking at my legs before his head snapped up, and he stared into my eyes. "You're wearing yoga pants." He pointed to my lack of proper Christmas Eve attire.

That was not where I thought this conversation was headed.

I looked down, and embarrassment slugged it out with anger for the spot in my stomach. "Well, it's not like I knew you'd be coming over. I went for comfort, not sex appeal since I figured I'd be alone tonight." Arching a brow, I stepped closer to him near the tree. "So you decided to come here and criticize my poor fashion choices, along with making me feel bad for running out after I kissed you?"

Silence hung thick in the air for what seemed like forever as he stood perplexed, mulling something over. "Wait, you kissed *me*?" He pointed to me and then at himself. "I thought *I* was the one who kissed *you*."

He closed the space between us. The warmth of his body radiated off him. I wanted to get closer, soak it in, bask in it. Instead, I turned my back to him to try to form a complete sentence before I broke down. "I guess we both kind of kissed each other." I shrugged. "But I was the one who ran out on you, and I'm sorry I freaked. I just..."

"You asked me yesterday what I was. What did you mean?" He brushed the hair from my shoulder before sliding his hand along my back, turning me to face him.

I forced back a shiver of delight at his touch, my body aching for more.

I shook my head, unsure of what to tell him. *Do I sound like a crazy idiot and say "I saw every single time you visited me as a child"? Do I tell him that I think he's my invisible friend from my past? Do I ask him what kind of immortal being he is?* He'd have me committed.

He lifted my chin with his finger, forcing me to look into his eyes. "I'm going to tell you something, and it's going to sound like the most insane thing in the world, but please, just listen before you run, okay? Because I have to know something, and I'm pretty sure you're the only person that this may make sense to."

I blinked and nodded. "Okay."

His eyes shifted, as if he were drinking me in with his gaze. That sexy wordless moment went beyond even our kiss, because it was as if he saw me for the first time, and the adoration and desire in his eyes was unmistakable. My heart thundered in my ears, and I prayed he couldn't hear it.

"When we kissed yesterday, it was like a veil lifted for me. For a year I've floundered, wondering who I was, where I came from, searching for answers and aching to know my past. From the moment I heard your voice, something in my heart told me I had to find you. When I did, everything changed for me. I should have kissed you on Thanksgiving. I regret that night, that I didn't take the chance sooner."

My heart lurched into my throat. I forced myself to keep the tears at bay, but I had a feeling before his speech was over, one or both of us would be in tears. Because I knew he was about to lay on me that he'd be leaving with Tera to go back to his old life. I had to cut him off at the pass, or I'd crumble under the weight of his words. I thought back to my chat with Mom and how I needed to fight for what I believed in.

"I know what you're going to say. I know Tera's your fiancée, and you want to be a good, faithful man. But I'm not going to tell you I regret our kiss yesterday. I don't. I loved every minute of that amazing kiss. I don't care what crazy things happened as a result in my head, but I'm trusting my heart, and my heart cares for you deeply. And I know after tonight, you're going to walk out that door and go back to your life with her, because you're just that good of a person. Well, I'm *not*." I shook my head and the ornament from Pete swung slowly, side to side.

Believe.

In those few seconds, I had to decide if I wanted it more than I was afraid of it.

I turned and faced the most beautiful man I'd ever met and launched myself at him. Cupping his cheeks, I pulled his face to mine and crushed my mouth to his. He didn't even pull away, but welcomed me, folding me into his arms as our lips twisted, deepening the kiss. His hold around me tightened as he cradled the back of my head with one hand, and the other splayed over my lower back, curling his fingers into my flesh as our tongues met.

Time stood still, just like with our first kiss. We were no longer two separate beings, but one. Peace settled in my soul as his warmth wrapped around me like a blanket of joy. Nothing felt more right in the world than being in Teddy's arms, joining our lips, locking together the missing pieces of our hearts. His kiss gave me life. My kiss gave it back to him.

We parted lips, needing air as we panted for breath.

"I don't want Tera," he said between two breathy gasps.

"You don't?" I choked out, fumbling with the edge of his sweater in a nervous twitch.

He pressed his forehead to mine. "After our kiss yesterday, I saw things. Every time I've had a memory come back, it always came with a painful headache, and then it would be tiny bits and pieces of memories, never one complete with a face, or a name, or anything other than a clue. But after kissing you, there was no pain. There was only joy, complete soul-filling happiness, and a lot of memories. They all included you."

I stepped back in a gasp, throwing my hands over my mouth. He saw them too.

"I know. I know. Please, hear me out," he said, grabbing my hands from my face, holding on to me, probably so I didn't run. "Every single thing that came back to me revolved around you. But it was you as a child, you growing up, high school, college...your life. I don't understand, though, because how could that even be possible?"

My lips trembled, and I wasn't sure if the words would actually make it out of my mouth or not. "Because you were my best friend."

"What?" He canted his head. "I could understand if we grew up together, but you were a child. I was an adult in these memories. Did you see them, too?"

I bit my lip and nodded. "Yes."

"You don't think I'm crazy?" His eyes lightened, and a smile twitched his lips.

I shook my head. "If you are, then that makes me crazy too. Or drunk, and I haven't had any rum, so it would be divine inebriation."

He chuckled and entwined his fingers with mine at our sides as we stared at each other. "Well, we've established we're not crazy, but what do you think it means?"

"It means you're either a ghost, a time-traveler, or your immortal. Because all those memories happened. I had them before the kiss."

He tilted his head. "What?"

"Remember when I told you that you reminded me of someone who didn't exist? Well, you did exist, but only to me. I was the only one who could ever see you. I saw you everywhere. You never left my side. My mom called you my invisible friend, because I would always tell her about the boy with the blond hair who protected me. I never mentioned it was a man, because that would have been creepy. But it was never remotely creepy. You were my protector, my friend. She thought it was my imagination. But to me, you were real. Until I got older, and I thought I was crazy and you stopped coming to me in person."

"Wait, you mean...I was really there with you when you were young? But I looked like I do now?"

I nodded. "Yes. The exact same, except your hair was longer." I ran my fingers through his hair, letting my hand fall to his shoulder and down his chest.

Confusion colored his eyes as he struggled to understand. "You said I stopped coming to you in person. Did I just disappear?"

"No," I whispered. "As an adult, you came to me in my dreams."

"For how long?"

"For the last ten years. Every night. But when I woke up, you were gone. I would try so hard to remember what you looked like, what you sounded like, what you felt like, but it all blurred until you faded completely from my waking mind. Only at night, in my dreams, could I see you again. But after our kiss, I remembered those dreams, remembered you."

He swallowed, and his Adam's apple bounced in his throat. "May I ask what happened in your dreams?"

Tears pooled in my eyes. It was too much. A quiver hit my lips, and I stepped back from him. Pain welled in my chest as air wedged in my throat, and I struggled to contain the sob wanting to rip through my body.

"Eden, what's wrong? Did I hurt you?" The same pain in my heart stirred in his eyes. "Please, don't tell me I hurt you."

"No," I choked out and tilted my head. With a trembling hand, I cupped his cheek, running my thumb over his soft skin. "You loved me."

His eyes glassed over, turning his gorgeous blue eyes a watery gray. "We..."

I nodded and sucked back a blanket of tears.

He raised a hand and caressed my cheek with his warm fingertips in return. "Did you love me?"

"Yes," I whispered. "I never stopped."

He stared into my eyes, through me and into my soul. He dropped his hand to the back of my neck and tugged me to him with force, crushing his lips over my mouth. He slid his other hand along my back, pulling me flush to his body as our mouths continued to tell each other what we needed to know without words. I pressed my hand against his heart, like in the office yesterday, and it thumped hard and fast against my fingers.

None of it made any sense, yet everything felt real, as real as Teddy's lips on me at that exact moment. It was just like in my dream. Did dreams come true? If they didn't, then I didn't want to ever wake up.

21

THEO

I HELD MY LIFE IN MY ARMS. SHE WAS MY YOGA GIRL. THE KEY TO MY past. I needed her kiss like air in my lungs. The feeling of wholeness she provided was all I craved. I wanted more of her—of us.

Our lips parted, and I pressed my forehead to hers. "In my memories, I loved you too. With every kiss, it proves to me that I still do."

A small smile curled over her beautiful kiss-swollen lips. "I don't know what this all means."

"Me either, but maybe together, we can figure it out." I caressed the back of her head with my fingers as I stroked her jawline with my thumb, staring into the eyes of my future. "Are you scared?"

She tilted her head into the palm of my hand and she closed her eyes. "Yes. Scared that I'll wake up again tomorrow and you'll be gone. Faded away again. That this was just another one of my dreams."

Her words were like a punch to my heart. I never wanted to cause her pain. I didn't understand what happened in the past, nor could I control it. But I could control the future. "What if you woke up *with me* instead?"

Her eyes popped open wide and sparkled with delight at my

words. The one thing I needed affirmation on shone within them
—hope.

I closed my eyes, and my heart thundered with a raging mix of
excitement, anticipation, and a twinge of fear. Though my memories started coming back, none of them included sex, with anyone,
let alone her. But I craved Eden, longed to be one with her, and I
prayed my body would instinctively know what to do. With my
hand on her jaw, I tilted her head back and slid my lips along hers,
sweeping her tongue with my own. A soft moan floated between
our joined mouths. I picked her up by her thighs, and she wrapped
her legs around me as I carried her to her bedroom.

Easing us onto the bed, I rolled her to her back and hovered
over her. She worked her hands up my chest and lifted my sweater
over my head. I dipped my head to her neck and pressed my lips to
her supple skin. Her nails grazed the skin along my bare arms as
she dragged my shirt off. It drilled ecstasy straight to my center.

I slid my hands under the edge of her shirt, stopping to indulge
in the warmth of her skin against my fingers. She guided my hands
up her stomach, and I took over, pulling the shirt over her head.
Her beautiful olive skin peeked through the lace of her black bra,
and another spike of desire shot through me as I cupped my hands
over her breasts, strumming my thumbs over her erect nipples. The
moan that floated from Eden's lips was the sexiest sound I'd ever
heard, and it drove me onward, wanting more as I slid my fingers
beneath her back and unclipped the garment from her body.

I stood and stared at her naked flesh before me, all soft skin and
gorgeous, generous curves, like a work of art my eyes feasted upon.
Sucking in a breath, I dropped my jeans, baring myself to her as
well. Her gaze raked my body, and the most seductive smile curled
over her lips, begging me to claim her mouth. I tore off her yoga
pants and kissed my way up her body, relishing each time she
flexed beneath my lips, until I captured her mouth with my own.

The minute our bare skin touched, a fire roared through me.
Our breathing became one as we lay together, our bodies coming

alive with each other's caresses. Two bodies, one heart, writhing, aching to touch and be touched everywhere at once.

My eyes closed as I let my body feel each movement, hear each gasp and soft moan, taking in all she gave me and giving her all I had to give. But my hunger for her grew beyond kisses. As if she knew, she slid her hand between our bodies, reached between my legs, and curled it around my cock. A fire blazed inside my veins. I opened my eyes and found her eyes open as well, not looking at me, but into me, into my soul. Locked in each other's gazes, she guided me where she wanted me to go, and I buried myself in her, body, mind, and soul.

We joined as intimately as any two souls could, uniting in rhythm with our thundering hearts. Natural instincts took over as our bodies moved in time with each other, like a choreographed dance, pushing and pulling every emotion in and out of us, slow and with care. She'd never looked more beautiful than she did with pleasure flushed upon her cheeks, parted kiss-swollen lips, and eyes pressed closed as she took what I gave and, in return, gave me what I needed.

Her body arched, and her soft moans turned heady and hungry as she writhed beneath my movements that urged me to take more of her. I drove faster, my own hunger speeding my heart and strides until a wave of euphoria burst through my lips as a growl.

I loved this woman. I didn't think I knew what love was, but now I knew. She was my everything, my world, and I didn't want it to stop. In that moment, I knew I would fight for her. I would do everything in my power to make sure she was happy. I would love her until the end of time. I would die for her.

My heart had never felt so full, and I had never had such peace in my soul as I did when she cried out a name like a prayer on her last breathless moan, "Theo."

We stilled, eyes locked and both heaving for breath as we lay with our bodies entwined, one hand connected above our heads, one hand connected to our hearts.

"You called me Theo," I gasped.

Her chest heaved beneath mine, brushing her erect nipples along my skin. The feeling launched another wave of desire through me, and I ached for more of her already.

"I don't know where that came from. It just burst out of me," she whispered, partly from breathlessness and partly from fear, for the stunned look in her eyes sent a ping of fear to my own heart.

Tera had called me Theo, and it was the only thing that felt right in any of the things she'd said.

"I'm sorry," Eden said, and she closed herself off from me by pulling out of our embrace. "I totally just called out someone else's name in the throes of passion with the man of my dreams. I want a hole to open up and swallow me."

I rolled her back to face me and took her in my arms. "Don't be sorry. I think it's my name."

"What?" She blinked, and the innocence on her face made her even more adorable. I was so completely and irrevocably in love with this woman, there was no doubt.

"Well, my legal name is Theodore. At least that's what I chose to go by when I woke up. When I saw it on the side of a school that first day, it just clicked with me. But Pete told me it sounded stuffy, so we decided to go with a nickname Teddy. So maybe Theodore really is my name, if that's what you called me. Did you call me that in your dreams as we made love?"

Quivers shook her body against mine, and I tucked her closer to me. "Yes. But for some reason, Theodore doesn't feel right to me. Theo does, but your full name doesn't. I don't know why that would be."

Her face flushed, and I longed to make love to her again and again until we were absolutely spent and sated. "I cannot get enough of you. You're like a drug, Eden. You have such a power over me that I just want to succumb to. So tempt—"

The word tempting caught in my throat, and my mind spiraled back to the conversation with Pete about temptation. Was he talking about Eden, the one tempting me away from Tera? Maybe that's why nothing felt right with Tera. Panic dampened the wave of pleasure coursing through me. Was Eden really the woman I cheated on Tera with? How else would she have known to call me by that name?

Dear God, what had I done?

She snuggled closer, pressing her lips against my chest over my heart. I brushed the back of her head with my hand, fighting back the urge to leap from the bed and flee. My heart and body ached for Eden. I didn't doubt my love for her, but my head still tried to put Tera into the equation, tried to make me rethink things and feel guilty.

"I think I need some water. Do you mind if I run to the kitchen?" I said, easing away from the comfort of her body that clouded my every thought. Maybe with a few minutes of clarity in the kitchen I could figure out what to do.

Moments ago, I was so sure it was Eden. Everything about her fit everything about me. Yet when I admitted my love for her, the doubts came spiraling back. One simple word, my name, threw me for a loop. How would both of them know it if I weren't involved with both of them somehow?

I slid my jeans back on and made my way to the kitchen. Eden's soft footsteps followed, and I turned around, finding her back in a tank top and yoga pants. My yoga girl. How could that be wrong?

She filled a glass of water and handed it me before she curled up on a chair at the kitchen table, trying hard to hide the worry in her eyes at my sudden change in demeanor. As I sipped the water, doing my best to mull over where I should go from there, I watched her shuffle through pictures on the table.

"What are those?" I asked, eyeing a stone tablet in one of them.

She glanced up. "Oh, these are the pictures from my last excavation. I'm trying to translate this one. I've gotten pretty much everything except the last word, which is kind of cut off."

"It's ancient Greek," we both said together, looking at each other and smiling.

She nodded, and I bent over her and studied the word. The last few characters were blurred, almost like they were scratched off on the original tablet, or someone had tried to.

The longer I looked at it, the more familiar it seemed until I blurted out, "*Pisteúō*."

We turned and locked eyes.

She repeated the word. "*Pisteúō*."

We both said together, "Believe."

My hands shook, and I dropped to my knees in front of her, the glass of water crashing to the floor beside me.

"*Pisteúō*." I closed my eyes and pictured myself saying that very word one time before.

When I opened my eyes, the world spun around me, throwing me back in time to the night I said it to Eden, one year ago. "*Pisteúō*." The night I was taken from her. The night I became human for her.

"Eden," I choked out with newfound eyes, or rather my old ones. The ones where I remembered who I was, Theliel, her guardian angel. All my memories slammed into my head at once. Everything, including her. How could I have ever forgotten her? How could I have ever believed it could be anyone but her?

She shook her head, confused. "Teddy?"

"No, not Teddy. Theo."

She tilted her head. "Theo." But the lost look in her eyes told me she didn't remember yet, or if she did, she didn't believe it.

I tightened my grip on her hands and pulled her to the floor with me. "Believe, Eden. Believe." I closed my eyes and believed hard enough for the both of us. "Believe in us. Believe in what your heart is telling you, no matter what your head says. Believe in love. Believe in me. *Pisteúō*. I love you, Eden. I always have and I always will. Believe."

I opened my eyes and watched her mouth the word *Pisteúō*. Her body arched backward, and her head lolled. I dived around her, catching her like I always did when she fell. Clutching her to my chest, a tear slid down my cheek and plunked against hers. "*Pisteúō*."

She fluttered her eyes open, and her own tears streamed across her cheeks. "Theliel."

I nodded and brushed a lock of hair sticking to her cheek from the tears. "Do you remember?"

Sobs consumed her, and she threw herself against my chest, hugging me so tightly it knocked the air from my lungs. I sat back and pulled her onto my lap, cradling her in my arms. "My Eden."

"Theo, my angel. My guardian. My love," she whispered against my ear as her body convulsed in my arms between sobs. Her grief, fear, and love poured out of her in waves. I soaked it in, letting her give it all to me.

༄

Eden

We sat there, clinging to each other on the floor, afraid to break apart ever again.

Theo kissed his way up my neck. I leaned back as he claimed my mouth with his own, reminding me who he was, who I was, who we were, and what we could have again. When all breath finally left me, I pulled back and held his face in my hands, and he took mine in his.

How could I have forgotten my angel, my best friend, who stood by my side my entire life? He held me and never let go through everything, then came to me through dreams until he could no longer hold back and came to me in human form again, this time as more than a friend, but as a lover, the love of my life.

Only it wasn't the first time. Memories flooded back of every time he'd come to me in human form, only to have our memories stripped each time they caught him. But still, he broke through and continued to come for me, to find his way back to me. Each and every time.

Worry flooded me that they would come for him, again, and rip him from me once more. But something about this time seemed different. Theo was no longer an angel in human form. He *was* human. He must have given up being an angel for me.

I believed in him, in us. I believed in love.

My heart was so full it could have burst as I looked into those big blue eyes of his.

"Hi," I whispered. How lame. Of all the things I could have told this man, that was what came out?

His smile took up his whole face, beaming with happiness. "Hi."

"Is this really happening?" My lips trembled as I touched his human face.

He nodded. "They gave me a choice. I chose you."

Tears cascaded over my cheeks as I stared at my other half, the missing piece of my heart. "What if they come for you again? This isn't the first time, Theo. I see all the memories now."

"I know, but I think this time is different. I see them too. Each time I went corporeal, we ended up falling in love, then punished by having our memories taken. I think they thought it would be enough to keep us apart. But we proved them wrong. Each time, I was drawn to you, no matter what they did. Even now, they gave me a choice, a choice to be fully human. Once again, memories taken but never truly forgotten as we found our way together again. This time, I can't go back to being an angel."

"Believe. If that was what this was all about, then I believe. I believe you and I are meant to be. Nothing can keep us apart."

He pulled me to him and swept me into a kiss that burned all the way to my core. His lips told me without words what was in his heart. His tongue swept away the lingering doubt. He made me believe in him, in our love.

We pulled back, and something cold pressed into my skin. I glanced down, then back to his eyes. "I'm wet."

He arched a seductive brow. "Are you now?"

I laughed and swatted at him. "Well, yes, always when you're around. But I mean my clothes. I think I sat in the water from the glass you dropped." I pulled at my soaked yoga pants.

"I can help you out of them." He gripped the waistband and ripped them from my body.

I gasped, and a laugh bubbled in my throat. The hunger in his eyes fed my soul. He needed me, and I needed him.

Sliding his hand behind my neck, he cradled the back of my head and kissed me, holding me simply with one hand as he eased us from the floor back to standing. He caressed my cheek with the back of his other hand as he tilted my head, taking the kiss deeper. His hold over me was intoxicating, and I gave myself completely over to him, letting him take me where he needed to go. The longer we kissed, the stronger his movements became as he claimed me, physically, emotionally, and spiritually.

He picked me up with one arm hooked around my waist, the other entwined in my hair. Setting me on the table, he kissed me harder, and I matched him, afraid that if we stopped he'd disappear again, and we'd forget, lose our other halves. I pushed his jeans over his hips before wrapping my legs around him, aching for us to be one again, this time with all our memories, with both of us being whole.

Our bodies joined, and we both gasped into the kiss. Every single memory of us together flooded my head, through my dreams, last year, and tonight, all swirled together in my mind as we expelled our grief over losing each other, our joy over finding each other, and our love demanding we never be broken apart again. Our agony faded away, and love filled us with each move-ment, each kiss, each touch spiraling to a climax, and his name left my lips once more, not as a prayer, but a declaration, that he was mine, and I was never letting go again.

I had my Theo back. My heart restored.

He picked me up from the table and carried me over the broken glass to the living room, easing us onto the sofa. We covered up with a blanket, and I laid my head on his chest, listening to his heartbeat in front of the twinkling white lights of the tree.

He kissed the top of my head. "I love you, Eden."

I pressed my lips to his heart. "I love you, Theliel."

He traced patterns along my back with soft fingertips, and I sank into his embrace, soaking up his essence, his warmth, his love.

"Do I dare ask what happened to make this time different?"

"Not tonight. Tonight, I don't want to think about anything other than you and me, sharing this moment. Tonight is about us and no one else. Tonight we just believe, in each other, in love, in soul mates." He tipped my head up and dotted kisses on my lips. "We found our way back to each other."

I snuggled closer to him and let my mind wander as I soaked in his warmth, his goodness, his essence. "So where does that saying 'every time a bell rings, an angel gets its wings' come from?"

"Probably the seraphim. They love the publicity." He laughed and curled his fingers along my hips.

"Did you ever have wings?" I lost myself in the depths of his eyes as they turned the deepest shade of blue I'd ever seen.

He caressed my cheek with the back of his hand. "I never needed wings, Eden. You made me soar."

22

EDEN

MY EYES FLUTTERED OPEN AS I TRIED TO FIGHT THE LURE OF SLEEP attempting to pull me back under. I had the dream of all dreams, and I lay there smiling like a damned fool as I tried to relive it. My dream man had come to life.

I scanned the room around me as the dream faded away, as usual. Panic flooded my heart as I realized it was Christmas morning, and I shot up. Something was wrong, way wrong. Everything from last night came hurtling back to me.

Theo. Theliel. My angel.

Last I remembered, we had fallen asleep cuddled on the couch, but somehow I ended up in my room, alone. Again. I slid out of bed and realized I was naked. After scrounging around for a pair of fuzzy pajama bottoms and a shirt, I dashed out of my room.

The smell of coffee, pancakes, bacon, and eggs all hit me at once, and I glanced at the kitchen to find a half-naked Theo flipping a pancake in the air, doing some amazing dance move that would have made Gene Kelly jealous. I clasped a hand to my heart and blew out a thankful breath.

"Hey, sleepyhead," he said with a smile as he flipped another pancake.

I folded my arms and stared at the man, shaking my head. "You scared me. I woke up alone in a panic."

He set the pan down and sauntered over to me with the biggest, poutiest lips. "Forgive me?" Slipping his arms around my waist, he whisked me sideways and dipped me over his arms. He brushed his soft lips against mine in a quick kiss before he lifted me back to standing. "I woke up starving, and you were sound asleep. So I thought I'd let you sleep in while I made breakfast. Plus, I had to clean up the glass and water from last night before your mom gets home."

"Speaking of," I said, glancing at the clock on the wall showing ten a.m. "She never came home last night. Guess she had a sleepover at Pete's."

Theo snorted. "Is that what kids call it these days?"

I smacked him on the ass and slid my arms around him from behind as he flipped the last pancake. He smelled wonderful, like cologne, soap, and Theo. I pressed my cheek to his back and hugged him tight, thankful he was still here.

"Do you miss me already?" he said with a chuckle over his shoulder.

"Yes. You promised me I'd wake up with you, remember?" I took my turn pouting my lips.

He spun in my arms and slid his around my back. "I did, didn't I? I'm sorry. How about we try again tomorrow? And the day after that. And the day after that."

I nodded and bit my lip.

"Don't do that. It's so stinking sexy it makes me want to take you right back to bed and bite it myself."

"Why can't we?"

"Because your mom and Pete will be here any minute."

I arched a brow. "How do you know? Do you still have your angel powers or something?"

He shook his head. "Naw, Pete sent me a text about thirty

minutes ago and asked if we were decent because they were headed this way."

I giggled. "I guess I should go shower then."

"Want to conserve water?" He wiggled his brows.

I narrowed my eyes. "Environmentalist is now added to your list of can-do-no-wrongs?"

"Not yet. This one is purely selfish. I was hoping for shower sex."

"Points for honesty."

He laughed and brushed my lips in a long, slow, swirling kiss that tingled all the way to my toes. But it was short-lived as the front door opened, and we broke our embrace as my mom and Pete walked in the door.

"Go get your sweater on," I said, nudging Theo toward the bedroom. He dashed off, and I stood with my arms crossed, one hand awkwardly twirling a strand of my hair. "Hey, Mom, Pete."

"Merry Christmas," they said in unison, with a little too much merry in their voices. I wondered if Mom dipped into the brandied fruitcake already.

They shook off the snow and brought in two bags full of wrapped presents. Pete slid them under the tree as Mom took off her coat. Theo jogged back out, still barefoot but with his white sweater on.

"Merry Christmas," Pete said, extending a hand to Theo, pulling him into one of those manly half hugs with a pat on the back.

"It smells wonderful in here. Theo, did you cook all this?" Mom asked, walking out with a mug of coffee for her and Pete.

"Wait, did you call him Theo?" I stared at my mom, who shot a smile to Pete, who shot a smile to Theo, who stood just as confused as I did.

"Well, that's his name, isn't it? Why wouldn't I?" Mom took a sip of her coffee and sat in her favorite chair.

"Yes, but..."

"Madeline, my love, why don't you go change into that lovely dress you bought? I'll fix us some plates in the meantime," Pete said with a smile.

"Oh, you're such a dear. I think I will. If you'll excuse me for a few moments." Mom scurried off to her room and closed the door.

Theo and I both stood and looked at Pete with our arms folded.

Pete chuckled to himself. "Something wrong?"

"Actually, for once, no. But I don't understand why Mom called him Theo."

He smiled. "Because that's all she's ever known him as."

"What happened to Teddy?" I tilted my head as a thousand and one questions rambled in my mind.

"He never really existed, now, did he?" Pete said, rocking back and forth on his feet, fighting a ridiculous grin twitching on his lips.

"What?" Theo asked.

Pete walked to the tree and slid the ornament he gave me last night against the palm of his hand. "Seems as if everything's back to how it should be. Christmas morning, a rebirth of faith—whether it's in humanity, God, or ourselves. All we have to do is believe in something hard enough to make something happen." The ornament slid off his palm and swung side to side as he walked back over to us. "Now, it may not happen how we pictured it in our minds, but then, we're not always given what we want. But we're always given what we need. What we so often fail to see is just what that need is. Sometimes we must learn a lesson first."

"Who are you?" Theo asked, grasping Pete's arm.

Pete turned and smiled, placing a hand over Theo's. "You already know. I'm a friend."

"You're one of them," I gasped and threw my hands over my mouth.

Theo looked between me and Pete. "Kasbiel?"

Pete smiled and placed a finger over his lips in a hush.

Tears glassed over Theo's eyes as he threw his arms around Pete, aka Kasbiel. "Thank you, for everything, old friend."

"Took you long enough. You're as stubborn a human as you were an angel." He folded his arms.

I clasped a hand to Pe—Kasbiel's elbow. It would take some getting used to calling him Kasbiel and not Pete.

He winked and wiggled his finger. The angel leaning at the top of the tree righted itself, sitting tall on the top branch. "You know, every time a bell rings, a seraph gets another set of wings."

"A new set?" I arched a brow.

Kasbiel turned and smiled. "They can have up to six."

I nodded and pursed my lips.

Theo shrugged. "Well, they are the higher sect of angels. So they get all the notoriety." He stepped closer to Kasbiel, leaning toward his ear. "What do I do about Tera? She was obviously lying."

"Oh, you'll find she's left town." He nodded and pointed outside.

"How do you know?" I asked.

"Once goodness and love prevail, she must find a new target to try to corrupt." Kasbiel smiled. "She seduced Grayson to hire her to put a wedge between you both. He had no clue what she really was, of course. He wanted revenge for some pictures sent to his mom or something?" He raised a brow at me.

"What? I just felt his family should know what a lying, cheating pig he was." I shrugged, and then my eyes shot wide open like saucers. "Oh, it all makes sense! My mom mentioned that one of her friends saw someone at the store talking to Grayson. That must have been Tera!"

Theo shifted his hands to his hips. "You knew who she was from the start, didn't you? I wondered about your interaction with her the other day in the office."

He chuckled again. "Oh, yes. But I couldn't tell you then, now, could I? You remember how it's easy to recognize a soul with no hope. They can disguise themselves all they want, even impersonate an angel of light. But they can never hide their black souls, the dark angels." He turned and faced me. "She was merely one of a legion of dark souls who work to break apart love. For without love, there is no hope. Without hope, there is no light. Without light, there is only darkness, and that is what they thrive on. Once they heard that Theliel fell and would have a chance at humanity and love, they set out to stop it."

A shudder tore through me, and Theo wrapped his arms around me from behind.

"What about my mom? I thought you guys..." I made a motion with my hand, not wanting to finish the sentence. My heart hurt, knowing my mom would be crushed if Pete left. I was so happy for her that she'd found love again and wasn't lonely anymore.

"Oh, I'm not going anywhere. I can't very well leave my Madeline now, can I? She was a tremendous help to me. That smile of hers gives me great joy. And the things she taught me." He whistled and shook his head with a sly grin.

I didn't even want to know what it was she taught him.

"What do you mean, you're staying on earth?" Theo asked.

"I may have made a deal with Phanuel. He bet me you wouldn't find Eden and get your memories back. I, however, believed in you. So we made a little wager. I couldn't interfere by telling you anything, but if you pulled it off, I'd earn my humanity and be able to stay on earth with Madeline."

Theo and I stared at each other and then at Kasbiel, and he shrugged. "What can I say? I finally understand this love thing you taught me about."

Theo tossed his head back with a hearty laugh.

Mom came out of her bedroom in a gorgeous flowing red A-line dress. "Well, what do you think?" she asked as she twirled in a matching set of red pumps.

"It's beautiful, Mom. You're stunning. Did Pete pick that out?"

"Yes, isn't it gorgeous? We're heading out to meet Thandie and the kids at church for the children's Christmas program."

I zipped Mom up and turned around, catching Kasbiel/Pete, looking at my mom with such adoration. It was adorable. Though it would be tough not to accidentally call him Kasbiel.

"Pete told me I look beautiful in red." A giggle laced her words that bloomed into a full-on blush.

"And I was right." Pete kissed the back of her hand before curling it over his arm to escort her toward the door.

"You're stunning, Miss Madeline," Theo said as they headed out. "Merry Christmas."

"You hang on to this one, Eden," Mom said, thumbing over her shoulder as she slid into her coat. "You guys sure you don't want to come?"

I glanced at Theo. "I think we want to spend Christmas morning together at the house."

"Suit yourself." Mom kissed my cheek and leaned into my ear. "Thandie and I have been talking, and instead of selling my old house, we've decided to move her and the kids into it. I think I'm going to move in with them as well. Together, we're going to open that bakery I've always talked about. You and Theo don't need your mom hanging out all the time. So I'm thinking after the holidays we'll make the move back."

"Are you sure?" I clutched her elbows as she pulled back from the hug.

She nodded. "Merry Christmas, darling. I'm so happy for you two."

I tilted my head, and a twinkle sparkled in her eye. She winked and headed out the door.

"So do you think the town remembers you naked in a snowbank?" I spun around to face Theo, but he wasn't where I left him.

Instead, he knelt in front of the Christmas tree on one knee and held open a red box with a diamond ring the likes of which I'd never seen. A light gleamed off one of the edges of the rock, and it painted rainbows on the wall in reflection.

"I don't want to lose another day with you, Eden. You proved to me last night that you would fight for me and our love just as much as I would for you. Even without my memories, I knew in my heart you were out there. Though it turned out we weren't actually married, my heart loved you like we were, and I fought to stay true to that. I loved the idea that I had a fiancée and possibly kids out there waiting for me. But I love the idea of building that family with you even more. I don't want to lose another day with you and hope that you would do me the honor of becoming my wife. My real wife."

Tears flowed down my cheeks in waves as I nodded. "Yes. Of course. Yes!"

He stood, and I leaped into his arms, covering him in kisses. With a laugh, he set me back on the floor. "Can I get the ring on you first, and then we can celebrate?"

A giggle popped from my lips as I held out my left hand for him to slide the ring over my finger. "It's stunning."

"It doesn't hold a candle to you." Theo brushed a lock of hair behind my ear.

"How did you...?" I pointed to the ring and shook my head.

He shrugged. "Kasbiel may have helped me a little on this one. I can't give away all my secrets, now, can I? Call it an angel thing."

I grabbed his hand and led him to the bedroom. "Come on, angel, I'm about to make you soar."

෴

Thank you for reading! Did you enjoy? Please add your review because nothing helps an author more and encourages readers to take a chance on a book than a review.

And don't miss book two of the *Heaven on Earth* series coming soon and find more from Wren Michaels at www.wrenmichaels.net

Until then, find more Mystic Owl books with <u>PINK GUITARS AND FALLING STARS</u> by Leslie O'Sullivan. Turn the page for a sneak peek!

You can also sign up for the City Owl Press newsletter to receive notice of all book releases!

SNEAK PEEK OF PINK GUITARS & FALLING STARS

BY LESLIE O'SULLIVAN

JUMPER

You only get one parachute. There's no point packing two for a B.A.S.E. jump since you'll be pavement art before the second chute blossoms.

"Justin!"

Startled by a bellow from my jump leader/uncle, Timmer MacKenzie, my toe jerks to a stop half an inch above the trigger pedal of my launcher. Is his gray matter shredded, distracting me during a safety check? There's no chute on my back. One accidental tap on the business end of this launcher, and I'll be eye to eye with the flock of seagulls patrolling the Hollywood skies. I retreat onto the non-ballistic end of my perch. Peering over the edge of the Rampion Records Tower, I analyze the antics of the wind.

"Join us," Unc calls, teeth clenched in a P.R. smile. He hosts a cluster of reporters near the center of the circular roof. "Meet the rising star of the Slinging Seven."

Their faces morph into a collective portrait of panic as I leap more dramatically than necessary from launcher to the terra firma of the rooftop. After a salute to the Hollywood sign, a photo op my uncle will appreciate, I join the party. Pre-jump interviews are not my happy place, but keeping a smile on Timmer's face is essential. He leads our B.A.S.E. jump troop, giving the green light for my carcass to launch off skyscrapers, bridges, and cliffs in a wing suit.

"This Rampion Records Tower may rival Mount Olympus for acceptable jump altitude," Timmer tells the press jam sandwich. "Even so, I believe in enhancing the safety zone for my lads."

I sweep an arm across the roof. "Thus, the launchers."

"Your latest exhibitions of low altitude B.A.S.E. jumps have raised serious concerns," says a fresh-out-of-journalism-school reporter. He rocks a Channel Six pin on the lapel of a blazer clearly tailored for someone else. We get his type all the time: low man on the news roster, usually stuck with covering mudslides or C-list celebrity screw-ups.

I grunt at the question. Timmer's a walking archive of aerodynamics. His B.A.S.E. jump designs adhere to a superhuman canon of safety. Even Unc can't control the wreath of clouds descending on the tower. Humidity makes trickier conditions. My bangs congeal into a sweaty clump. Twenty-three is too young to die when you have plans, and I have plans.

"To you, B.A.S.E. jumping is an extreme sport. To me, it's a science." Timmer slings an arm around my shoulder. "Would I risk my own nephew's life?"

A grandfatherly dude slides square-framed sunglasses to the end of a nose in serious need of a good hair plucking. "Come on, Mr. MacKenzie, that kid can't be eighteen."

I wince at the familiar speculation my youthful image always dredges up. Satan's roadies have prepped a new circle of hell for Timmer's perpetuation of the lie about me being eighteen. My B.A.S.E. jumping talents at twenty-three are PDG – pretty damn great—but a fresh out of high-school dude rocking my moves is prodigy wonder boy territory, great P.R. fodder.

I keep my lip zipped over the deception. I'm not going to lie, it does not suck being a prodigy wonder boy.

Unc spins me to display the product emblems plastered all over my banana-colored wing suit. "Endorsements like these don't come from launching children into the sky. Justin jumps one-hundred percent legally."

The reporter's skepticism settles at the edges of his mouth. Metallic coating on his sunglasses turn my gray eyes silver as I catch my reflection. The gloaming breeze plucks strands of my tawny mane free from the generous layer of product I always apply before a jump. I'll have to retame those suckers to restore my roguishly hot vibe instead of the young and soft look Timmer prefers. I'd give my right nut to have a growth spurt on the spot. Sadly, thanks to MacKenzie short man genes, there probably aren't any in my future.

A gust of wind blows the press a tiptoe closer to the curved edge of the roof. Timmer and I hold our ground with matching "no big thing" expressions.

A babe in a raspberry-colored lady suit pushes toward me, eyes bulging with concern. Twitchy fingers alight on my shoulder. Next to my banana wingsuit, we're a fruit salad. Here comes the *concerned auntie* vibe.

"Justin, why take risks B.A.S.E. jumping with the Slinging Seven Troupe even for someone as enchanting as Zeli?"

I bite back a groan at the mention of the pop queen.

"Is glorifying her platinum record worth your life?"

Truth rumbles in my throat. *Yes, ma'am, B.A.S.E. jumping is worth the moon. It got me to Hollywood, the land of my music dreams. Dreams that will free me from Timmer's whims so I can make my own destiny.*

Timmer's glare scorches a hole in my suit, cueing the trained monkey answer he expects.

I open my arms to the clouds. "Who doesn't want to fly?" Every person on this roof does. I see it in the way their eyes brighten.

My stomach loops into a knot. Unc may piss himself when his prize canary asks to go AWOL. I've jumped off everything Timmer asked of me on our jiggy pathway around the country to make it here. My gaze drifts to the Hollywood Sign as I press toes into the roof of Rampion Records, the touchstone by which all music greatness is measured.

Tonight, this bird will fly off the Rampion Tower. Tomorrow, I dive into the audition for Rampion's annual singing competition, The Summer Number One. It's the U.S. Open of music, amateurs vs. pros, where Rampion Records dangles a chance for nobodies like me to go mic to mic with their current stable of rock stars. According to the Rampion P.R. machine – *Even the little people in this world have a shot at the Summer Number One dream.* This ammie is going to kick some serious pro ass and score a Rampion Records contract. I've got everything I need for the audition: demo tracks, my guitar, ass-hugging black jeans, and a sexy aviator jacket.

For the last five years, in every crappy rent-a-room the Slinging Seven have crashed, I've done dozens of online music courses. I study. I practice. I'm ready.

Unc laughs at one of the reporters he's chatting up, and I see Ma's smile here on the rooftop. Our signature MacKenzie smile packs serious wattage. I should know, I've busted it out often enough to sway, play, and dazzle females of the species.

Once I grab the top spot in the Summer Number One, my pile of gold for winning will be enough to snag my own digs here in L.A., the last place I remember Ma smiling. The cold burn of loneliness flares when I think of her and wonder if she's safe.

Clouds thicken as I watch the sun dip into the Pacific Ocean. I ignore a stitch of concern at the base of my neck as the jump difficulty ticks up a notch and think in my language of future Justin merch.

T-shirt moment: Music Dreams Sucker Punch Death.

Channel Six pushes in front of his colleagues. "Justin, does Zeli have a lock on the top pro spot in the Summer Number One?"

Lady Suit bumps her shoulder into mine. "Is Zeli your dream girl?"

My lips twist into a frown. Zeli is my nightmare.

Timmer digs his fist into my back, my cue to fix my pissy face. I manage to upgrade to a grimace dressed as a smile. By their winks and snickers, the reporters take my tension as embarrassment. I'd like to water cannon them all off the roof. I'm entitled to a dream girl, but it will never be the plastic diva with her bubblegum diluted pop crap. That chickadee is an affront to everything I love about music.

Unc hasn't run out of bluster. "It's an honor for the Slinging Seven to be part of Zeli's platinum record celebration."

My temple throbs. I'm more than half nuts to risk a concrete sandwich for that over-hyped female commodity with a pink guitar.

Don't stop now. Keep reading Mystic Owl books with your copy of PINK GUITARS AND FALLING STARS by Leslie O'Sullivan.

And don't miss book two of the *Heaven on Earth* series coming soon!

Don't miss book two of the *Heaven on Earth* series coming soon and find more from Wren Michaels at www.wrenmichaels.net

Until then, find more Mystic Owl books with PINK GUITARS AND FALLING STARS by Leslie O'Sullivan.

∽◦◦∼

Zeli's signature pop diva sound and image are nothing short of magical—literally. Her fame comes with hidden costs, a curse that could ruin her voice forever.

Aspiring indie musician, Justin MacKenzie, is determined to kick it to the top of the Rampion Records' Summer Number One professional vs. amateur singing competition.

The favorite to beat in the annual televised contest is none other than the label's smoking hot superstar, Zeli, whose crazy extensions flow the length of a football field. Those ridiculous extensions, coupled with her bubblegum brand of pop, are an affront to everything Justin loves about music until a stolen kiss blazes into a romantic encounter.

Once inside Zeli's world, Justin discovers things are not as they seem. In their quest to allow the real Zeli, to step into the spotlight, the pair must confront the mysterious force behind the dazzle of Rampion's success. If these star-crossed lovers can't rally their own magic to defeat the darkness, they will lose everything—including each other.

∽◦◦∼

special subscriber-only contests and giveaways as well as receiving information on upcoming releases and special excerpts.

All reviews are **welcome** and **appreciated**. Please consider leaving one on your favorite social media and book buying sites.

Escape Your World. Get Lost in Ours! City Owl Press at www.cityowlpress.com.

ACKNOWLEDGMENTS

Thank you to Heather McCorkle for first taking an interest in my manuscript, and a big thank you to Lisa, my editor, for helping me make it the best it can be. Thank you both for your faith in me, for dialoguing and always making it a team effort. Your support and professionalism have been outstanding. I'm blessed to have you both in my corner. Owls to the end!

Thank you to my BB girls, my CPs and my best friends, Kristy and Jen. You are the wind beneath my wings. The marshmallow to my fluff. The wine to my cheese. Your honesty and enthusiasm mean the world to me. Through thick and thin, good times and bad, you've been there through it all. I would be nowhere without you guys. So incredibly blessed to call you my friends. I love you both!

Thank you to my buddy Margaret. Wow, we've been through it all, huh? Ups and downs, and all arounds of this business, but at the end of the day I can still call on you to pick your brain, you never turn down a favor when I need it, and we can always pick up right where we left off without missing a beat. Friends forever, Nerd. Love you.

Thank you to my friend, Nicki. It's been a long time since that first tweet that brought us together. Thanks for the laughs, the BBQs, the coffee dates, the encouragement, the talks and the understanding. Going to miss having you so close. Glad we had the time we did and that even though you're back down under now, you'll always be only a tweet away.

Thank you to my Misfit Squad! Lots of laughs, hugs, tears, and cheers, you've been there for me through the query trenches, thick and thin. Especially, M, I adore you to the moon and back. Thank you for your encouragement and pics that get me through the days. Love, Mompire.

To my family, my wonderful husband Michael and beautiful daughter, Elissa. Your constant support of me means everything. I'm blessed beyond measure with you both. I love our family and love our life. Thank you for all you do. Love you 3000.

ABOUT THE AUTHOR

WREN MICHAELS hails from the frozen tundra of Wisconsin where beer and cheese are their own food groups. But a cowboy swept her off her feet and carried her to Texas, where she promptly lost all tolerance for cold and snow. Fueled by coffee, dreams, and men in kilts, Wren promises to bring you laughter, heart-fluttering romance, and action that keeps you on the edge of your seat. The easiest way to her heart is anything to do with the Green Bay Packers, Doctor Who, or Joss Whedon.

www.wrenmichaels.net

 facebook.com/authorwrenmichaels

instagram.com/wren_michaels

twitter.com/AuthorWren

ABOUT THE PUBLISHER

City Owl Press is a cutting edge indie publishing company, bringing the world of romance and speculative fiction to discerning readers.

Escape Your World. Get Lost in Ours!

www.cityowlpress.com

f facebook.com/YourCityOwlPress
🐦 twitter.com/cityowlpress
📷 instagram.com/cityowlbooks
📌 pinterest.com/cityowlpress